D1527535

ROUGH JUSTICE

Tor Books by Ken Gross

A Fine Line
Rough Justice

ROUGH JUSTICE

KEN GROSS

TOR

A TOM DOHERTY ASSOCIATES BOOK
NEW YORK

ROUGH JUSTICE

Copyright © 1991 by Kenneth Gross

Excerpt on page 58: Reprinted with permission of Charles Scribner's Sons, an imprint of Macmillan Publishing Company, from *The Great Gatsby* by F. Scott Fitzgerald. Copyright 1925 by Charles Scribner's Sons; renewal copyright 1953 by Frances Scott Fitzgerald Lanahan.

A Tor Book
Published by Tom Doherty Associates, Inc.
49 West 24th St.
New York, NY 10010

Library of Congress Cataloging-in-Publication Data
Gross, Ken

    Rough justice / Ken Gross.
      p.   cm.
    "A Tom Doherty Associates Book."
    ISBN 0-312-85018-2
    I. Title.
    PS3557.R583R68   1991
    813'.54—dc20   90-48776
                                              CIP

First edition: February 1991

Printed in the United States of America

0 9 8 7 6 5 4 3 2 1

TO MY FAMILY—
You Know Who You Are.

1

December, 1986

"It's okay," and the man in the leather jacket, starting on his third whiskey sour in fifteen minutes. "I'm a professional."

"Oh, good," said the woman on his left, "I'd hate to see an amateur try that."

The man in the leather jacket thought: why do I bother? He was standing at the teak-wood bar in the yuppie staging area on Manhattan's Upper East Side. The long row of pinstripes was clustered just below the dinner specials, which were posted in fine bold script. The specials, not unlike the slick MBA's and corporate consultants letting off steam, sounded better on paper. The bar was moist with slippery eyes rolling from group to group, seeking a better, greener place to land. The young man in the leather jacket couldn't tell whether it was a sign of relief or a hiss of ambition he heard as they called for more liquor and recounted the office tales as if they were establishing legends around a campfire.

He was making half-hearted quips to the woman he found on his flank when he filled the opening in the solid block of pinstripes at the rail. Openings at the bar appeared like seats on the subway—they were snatched up shamelessly. Jay's was one of those dedicated, trendy, upscale spots on First Avenue, the kind that twitches with unspent energy on a Friday night. The man in the leather jacket had started out with notions of seducing the businesswoman; she had an inviting blush of intensity in her face, but each time he began to make his move, each time he uttered something winning yet ironic, he was blown back by another gust of her grievances. She was underpaid, overworked, passed over for promotion and beset with unfair demands on her time at whatever corporation was paying her bar bill. The professional insults left her seething and vengeful and a little unglued.

Not that she was alone. After a week of corporate smoke and fire, there were a lot of working-class casualties prowling First Avenue, looking for revenge. The young man in the leather jacket did not feel up to playing scapegoat, although she was tempting, and he could feel her inclination and knew that it wouldn't take much—a little overt sympathy, a few understanding grunts in the right places—and he could take her home.

But something happened. For no apparent reason he went sloppy and weak. One minute he was busy plotting, debating, weighing, the next he felt dangerously exposed. Watched. Not just watched—carefully and maliciously measured. It had a sickening effect on his legs and he sagged as if someone had struck him from behind the knees. He made a quick sweep of the bar, but he couldn't pick out the enemy eye. Everyone seemed bent into his own drink, preoccupied with his own specific melodrama. But the chill that crawled up the young man's back was unmistakable. There was no doubt that he stood dead center in someone's bull's-eye. Suddenly, he was short of breath and slightly dizzy. And the woman on his right held no more appeal—a sure sign of an altered state of consciousness. She didn't notice the change in seasons.

"I don't mind," she was saying to the image of herself in the mirror, "except you know that if I was a man I'd be making six figures. I'm talking big six. I put that deal together, top to bottom, and it was elegant. Fucking elegant!"

She was hurt, genuinely wounded for herself, and the look in her eyes was a combination of sorrow with admiration, for what she saw coming back from the mirror with the speed of light was a brave, wronged woman. Inside that pearl-gray suit with the assertive shoulder pads stood a handsome, undaunted person who, because of her innocent gender, was oppressed.

"They didn't even mention my name at the meeting," she said, her voice broken with anguish. "Assholes!"

"Uh," began the man in leather, looking around frantically, digging down in his pocket, slapping a twenty-dollar bill on the bar, "you'll have to excuse me."

"The john is that way," said the woman with the whiskey sour, jutting her head past the dining area. The young man stopped for a second, wondering how she knew he was searching for something since she never took her eyes off the mirror. But then he knew she could see him in the mirror. Like all the other sharks that swam these waters, she had eyes that rolled around in the back of her head.

"Yeah, thanks," he said, pulling away.

She moved her head to watch him when he went the other way and bolted out of the bar. She turned back to the mirror, then frowned. She couldn't see anything there that would drive a man half running into the night. She shrugged. Nowadays, with offers popping up like shooting-gallery targets, things that slipped out of your grasp had to be counted worthless. And she felt something else: relief. Not because she found the young man uninteresting or unap-

pealing. Not that he didn't measure up to all the other young
men who bounced in and out of her bed. But it was nice,
even for a moment, to have a reprieve from the strain and
effort of constant movement. Just a pit stop in the long race
seemed a sweet and cherished luxury. Nevertheless, she
couldn't ignore the sting of rejection—if that's what it was.
She dealt with it in her usual fashion: "Asshole!" she muttered, holding up her empty glass for a refill.

The young man walked quickly down First Avenue,
checking for dangerous reflections in the store windows, dizzy with fear. He was huddled, but it wasn't against the
wind or the cold. He turned every few feet to see if he was
being followed, to see if anyone had trailed him out of Jay's.
No one had left the bar. No one looked like a tracker. There
were women exercising poodles and men who appeared to
belong to the neighborhood taking their territorial after-din-
ner walk, marching off the boundaries of their domain. The
streets looked as they usually looked in this pampered section
of the city—secure and benign. Even the derelicts were neat
and compact, piled like dustballs in the doorways of the
closed shops, wisps of steam coming out of the layers of their
clothing. The young man in the leather jacket stood on the
northwest corner of First Avenue, at 78th Street, in the entryway of a dark dry cleaner, looking for some tangible clue
to the vivid attack of nerves. He could not see what it was
that his intuition saw. He knew enough not to trust his own
eyes. He knew that much.

He was a big man, well over six feet, and his shoulders
were broad and sturdy. His hands were thick and rough
from use. Not a handsome man, but he had things going for
him. At thirty, he was physically impressive. He told himself that he was obliged by career demands to keep himself fit
and so he watched his diet, lifted the weights and ran the
gruelling miles. Working out became a matter of honor. He
had made a bargain with himself and he couldn't rest until

he'd paid his dues. He had always been active, in the physical sense, always able to defend himself in a fair fight—and
he had had his share. His flattened nose attested to his
willingness to take up a challenge. But it wasn't a fair fight that he feared. In his line of work,
no one fought fair. They snuck up behind you and crushed
your skull with an iron pipe. They lay in ambush in dark
alleys, like hunters in a blind, and shot you dead and even
then, pumped bullets into the corpse. They used knives and
guns—anything—to annihilate you in a fashion that would
expose them to the least possible danger while leaving you
mashed and mutilated, dead and gone. Fair play had nothing
to do with it.

And now, for no apparent reason, he felt the hairs on the
back of his neck come alive. He was certain beyond all doubt
that someone was stalking him.

There was a public phone on the southeast corner, but the
man found that he had no change. He went through his
pockets again. "Shit," he said out loud. He always remembered to keep a quarter for the phone. It was a survivalist
habit. But he had handed his last quarter to the woman in
the bar. She had needed it for cigarettes. "Oh, God," he
groaned at his mindless lapse.

He looked around and saw an all-night Korean deli in the
middle of the block, lit up like opening night. Outside stood
the old man of the family, Mr. Ku, an urban scarecrow. The
geezer was lean and full of suspicion. The drunks and homeless staggered by, but left the displays of fresh fruit alone.
They could see that Mr. Ku was sizing them up, watching,
looking for something, prepared to make them pay.

Inside, the old man's wife stood at the register.

"I would really appreciate some change for the telephone,"
the man in the leather jacket, the customer, said to the
woman at the register. He opened his wallet. He had two
twenties and a single.

She didn't reply. But the customer saw a sign behind her:

"No change without purchase," it said. It was final, no appeal. The customer didn't argue, he knew the futility of that; he handed her the single and bought a candy bar. He grabbed the change and didn't notice until he was halfway out the door that he held only twenty-one cents in his hand. The phones took quarters.

"Let me buy something else," said the man, trying to hand back the milk-and-nut bar. The woman, trained to inflexibility, shook her head. Mr. Ku had come in off the street and had taken a blocking position at the door.

The man in the leather jacket still needed change. But he had spent his last single. Now he only had the twenties and there was another sign behind the counter: "No change for $20 bill unless purchase is $10 or more."

The customer took a cart and gathered up a milk container, a package of cheese, a loaf of bread, two Cokes and a package of cookies. It came to $11.98. "Could I have one of the singles in quarters?" he asked. The wife handed him three singles, a five-dollar bill and two pennies. The husband folded his arms and kept his unblinking vigil.

"How much is this?" asked the young man, holding up a pack of chewing gum.

The husband and wife exchanged some harsh words in Korean. Then the old man said, "My wife does not understand. You are seeking change for the telephone." The wife smiled sweetly and held out four quarters. He handed her the dollar bill.

The customer took the quarters. As he passed Mr. Ku on his way back out to the street, the fierce, craggy face of the old man broke into a friendly grin.

"You have to speak up," said the old man. "My wife is hard of hearing."

The customer nodded, then ducked back out onto the street. It was emptier now—no one in either direction. A cab whizzed by. He didn't see the stranger watching him from an unmarked car on a sidestreet.

The stranger in the unmarked car cupped his cigarette, like a soldier on sentry duty. A police radio played softly in the car. The focus of his attention was complete and terrible. And the young man in the leather jacket was in the center of his gaze.

The telephone stand was empty. The young man made certain that his back was to the wall. He slipped in the quarter and still his eyes kept tracking up and down the street, looking for the ambush. His fingers were cold but they hit the right numbers on the phone. It rang twice.

"Sanders," said a voice on the other end.

"Bring me in," whispered the man.

"What? Who is this? I can't hear you," said Sanders, who knew that an automatic switch had already been activated, that the man's voice was being recorded and that a trace had begun.

"This is your guy, this is Highway, one of your people," he hissed. "I need to be safe. I am in big fucking trouble."

"Calm down."

"Listen, don't tell me that. This is way over my head. Someone's after me. I'm scared shitless. I didn't bargain for this. I want out. Now!"

Sanders had been in the business long enough to distinguish among the various kinds of panic. He could read the difference between unfounded hysteria and something else. He heard something else on the line.

"Where are you?" he asked gently.

"Seventy-eighth and First," whispered Highway, looking around.

"Is there anyplace safe, somewhere you can wait? Is anything open?"

"A Korean deli. On First."

"Go there. Wait. We'll pick you up."

The young man heard the click and started backtracking to the Korean deli.

The stranger in the unmarked car, who had his own

scrambler line, also heard the telephone click. He stubbed
out his cigarette, put on his gloves, and took a small attach-
ment out of the glove compartment and screwed it onto the
.9-millimeter pistol he kept under the car seat. He waited
until the man was inside the deli, then he got out of the car
and, as he was locking it, checked the street for signs of in-
terference. He didn't want a stray garbage truck interrupting
his work. Or a delivery van. Or some heroic cop on a night
patrol. He was satisfied. The street looked clean and empty,
washed down, it seemed, of all other life for his convenience.

Highway was filling up the shopping cart—frozen foods,
cakes, donuts—anything. The deli owners were watching,
baffled. They recognized fear, some elevated level of energy
that signalled danger, but they had no idea what was taking
place. So far, it could be anything.

The stranger from the unmarked car came in quickly, and
made a quick survey of the store. He looked for security
cameras or guards, and counted the house. He was compact
and composed and had a cashmere coat, one of those lush
double-breasted topcoats that fold around and tie closed with
a belt. He walked near the end of the aisles, never glancing at
the displays of fruit or salad. Mr. Ku knew that he was not a
customer. He walked like a warlord. The stranger made his
way across the length of the store, then down the far aisle,
keeping everyone in the store in sight. He vanished into the
aisle with the stacks of bread and breakfast food.

Highway was blindly stuffing his cart with boxes of rice
and cereal. At first he didn't notice the smaller man, the
stranger in the cashmere coat and Italian suit. But then he
heard him and jumped when he looked up. The smaller
man's hand came out of his coat pocket. It had a leather case
with a detective's gold shield flapping in front. "District Attorney's Squad," said the stranger.

Highway was hyperventilating. He held up a hand, put
the other one on his chest and smiled. "Boy, am I glad to see
you. How'd you get here so fast?"

The stranger didn't answer and Highway's relief turned into terror. For he noticed something. This one was alone. Where was the backup? New York City didn't send its detective out alone. There was always a backup. Especially DA's detectives, especially on a dangerous assignment like this. Highway started to ask for the detective's ID card, but he never got the chance. By the time he opened his mouth, the "detective" had picked up a box of Wheaties to shield his .9-millimeter gun. The young man in the leather jacket, the mob informant known as Highway, saw the barrel and saw two quick puffs of smoke. He heard nothing much—the quick splat, splat—because the stranger had his silencer attached to the gun. He felt the first thud, followed quickly by the second. No pain, just wild surprise that it was so easy, so quick, so final. His chest exploded and he fell unseen among the boxes of rice. He knew that he was a dead man before he died.

Mr. Ku was still trying to understand what was happening in the back of his store. His wife started to ask, but he held up his hand, silencing her. He had seen the second stranger walk to the back, as if he knew the first one, the tall Caucasian. This second man, the smaller one with the expensive coat, was purposeful, confident and intimidating. Mr. Ku stood on his tiptoes, but still he couldn't see, and after noting the bold stride of the second man, he was not certain that he wanted to see. Of one thing he was certain, they were not out to rob him—not men dressed like that. His wife tried to speak, but he put a finger to his mouth and shook his head. Wait here, he told himself. It could be nothing. But he didn't think so. The two Americans spoke—he could hear the voices, but not the words.

The smaller man came back, alone to the front of the store. He walked straight up to Mr. and Mrs. Ku; he was smiling. He had a handsome face and the smile was reassuring. He carried a box of Wheaties. It had holes in it and the cereal was leaking out. It had a hypnotic effect on the couple.

Then the stranger turned the box of Wheaties and shot Mr. Ku once in the head. It was a straight, deadly shot that took Mr. Ku's scalp away, exposing the brain pan. Mrs. Ku started to say something but the stranger blew off the back of her head as she turned away. The stranger made certain they were both dead—his rule was to leave no witnesses. He seemed to be in no hurry. Mistakes were made in haste, he knew. Better to take your time and think of everything. The stranger walked back to his first victim and carefully planted the .9-millimeter gun in the dead man's hand, wrapping the fingers around the handle and on the trigger, leaving fingerprints. He picked up the shells, then looked around, making certain that there were no witnesses, and took a sponge from a fresh package on display in the household cleaning section and spread some blood from the first victim toward the front so that it would look as if he had killed the two owners, and been killed himself, in a botched robbery attempt. A precinct detective trying to reconstruct the events would be confused.

The stranger checked to see that he was not damaged—in the heat of these things men have blown off fingers and not known it for hours—then, satisfied, calmly made his way across the avenue, opened the unmarked car and drove away, circling back north. Still no sign of activity in the street.

Three blocks north, he noticed a man in the passenger seat of a car parked along First Avenue. The man had his head outside of the car window, and was retching over the side of the car. The drunk looked up and their eyes met, just the blink of an eye, but it was enough.

2

Jack Mann's head was stuck out of the window on the passenger side and he was roaring into the night—a disproportionate sound for the amount of spittle that emerged from his lips and dribbled down the door of the car. "Oh, God, please let me die. Awwwwwrr! I won't ask for anything else, I swear; just lemme die."

The thin noodle of bile was all that was left of the three bottles of wine and the parade of beer and whiskey that Jack had swallowed in a futile attempt at numbing himself. The news about his wife was final, hopeless and unbearable. Since he couldn't go to her for consolation—they both preferred the pretense of hope to a gloomy countdown—all he could do was douse himself with liquid anaesthesia. Unaccustomed to the echo of pain and nausea that came from out of the bottle, Jack wound up suffering surprise as well as misery. He had left his spoor all over Manhattan.

His friend and partner, Moe Berger, held Jack so that he wouldn't bash his head on the metal frame of the car window. Jack's head rose and fell in its violent heaves, and Moe didn't notice the unmarked cruiser go by with the single occupant in the cashmere coat. Jack saw something. His head was rising when the cruiser passed and he saw the profile of the driver, then the flame from the eyes when the driver turned and looked him in the face. He saw that, but the world was in fluid motion and whatever he saw didn't seem to matter as much as the fact that he was in the midst of trying to die.

Watching the back of Jack's head, Moe saw an opening to win a round in their long-standing duel of jokes. It could also serve as a distraction, something Jack badly needed. While Jack was roaring and heaving and dying, Moe would finally stump him, beat him to a punch line, thus winning a dollar and boasting rights:

"Listen, Jack, you know this one? This guy orders a bowl of soup and he calls the waiter over and he says, 'Waiter, taste this soup.' The waiter says, 'What's the matter? Is there something wrong with the soup?' And the guy says, 'Just take a taste of the soup.'"

The mention of food triggered a fresh wave of nausea in Jack. "Arrrhhh!"

Moe heartlessly continued: "So the waiter says, 'What's wrong, too salty? Is that it?' 'Just taste the soup,' says the customer. And the waiter says, 'Is it too hot, too cold, what?' The guy says, 'Just taste the soup.' Finally, the waiter says, 'Okay, okay, I'll taste the soup. Where's the spoon? . . .'"

Jack turned his head and from the depths of his misery beat Moe to the punch line: "'Aha!'"

Moe hesitated. It was, after all, a tragic evening in Jack's life. "I thought you were dying," said Moe after a moment.

"Death is my only hope," replied Jack, once again drooling down the door.

"Don't let me stop you."

Jack began gagging.

"You gonna be long?" Moe asked.

"Oh, I hope not!" Jack moaned, looking down at the streaks on the door. "I think maybe we need a new paint job," he said, sucking in air, his head bobbing up and down in the cold.

Three and a half blocks south, a homeless beggar hid in the shadows near the Korean deli. The man, who had his turf, if not a home, knew the neighborhood and, not seeing Mr. Ku standing guard, intended to pilfer some food. He was at that far edge of hunger where he would take desperate chances. He knew that the market was open because it was always open.

A short man with a striking face had left the deli. The homeless man had lost track of most things—streets, years, his own identity—but he noticed that the man left the deli in a controlled hurry. Didn't look like a customer. He wasn't carrying a bag. The homeless man couldn't pigeonhole his business—maybe an operative of some secret agency bent on destruction, maybe an arm of spiritual vengeance sent to punish the secular apostates from a religious cult. That would explain the terrible heat he sensed from the man. Maybe someone employed by his father looking for him.

The homeless man hid in the shadows until the short man was gone, then went into the deli. As he came through the thermal layers of the doors, he sensed something wrong. There was no one behind the counter, no one tending the register, no one watching the merchandise! Maybe it was a trap. But maybe not. He fought off the urge to retreat. It might be dangerous, but there was a cornucopia of fresh food here. The homeless man survived on day-old bread and spoiled apples and the soup-kitchen stew made out of unsellable meat and borderline potatoes and limp carrots. Everything donated, all of it compromised. It tasted of contempt. He knew that the food he ate was considered garbage by the bourgeois clerks and secretaries and market ana-

lysts who filled up their plastic, see-through dinner
containers of salad with the carefully picked vegetables on
display. The homeless man had watched them in their grim,
focused rounds, selecting this pea and that carrot, rejecting
the wilted remnants that would wind up as his dinner. He'd
endured the grudging, sanctimonious donations of those who
wouldn't touch his hand, dropping their quarters into his
outstretched palm. And so it was with a wild sense of vin-
dication that he began to stuff his pockets with crisp apples
and solid grapes and unripe bananas. His hands were so busy
that he crushed the grapes and squashed the bananas. It
didn't matter. They would still taste like rain in his parched
mouth. He gave a quick glance over at the cash register, but
he rejected the notion. That was theft, and he was not a
thief. He would steal food, but that was survival. He felt no
guilt about stealing food.

Then, as he turned, he spotted the blue-gray glint of metal
lying in the aisle by some spilled boxes of cereal: a gun.
Something stirred in him. A kind of slumbering pride. To
survive, he had had to cringe and slink from door to door, to
appear humble and meek. To seem pathetic. But he didn't
feel pathetic. He felt a constant and smoldering rage at having to beg for food, at having to eat off paper plates with
plastic spoons. He was furious that his bed was an unyield-
ing metal grating. He was bitter at always being hot in summer and cold in winter. He resented the casual, thoughtless
prodding of the police, who regarded him as some kind of
self-propelled eyesore. To have a gun would change all that,
even if he never used it. He would know he had the power
and that might be enough. There were practical possibilities
to consider, as well. He wouldn't have to worry about pro-
tecting his belongings from the packs of organized predators
who came through the streets flashing knives, stealing shoes
and sweaters and whatever sorry possessions the shifting
mass of homeless could stuff into their plastic and appropri-
ated garbage bags. He could show his gun—he might not

even have to use it—and they would retreat and he would sleep in peace.

He didn't see the dead man behind the spilled boxes of cereal. Looking around, expecting someone to lunge out at him, he inched his way down the aisle, his eyes busy and blind with fear. And then he reached down and lifted the gun. It was heavier than he expected. Good. Substance. Weight! He had half expected the playful heft of a plastic gun, which was all that he had lifted until that moment. This weight had to be taken seriously. It seemed to give him substance. He stared at it, then stuffed it inside his pants, under three layers of shirts and two sweaters.

It was at that instant, when he was looking down to smooth the bulge of the gun under the rope belt of his pants, that he saw the dead man, or rather the stream of blood that led his eyes to the dead man. He jumped back, knocking down more boxes of cereal and rice. He told himself: run, get out! As he passed the front, he noticed Mr. Ku and then Mrs. Ku—half hidden by the counter near the register—and the sight boosted his fear and he half-ran out of the door. He turned south, sprinting for the park at the corner, holding the gun in place as he ran so that he wouldn't lose it.

The call came over the radio as a ten-thirteen—policeman in trouble. Moe pulled away from Jack, settled behind the wheel, put the car in gear and, once Jack had tucked his head back inside, mashed down on the gas pedal. Without a word, Jack pulled his silver police shield out of his back pocket and hung it on his breast pocket. He took deep, sobering breaths as Moe whipped the car around in a U-turn, going the wrong way down First Avenue. They might be plainclothesmen, but they were cops and a ten-thirteen call for help meant everyone. No holds barred. It took them barely a minute to go to the deli and by that time two sector cars were already there, doors flung open in haste as cop

rushed to help cop. There were also a couple of unmarked
DA's squad cruisers.

When they got to the deli, the call had been clarified. It
wasn't a ten-thirteen after all, and the wind went out of everyone. It was only a triple murder.

Deputy Inspector Ray Monahan, a tall, thin man with ice-
blue eyes and military bearing, was on his dinner break
when the first, erroneous call went over the air. It was his
night as acting borough commander of Manhattan and he
was just starting on a thick steak at Bill's Restaurant, a garment center secret hidden between garages on West 40th
Street, when his beeper went off. A few eyes inside the restaurant flickered, hearing the beeper, then, ascertaining that
it was not for them, bent back to their meals. The meals at
Bill's were worth attention—juicy steaks and fresh fish and
mashed potatoes that tasted fresh, chemically pure, toxically
safe. Even the style seemed authentic, like an old speakeasy
out of the thirties, with its polished wood and old mirrors
and wisps of cigar smoke hanging in the air. It belonged to
the aging clothing moguls who brought in their ingrate sons
for a taste of something finer than food. These inarticulate
old-world garment kings, unable to explain what it was that
they treasured in the portraits and photographs of legendary
manufacturers, stars of the rag trade, which were sprinkled
like family trees on the walls of the restaurant, wanted to
pass along some understanding of tenuous values by introducing their dense and spoiled heirs to a temple of European
craft, as if, contained in the hand-mashed potatoes, was some
secret of untampered quality. At Bill's, the chef cooked like
the endangered Latvian tailors sewed—with infinite care,
with patience, with attention to the work and with some
memory of an ethic and a bottom line other than profit.

But such lessons were wasted on the idiot sons who would
eventually run their fathers' businesses into the ground. At
night, freed of the frustrating attempt to educate their sons,

the old-timers came back to Bill's to unwind, to sit unhurried, and talk the way men talk when they are not rushed, when they are relaxed into a kind of everyday philosophical mood. Dangling on their arms were the young models with their faces cast in professional indifference, enduring the repetition of stories and industry parables with the same stone patience with which they would endure the endless poses and changes of clothing for photographers and designers. Over and over, they heard the desperate saga of the missing bolts of cloth that almost stopped production (as if production was a heart that could never be stopped), or the crazy buyer who didn't understand the shifting market and tried to corner Nehru jackets, or the thick-witted partner who had money but no common sense and had to be restrained from throwing away a whole line of goods on an iffy miniskirt. Such stories were told in the grand, expansive manner of generals who have survived close battles, of skydivers telling of long falls, of mountain climbers remembering broken ropes, of garment center plungers living as if each season were a last breath of air.

Deputy Inspector Monahan enjoyed eavesdropping on the high-wire merchants. He thought of it as turning the pages of a novel. He listened as if he were overhearing the tales and sagas of the merchants in a kiosk in Minsk. The owners of the restaurant, always eager to accommodate important members of the police department, had come to understand his inquisitive nature and gave him a discreet table in the rear where he could listen and not be seen. And they always handed him the correct bill. Other high police officials accepted a discounted check, paying as little as twenty percent of the menu price for their meals and pretending not to notice. But Monahan was a prig when it came to his personal behavior. He did not take an unpaid-for cup of coffee, he did not accept the customary tickets to baseball games and football games, or venture into the swamp of untraceable cash that could have been left in his desk with a nod or shrug.

Monahan let it be known that he would report any attempt at graft or corruption. His shield was not for sale. There were such priggish men in the department and they were tolerated, like priests who were faithful to their vow of celibacy. For reasons that were not altogether pure, his demanding ethical code did not hurt Monahan's climb into the higher ranks of the police department. The older, compromised chiefs needed someone above reproach, someone of saintly virtue, in their midst. Who could question the moral rectitude of a department that had among its chiefs a man of Monahan's unassailable virtue?

When the beeper went off, Monahan saw his driver come in, making his way clumsily down to his table. The driver brushed aside the maître d', his face wet with worry. This was a street cop marching to the sound of the guns, thought Monahan. A bull in full charge.

"We got a ten-thirteen," whispered the driver, an old cop named Vince Toladano, who had been rescued from the rubber-gun squad by Monahan and who returned the favor with complete, unswerving loyalty.

"Where?" asked the inspector.

"Uh, I didn't check it out."

Monahan sighed. He left the uneaten steak, dropped two twenty-dollar bills on the table and led Toladano out of the restaurant. After radioing ahead and finding the location and the true nature of the emergency, they busted north through the park. The red light on the roof was waving off traffic, the siren crying, when the chief of detectives came on the radio. Chief Dennis McHue was senior ranking officer on duty citywide since the police commissioner and chief of patrol were in Europe on a junket.

"McHue," he barked.

"Deputy Inspector Monahan," replied the acting borough commander, who put his hand over the mouthpiece and spoke to the driver. "Slow down, Vince, this isn't a ten-thirteen."

"This is a Task Force case, Inspector," barked Chief McHue, who became even more of a martinet with each increment of power.

"Yes, sir," replied Monahan.

"You will turn over command and evidence to the senior Task Force officer on the scene. Is that clear?"

"What about uniform men, to sanitize the scene?"

"Fine. Fine. Just see that the uniform men understand that they are under Task Force direction."

"Yes, sir. Out."

The Organized Crime Task Force was a collection of high-quality investigators, the pick of New York city, state and federal detectives, who had one purpose: to eliminate the Mafia. It was an old idea with high-tech trimmings and media promotion. The public was treated to the sight—every now and then—of some low-level hood in handcuffs being led on what had come to be known as "the media walk" to be booked for some streetcorner slaughter. There were fifty detectives on the Task Force, not counting clerical help. They had their own offices and their own chain of command, and they even had their own district attorneys to present their cases to their own grand jury. They were accountable to no one but themselves and often left behind a scene riddled with dead victims and villains for local police to clean up. Monahan hated them. After watching their clumsy handling of several cases, he thought that they were all glitz and no substance. They offended his memory of camera-shy cops who performed their labors unsung. Cops were supposed to be modest heroes—or so he had grown up believing—not news hogs. Shy men outside the home precincts. Wordless, when it came to public comments. Their world was a defined sector, a specific foot patrol, and within that well-marked boundary, their deepest, most ardent wish was for a slow, uneventful passage. Anarchy and chaos and excitement were their sworn enemies. Monahan didn't understand these media cops with telegenic smiles and trigger-happy quotes.

And so he was in a bad mood when he came into the Korean deli and pulled aside a cop from the Manhattan North homicide squad.

"This is a Task Force job," he told Lieutenant Davey Press, who had been arguing with the Task Force team.

"Bullshit!" said Press, then, seeing that it was Monahan, calmed down. "Sorry, Ray."

Monahan nodded to the Task Force commander.

"It's from on high," said Monahan to Press.

"I hate these assholes," Press said.

Jack moaned, "Oh, God!" With Moe hovering over him, Jack was sitting on a plastic milk case behind the counter, within earshot, nursing a black coffee, trying not to vomit again. Nearby were the body bags where Mr. and Mrs. Ku had been placed side by side, awaiting the morgue meat wagon.

Monahan and Press jumped, as if the moan had come from the dead. Then, seeing Jack with his tin shield flopping out of his filthy breast pocket, smelling the vomit and the liquor, Monahan lost his temper.

"Who is this?" he said to Press.

Jack looked up, his eyes blood red, as if he'd been pickled in salt water.

"Uh, Anti-Crime Squad, Inspector," said Moe.

"What are you doing here?"

"Ohhhh!" Jack groaned.

"We were in the vicinity and responded to the ten-thirteen," Moe said, trying to pull the inspector aside.

"You're standing on some brains," Jack said, his head bent into the hot coffee.

"What?!? What did you say?" cried Monahan, practically screaming. Other cops began to turn around, paying attention to the commotion.

"Take it easy," Moe said, speaking to both Jack and the inspector.

"I said, you're standing on somebody's brains." Jack nod-

ded at the inspector's foot. Monahan looked down and saw
the green and pale pink teardrop of tissue that had been,
indeed, someone's brain. It was stuck to his shoe. He leaped
back, but the tissue clung to his shoe, and then he recovered
and stood on one foot. He motioned for one of the forensic
detectives. "Bag it," he said, though not so much for evidence but as a sign of respect.

Moe trailed after Monahan and whispered into the inspector's ear: "He's had some bad news tonight."

"Is he on duty?" Monahan asked.

"No. Technically he's on his own time."

"He's armed."

"His wife has cancer, chief," Moe whispered. "He just
found out today. She has six months to live, if she's lucky."

Monahan was stopped. He had lost his wife in a car accident ten years earlier and had never quite recovered. He
hadn't felt whole since.

"He's a good cop," Moe said, seeing that he had gained
Monahan's attention and sympathy. "The old school." He
nodded, punctuating the endorsement. "Good cop. He doesn't
drink. . . ."

"You coulda fooled me," replied Monahan, although the
steam had gone out of his anger. Monahan knew that the
good cops from the old school were rare. Solid men who held
out against easy ways, men who counted the leaves on the
trees, as he liked to say. Staunch guardians of the peace—
good cops. Humane cops who knew when to look away and
when to stand fast.

Moe was persistent: "He doesn't drink, Inspector; that's
why he can't hold his liquor."

"You should have looked out for him," Monahan said.

"I am," replied Moe forcefully.

Just then Special Assistant United States Attorney Marvin
Sanders pushed aside the yellow tape of the crime scene and
marched into the deli. The uniformed officers, who recognized the Task Force leader's pudgy face from the six o'clock

news, moved aside. Sanders stood for a moment surveying the store, while all the detectives froze in the midst of their assignments.

Jack concentrated, trying not to vomit a stream of hot coffee, like someone trying not to hiccup. He focused on a spot across the room where two objects caught the light and glowed back at him.

Sanders looked over at Inspector Monahan.

"I'm acting borough commander," Monahan said.

"Well, Commander," Sanders said, "in that case, get your people out of here."

Monahan turned to Moe and said softly, "You and your friend get lost."

"Thank you, Inspector," replied Moe, nodding, grabbing Jack under the arm and pulling him away. Monahan shouted: "Everyone but Task Force personnel, please report back to your duty stations."

A slow, reluctant shuffle began toward the front of the deli. Cops don't like being pushed out of a crime scene. It violates their notion of the trade off: they handle the psychopaths, but for a price. There is a certain rubberneck privilege that goes with the job.

One hard detective refused to budge, stopped in front of Monahan and placed his legs in a defiant stance, as if daring anyone to try to move him. "I gotta do some paper work on this, Inspector," said the detective. Monahan didn't remember the man's name, but he knew the type—first-grade detective with a lot of time on the job and a death grip on his own power.

"Forget it," Monahan said. "The Task Force'll handle it."

"Listen, Inspector, no disrespect, but that's bullshit. I was catching and this is my homicide, and I don't give a fuck about any task force or any federal asshole attorney."

Monahan smiled. He pointed to Sanders. "Go tell him that," he said.

The first-grade bulldog planted himself in front of Sanders

and began delivering his speech; Monahan couldn't hear, but he could see Sanders's face turning red. The Special Assistant United States Attorney practically ran over to Monahan, sputtering. "Get him out of here, Inspector!" he said, his voice rising out of control.

"Okay," Monahan said after a moment, "but lemme tell you something, Sanders, you could use a few men like that on the Task Force."

3

He woke up alarmed and disoriented. Jack Mann looked around. The things in the dank, fetid basement, though oddly unfamiliar, were unmistakably his own—the clean work bench, the crowded desk, the tools he had purchased with every intention of fixing and mending the chairs and tables he never got around to fixing and mending. The walls were covered with the usual American Legion and civic plaques delivered like junk mail at the monthly meetings to any policeman with more than ten years on the force and not under a cloud of corruption. Still, it took him a moment to connect it all to himself. So familiar and yet so strange. Maybe it was the hangover. His head was a thundercloud of pain. He couldn't remember how he got here—home—not from last night, much less from his tenement youth. It was one of those frightening mornings that jump out of clammy nightmares. Where were his clothes? He didn't remember getting undressed. What happened to the vomit? He remembered the retching that had turned his belly inside out. During his days on the force, he'd been shot and it hadn't made him feel as bad as the bout of nausea. At least there was something clean and heroic about getting shot.

Besides, Jack had something else to cope with on this cold, crisp morning. Something besides the pain and the confusion. He could handle his own misery, but he was not ready to face the big question of Natalie. His wife. His dying mate. The nurse would be upstairs, changing bedding, inserting needles, washing her down, taking her temperature, measuring her pulse. He was not yet ready to confront the mechanical ordeal of his wife's daily, morbid routine. Not that she was neglected, or mistreated. She was treated well, with care, even tenderness, by the succession of hired nurses and attendants, but ultimately, she was handled with the distance people devote to a lost cause. In the end, they were all going through the motions. He shook his head and the rattle of knives in there jolted him, made him almost clear-headed, and he groaned.

The sun was pouring through the window, flooding the basement with little particles of dust, creating a kind of sympathetic haze. The last thing he remembered was coming home, knowing that Natalie was asleep upstairs. He had stood on the lawn of his home in Rosedale—a bedroom community for working-class civil servants in the outer borough of Queens, a section technically within the city limits filled with cops and firemen and postmen—and had stared at her bedroom windows. The windows had looked like deep, empty sockets, like death, and he'd begun to weep. He'd blubbered soft drunken prayers—softly because he was ashamed to admit that he still held some small kernel of faith. And then the chain of memory led back to that drunken spree when he'd tried to forget the full granite truth. He could remember nothing else. Here he was in the basement cot, undressed, relatively clean, and no clue as to how he got that way.

Then, quite suddenly, he smelled the bacon and the coffee.

The smells wafted down from the kitchen, ghosts of other mornings when Natalie cooked for him. He could almost hear her chirping in her off-key, happy song. He had built up the basement as a present to her, to spare her the disturbances of his late-night shifts. So he would come home and watch television in the basement while Natalie slept upstairs. He'd fall asleep to a late movie, comforted by the thought of her upstairs, peaceful, and then be awakened to the smell of bacon and coffee. A perfume between them. She'd cook breakfast as a reciprocal gift because he let her sleep.

Their relationship, he had come to understand in this twilight of the marriage, had been an exchange of small gifts. They were always grateful to have found each other. Such an unlikely discovery—he a lapsed Catholic with blue-collar roots, she an intellectual Jew who taught English to indifferent high school students. Jack, with his instant passions and quick temper, was unable to understand why she would continue to read classic literature to kids who were only listening for the class bell. Because, she explained patiently, because patience was part of her nature, because sometime far down the line, maybe they would remember. A soft, subtle sound would come back and they would read a book. Maybe, he thought skeptically. A hard bet that one in hundreds would be struck by the music of high school English. But worthwhile. And he loved her for her high-principled optimism.

For a moment, on that cold sunny morning, as the odors from the kitchen descended into the basement, replacing the smell of wet cement, he forgot; his memory was overwhelmed, short-circuited by the sensuous trigger of breakfast smells, and everything was fine. He thought that he could sneak upstairs, grab her from behind the way he did when they first invented the game, and they would tumble together, groping out of their clothing, smothering each other with appreciation. For that flickering moment when the smell of food made him dizzy with her again, he forgot that Natalie was hopelessly bedridden. He was in thrall to the old sense memory of her upstairs, cooking for him.

He pulled on his threadbare robe, as he would have when she was healthy, and went up out of the basement. He didn't want to go, he didn't want to find her gone. But he had no choice. As he climbed the stairs and opened the door onto the living room, he could hear the bacon frying in the kitchen. Pans were rattling, dishes banging, the refrigerator opening and closing, and he could hear that thunking, hollow liquid sound of eggs cracking. But he couldn't see through the door into the breakfast nook.

As Jack pushed open the swinging door, it was like seeing a clock, being reminded that the hour was late. The cook was a large, lumbering twenty-two-year-old with a tendency to sudden bursts of kindness, acts that swept aside Jack's usual reservations about his weakness for fried foods and proclivity to get into mischief. Barry was Natalie's dead sister's child, an orphan since high school, lost without parents, vulnerable to bad company, yet winning in his lifelong role of playing the happy fool. He gambled badly, he dabbled in recreational drugs, he ran with worse characters who travelled in stolen cars. Jack was kept busy pulling Barry out of small jams. But he never hesitated. Barry was worth it.

Hearing the door move, Barry turned, smiled his lopsided smile at Jack, and waved his spatula in a kind of salute.

Jack couldn't help but smile back. It took an effort to return to the sad agenda. "How is she?" he asked.

Barry turned back to the stove, his voice turned up a notch, trying to reach some level of brightness: "The nurse is upstairs. All Aunt Natalie seems to want to do is sleep."

"It's the medication." Jack climbed onto the stool at the counter.

Barry kept his eyes on the stove. Then he handed his uncle a mug of coffee over his shoulder. Jack took it and sipped the scalding coffee, convinced that only hot, boiling coffee could break through his clogged, poisoned passages.

"You feeling okay?" asked Barry.

"My mouth feels like the zoo."

Barry turned, nodded and smiled at his uncle. "You were really stoned."

"Yeah, well . . ."

Barry dished out the food, put it on a tray and began to carry it out of the kitchen. Jack raised his eyebrows; Natalie certainly had no appetite for bacon, eggs, toast, coffee and juice.

"The nurse," explained Barry.

"The nurse," muttered Jack. Mrs. Graham. A cold woman with endless, uncompromising demands. Her own bathroom. A board under her mattress. Three carefully planned and detailed meals a day. Veal on Tuesday, steak on Wednesday, chicken on Thursday, and so on. Thin and middle-aged and bitter from spending her nights in strange homes on doomed missions. She looked at Jack, when she could bear to make eye contact, with a pinched, accusatory scowl, as if, somehow, he had set the outlaw cells loose, he was responsible for the illness, an irrational judgment with which he did not entirely disagree. As a result, he didn't mind the finger-wagging undertone of her conversation, even welcomed it. She spoke to him as if daring him to find a replacement, in crisp, clipped commands, like a Prussian Junker, like a misanthrope. Like a saint.

In a moment, Barry came back bearing the same tray full of food. "She's not ready yet." He shrugged. The nurse liked her food hot, but not reheated. A new breakfast would have to be prepared. Barry offered Jack the tray, but Jack shook him off. Then Barry pulled up the other stool and went to work on the meal.

"Somebody called," said Barry, his mouth full of bacon and toast.

"Who?"

"An inspector. I wrote it down. Says to call him at 10:30." Jack looked at the clock. It was ten; he still had time enough to shower and shave.

"You in trouble, Uncle Jack?"

"Why?"

"He sounded mad."

"Inspectors always sound mad."

Jack took a piece of toast, then remembered his stomach and just held it. "Mind if I ask you a question?" said Barry.

"I mind."

"Yeah, well, lemme ask anyway, Uncle Jack, 'cause you know I'm gonna get curious and I'm gonna ask anyway."

"This is not a good idea, Barry. Not today."

"I know. I know. But, listen, Uncle Jack, you know me, I can't help myself, lemme ask, it's been bothering me: how come you become a cop? I mean, a guy like you I don't think of as a cop."

Jack looked at him, trying to decide how to take it, whether it was a bad insult or a high compliment.

Barry tried to soften things. "Not that you're not a good cop. You're a great cop. The best. That's what's so bizarre. Nobody thinks of you as a cop."

"It's honest work, if you do it right."

"C'mon, Uncle Jack, you like busting guys?"

"I like busting bad guys. That gives me pleasure."

"That's why you became a cop?"

Jack took a bite of the toast, listened for a second to see if he could hear anything upstairs, then answered: "No."

"The gun," said Barry quickly. "That's why I'd become a cop. Yeah, I can appreciate that."

"No, it's not the gun."

"Yeah, well, with me it'd be the gun."

Jack shrugged. "It's very hard to explain." Not that he thought Barry lacked imagination. Trouble was Barry had too much imagination. And being a cop, being a good cop, required a kind of downshift of imagination. It required acceptance. In its finest form, being a cop was only an implied thing. The way Jack explained it to Natalie once, when she asked the same question, was that good police work was a kind of Zen exercise, something that triggered the other per-

son's conscience. A policeman reminded people of restraint.
He'd first recognized it when he was walking a beat in
Queens, a nasty street with competing Oriental and Hispanic
cultures. Men bullying their wives and kids on the sidewalks
in loud, brutal voices. An air of potential menace and violence spitting out into the atmosphere, like the spray from an
open hydrant. And then Jack came along in his police uniform and his polished brass and he noticed that a great quiet
moved along with him. Not that they made eye contact, or
even looked at him. He was like a tide coming in. He
smothered the broiling street with a kind of calm wave of
conscience. As if society itself was watching.

Natalie laughed. She called him a mystic cop. But she understood and respected it.

"So how come you became a cop?" persisted Barry.

Jack gave him that crooked, sideways look. "I liked the
way I looked in a uniform."

They could hear the nurse coming downstairs. She would
want her fresh breakfast. Jack passed her on the stairs as he
went up to visit his wife. "She's sleeping," said crusty Mrs.
Graham.

"I won't disturb her," assured Jack.

Natalie was lying on her back on the high hospital bed
he'd rented when he brought her home. Her face didn't look
much different from the day he met her almost twenty years
ago, although Jack wouldn't have noticed the difference anyway. The tubes were coming out of her nose and arms. He
could hear her breathing—labored and slow. He walked
carefully to the bed, then touched her fingers. She didn't
react. Jack was not a small man, but he could be delicate
when he had to be, and he climbed gently on the bed and
fitted himself into the few inches of spare room on the side
where there were no bottles and no tubes. He nuzzled next
to his wife, who smelled of alcohol and medicine. He closed
his eyes and smelled the bacon from the kitchen.

4

Tommy Day spent an hour and a half getting ready. It was his usual morning routine, performed with the slow, ceremonial care of a samurai warrior readying himself for battle. Tommy brushed his teeth, rinsed with a mouthwash, each act explicit, marking beginnings and endings, then he showered. It was a long, languid shower and he stood under the steaming spray of water, turning his face toward the nozzle, as if he was steaming out the wrinkles of his personality. He stepped out into a plush bathroom carpet and put on a thick terry-cloth robe.

He toweled his hair, a thick black pelt that he wore with pride. For some reason, he took credit for the hair. But the face underneath the hair made him uncomfortable. The trouble with the face was that it was entirely too handsome for a New York City police detective. Now that he was closing in on thirty, he studied it daily for signs of emerging character. There should have been a few lines, some wear around the eyes, a scar or maybe some imbalance between the brow and the chin, some deviation of the cheekbones, some doubtful accumulation of flesh—some sign that the face had been through the trauma and melodrama of half a lifetime. But there wasn't. The symmetry was perfect, and in the mornings when he shaved, as he smelled the soap and lotions and dipped into the hot water like a religious ceremony, he stared at the separate parts of his face, as well as the assembled whole, in sheer wonder that it had come through the chaos and melancholy, the violence and tragedy, without a telling mark. It wasn't vanity, because he hadn't earned his looks. It was surprise at the injustice. He never really believed that the attractive face gazing back from the mirror belonged to him. How could it? For one thing, he knew the ugly secrets that lay under that faultless mask.

Afterward, he brushed his teeth again.

The clothing was laid out on the bed. Fresh underwear. A clean shirt. Another of his score of hand-fitted $1,500 Italian suits. The shoulder holster with the .9-millimeter automatic went on before the tie so that the necktie would blend in with the creases of the shirt. The ankle holster with the .25-caliber Smith and Wesson went on before the shoes. The extra ammunition clips went into his attache case. He stood for a moment examining himself in the full-length mirror. He made some movements, raising his arm, lifting his leg, but nothing was exposed. His weapons were well-hidden. Then he called the Task Force and got Lieutenant Bill Lukash, his supervisor.

"You're still on vacation," said Lukash.

"Just checking in," said the detective.

"You picked a good time."

"How come?"

"We lost Mario last night," said Lukash.

"No shit! I'm willing to bet he didn't slip in the bathtub."

"It was definitely not an accident. Real professional. Go buy a paper, have breakfast. Don't worry about it. How's the vacation?"

"It's family, you know? Going to see my mother in a nursing home. She thinks I'm one of the attendants."

"Listen, Tommy, it's a blessing. She don't know. Only you feel the pain."

"My fucking asshole brother, Christ! He still blames me for putting her in the home."

"You had no choice, Tommy."

Tommy Day could tell that his supervisor wasn't listening anymore. Not in detail. He was moving paper, reading reports. Which is exactly what Tommy Day intended. To lull him into inattention.

"Couldn't leave her here alone . . ."

"No. No. Listen, Tom, I got people here, go buy a paper and catch up and call me back. I'll give you a fill. When do you get back?"

"Monday."

"Talk to you."

He took the pet carrier for the cats, then decided against the wraparound cashmere overcoat. Someone might remember, connect it. It was remote, but you never know. He wore the Burberry with the liner. He engaged the double locks, patted to make certain again that he had his keys, then left the apartment in the brownstone on West 95th Street.

It was a jittery moment on the Upper West Side of Manhattan. Eleven-thirty in the morning. Getting close to lunch time for the homeless; a soft shape of a line was beginning to form out of the clump of derelicts outside the soup kitchen that faced Tommy's apartment entrance on 95th Street. Every time he left his home, they were there, looking up at him with their expressions of defeated anger.

Men wandered back and forth, circled, established their presence, checked the turnout, calculated whether or not there would be large portions or even seconds. But they were not yet in line. Not officially. Once the line was established, men defended their spots. Sometimes, they fought with

knives over a place in line. They had little enough else to
fight over. Women, on the other hand, were given extra privileges. There was still an odd semblance of chivalry among
the homeless. Women were courted and teased; the broken-
down, unwashed toothless hags flirted with the men of the
streets, and spots which could cost a man his life were turned
over to them like bouquets.

Tommy Day watched them as he waited for his car in the
garage near Broadway. The scabby crowd stamped their feet
up and down, blew on their hands to keep warm. As it grew
closer to the time the door would open, their gaze grew
sharper. Soon it would not be possible to wander up close to
the front and claim a place. The line was growing hard.

Juan, the garage attendant, looked out with smoldering
hatred at the soup kitchen crowd. He had complained to Pastor Harold Morris, who ran the kitchen, about the men and
women who snuck into the garage when he was up on the
higher floors and defecated in the corners.

"Yes," said the pastor, an old timer who was beyond all
shock, "they have very little choice, you see."

"But they chit!" Juan had said. "In the garage!"

"Poor men," the pastor had murmured, missing the attendant's point.

"Listen, I have to clean it up!"

"Yes, oh, well, I do see your point. I am sorry."

"Why don't they chit in the damn church?" the baffled
attendant had asked.

"I don't really know," said the pastor, as if it was a good
question.

The attendant kept a metal pipe in the office, to chase off
the homeless he found trying to sneak into the garage. No
matter how many he chased, no matter how diligent he was,
every morning there were two or three piles of excrement on
the floor of the garage. He had tried a pooper scooper to
clean them up, but they didn't make them big enough for
humans, and by the time he got to it, the piles had adhered

to the floor and he was forced to use old newspapers and boiling, sudsy water to clean them off. The attendant would have quit his job, but he had a secret fear that if he did, he wouldn't be able to land another and he would wind up homeless, waiting on a soup kitchen line like the unwashed mass across the street.

"You have a cat, Mr. Day?" he said to Tommy, noticing the pet carrier.

Tommy looked down as if he were surprised to find the object in his hand. "Oh, yes," he said, slightly flustered.

"I got a dog," said the attendant.

"Well, I'm not home too much."

The attendant was looking across the street at the ragged, sullen line of homeless. "A mean son-of-a-bitch," he said. "Bite the ass off anybody." He looked at Tommy and smiled.

Tommy drove a Jeep. One of those high, off-the-road vehicles that was supposed to operate well on beaches and in untracked jungles but was, in fact, a delicate machine that would break down on a rough stretch of highway. Still, it gave Tommy pleasure to ride above the usual traffic, to look down and see the exposed thigh, the intimacies of the rest of the cars on the road. People were either shameless and didn't care what he saw—and there were scenes even he had trouble believing between men and women, and sometimes even between men—or else they were prim and paranoid.

Tommy drove east, out to the F.D.R. Drive and then along the Cross Bronx Expressway. He stopped on Third Avenue and moved the Jeep under the elevated girders. Trying to move in that street was like trying to walk in Calcutta—delivery trucks and double-parked cars were so thick and the noise was so deafening that life seemed packed in an endless, noisy gridlock. Tommy left the car in front of a hydrant, put his Police Department "Official Business" sticker on the dashboard, grabbed his pet carrier and walked briskly into the Bronx Animal Shelter. It was a chipped, off-white building crowded between auto body shops. The sound of crunching, blasted metal shook the walls. The receptionist was a pregnant black woman who was getting the last use for a while of a tight-fitting uniform.

"Detective Day, hey! hey! What do you say?"

He forced a smile. "Yo disey nada," he replied.

She had already grabbed the carrier through the sliding bullet-proof window and vanished into the back of the shelter. Two women who had been waiting for their turn smoldered. Tommy had broken the line, and even though he was a detective—which was why he got the greeting he got from the receptionist—and maybe even because of it, the people ahead of him were not pleased. "This is a police emergency," he said pleasantly, trying to turn the mood around. "Couple of cats wanted by the police." Neither of the women smiled. "Felonious felines," persisted Tommy, and still the faces of the women were frozen in anger at his privilege.

"Got three for you, to-day, De-tective Day," said the receptionist, opening the double-locked, bullet-proof door to hand him back the carrier—and even the suspension of the usual precautions annoyed the waiting women who knew that the bulletproof door would never unlock for them. "You got good homes for them?"

"The best," replied Day, hurrying out, because even a police sticker in the windshield didn't guarantee a car in this neighborhood. "Real cat lovers."

There was still a lot of traffic crossing the Bronx, even on a winter Saturday, but Tommy didn't mind. He had plenty of time. He drove past the tenements and public housing and drew his usual amount of pleasure from them. Nice not to be poor. Cozy. Tommy thrived on his perks and privileges, and the misery of the poor served to heighten his enjoyment. After all, he had once been poor, the child of a drunken lout. Tommy's childhood memories—memories he tried to blur— were sour. The sound of a fist hitting flesh, the sight of blood spurting from his mother's nose. His brute father standing over her, breathing hard, maybe about to punch her again, maybe done. Tommy was eight and cringing on the floor with his ten-year-old brother, Bill, and the sight of blood on his mother's face made them both sob.

"Oh, crying for the bitch!" and then his father turned his metal belt buckle on his sons. Live through this, he knew, even then, even that young. Soon his father would vanish again into that world of drinking and gambling and whoring, emerging after a few months, when he had a job, to board with the family. He never stayed more than a week, and even those few days deteriorated, after an initial moment of euphoria, into a hellish wait for the next explosion of temper.

Jack Day was a construction worker, or at least that was the grand title he gave himself. His trouble, he explained when he was sober enough and had the inclination to offer an explanation, came from the fact that his work was seasonal. He said that he took it hard when he was between the seasons, being the professional that he was. One day Tommy had to go down to his construction site and pick up some money—the family was on the threshold of eviction and the cash was required instantly—and his father was fetching coffee for the true construction workers, the trained men who worked on the high iron. It was a shock, seeing his father running errands, doing such a lowly job; Tommy was filled with hatred and pity and shame. The great household bully was nothing but a menial laborer—not even that, a gofer. The universe collapsed in upon itself. From that moment, his father was never the towering threat that evoked terror in his heart. But, then, all the boundaries and borders of his life were suddenly diminished. Even his mother seemed somehow less substantial, taking a beating from such a puny man. She should have been beaten by a monster, not a cur. Tommy was never humble after that. He was entitled to stretch, and thus he sought to afflict the world with his own measure of tyranny and fear. He wanted at least as much as a man who ran for coffee for construction workers.

*   *   *

City Island was separated from the mainland of the Bronx
by a small bridge, and the people who crossed that bridge
were watched by a small pocket of self-appointed neighborhood vigilantes. They did not stop blacks at the border,
but they kept them under surveillance until they finished
their business and returned to the Bronx across the same
bridge. There were restaurants and fishing boats and some
few residential neighborhoods in City Island, but above all,
the business of the people who lived there was security.

Tommy, who was known, stopped at a deli and bought a
ham and cheese sandwich and a bottle of water.

The house Tommy rented was remote, and the bay lapped
at the dock a few yards from the house. There were occasional floods when the drains couldn't keep up with the rain
and storms, but Tommy didn't rent the house to keep dry.
He had a small Boston whaler in the garage, some changes of
clothing in the closets, some money hidden in secret nooks in
the walls, along with some extra guns and ammunition.
There were navigation maps in the desk, as well as flashlights
with new batteries. The inside of the house smelled of wet,
moldy paint. A summer smell, even in winter. He put his
sandwich and water into his briefcase. He shivered out of his
suit and changed into jeans, a work shirt and boots. Then he
put on a leather jacket and a knit cap and got the whaler out
of the garage. He rolled it down to the water and secured it
to the dock. Then he went back to the house and fetched his
animal carrier and his briefcase.

There was a spare can of gasoline and the tank was full.
Tommy made certain that the oars were latched onto the side
of the boat and that the flotation vest was in the locker. The
engine kicked over after two jolts of the starter, and Tommy
rode into the waves out into the bay. The water was cold,
blowing in his face, and he could taste the salt of the ocean.

There was an old sandbar three-quarters of a mile off
shore. It was on the charts, but out of the shipping lanes.

Just an acre of sand and scrub where fishermen sometimes
picnicked. Tommy made certain that it was empty, circling
it twice, before he nudged the bow onto the beach and
dropped the anchor, pulling the boat up close inshore because the wind was strong without the breaks of trees or
buildings. He opened his briefcase and loaded his .9-milli-
meter pistol. Fifteen rounds in the clip. The action was oiled
and smooth. Then he attached the silencer to the front. One
of the new, smaller and more efficient models. It cost three
times what the gun cost. He strapped a pair of high-powered
binoculars around his neck.

The gun in one hand and the animal carrier in the other,
he got out and walked across the sandbar. There were wrap-
pers and empty beer cans in the sand. And thin disposable
plastic needles. They were probably also on the moon, he
thought.

At the far end of the island, he stopped, laid down the
carrier and, with the gun in one hand, searched the horizon
in a 360-degree arc. There were no witnesses. Then he
opened the pet carrier a crack and reached in and grabbed
one of the cats. It was an alley cat, young, but not a kitten.
Good. He didn't like too small a target. Tossing it away to
avoid the claws, he turned the cat loose. The animal immediately ran off, but there was no place to run. Every time the
cat broke into a sprint, it reached the water line and had to
turn around and make another break for freedom in a new
direction. It might as well have been in a box.

Tommy watched for a moment, to see if the cat established a pattern. Then, as the animal turned, twenty yards
away, he lifted the .9-millimeter, took it in the combat grip,
and fired one shot. There was a yelp and the cat sank flat
into the sand, the legs splayed out, dead in its tracks.

The second cat, a larger, older animal, ran in circles, a
confused and useless dance. Tommy winged it, knocking out
one of its legs, and the cat let out ear-piercing yowls. Instinctively, Tommy looked around, but realized that the sound

would be swallowed by the wind. He fired two near misses, just to see how the cat would react, then blew off the cat's head with one carefully aimed shot.

The third cat was the strongest. Tommy had been saving this one. He teased it with two shots on either flank and the cat ran as if it could run over the water. And then the cat turned and ran at Tommy. Straight ahead, like a cavalry charge. Tommy got down on one knee, sighted down the barrel, and blew the cat's head apart with the single shot. "Brave cat, I salute you," he said as he gathered up his victims by the tails and threw them into the ocean—a burial at sea. He boxed the compass again, making certain that no one had seen, then checked the time. He had an hour. He ate his sandwich and drank his water and then he got into his whaler and headed to his rendezvous.

5

Inspector Monahan was sitting in his habitual midtown coffee shop on Madison Avenue, talking to the waitress, Shirley. She was one of those middle-aged, dyed-blonde coffee shop mothers who know, after three mornings, what it is you take in your coffee. She spoke with unguarded plainness because she knew that she could not be fired, so rare was her willingness to perform the gruelling tasks of her job.

"You know, we got crack dealers coming in for coffee? You can tell. They got this wild, gimme-coffee-or-I'll-kill-ya look." She shifted her feet like a typist hitting a margin release.

Monahan shook his head, smiling ruefully.

"I'm tellin' ya, Ray, it's getting bad. They had to fire two cooks last week. Found them sneaking into the john with crack pipes."

"I'll speak to the precinct commander. Maybe they can put some undercover people in the area."

"I'd be real grateful, Ray, 'cause I'll tell you the truth, I'm seriously thinking of moving to Florida. Except I'm sure it's no better down there."

"Probably worse."

"That's what I say, probably worse. So what's a body to do? I got so that I carry a whistle. Now what-in-hell's a whistle gonna do when some crack fiend is grabbin' my purse?"

Jack came in. Monahan looked up and saw him check his watch and motioned to come and join him.

"Am I late? I thought you said 3:30, Inspector," Jack began. It was 3:15.

"It's okay, I'm always early," the inspector said.

Shirley poured coffee automatically, left another napkin, then moved off discreetly.

"You feeling better?" asked the inspector.

Jack grinned. "Shaky. Very, very shaky."

They drank for a moment. Shirley stopped by and left a grilled cheese sandwich for the inspector and a prune Danish for Jack. "On the house," she said. "Any friend of the inspector." Monahan gave a look of reproach. "It's okay, it's yesterday's Danish. They'd just throw it out."

"Oh, that really sounds appealing," groaned Jack.

They ate and drank and there was no palpable tension. Usually when Jack sat with a boss he felt the twin emotions of resentment and fear. Neither emotion was conducive to swallowing. But Monahan seemed decent. A fair man.

"I looked up your folder," said the inspector, finishing his sandwich, washing it down with his coffee.

"I don't usually get drunk."

"I know."

"It was just too much of a shock, about my wife. Although I knew it was coming. I shouldn't have been surprised."

"My wife was killed in a car wreck."

"I'm sorry."

"It was years ago. Feels like this morning. She was every-

thing." Monahan paused and sighed, then went on. "After-
wards, I fell apart. Took a month off, got drunk and stayed
that way." Jack shook his head, to show he understood.
"Worst thing I could have done," Monahan added. He leaned
on the table. "I dwelled on it. I had nothing else to think
about, nothing else to think about."

"Yes, well, my wife's not gone yet."

"I know. I know. It's very hard. I'm sorry. I just wanted
to offer some help."

"So this isn't to ream me out over last night?"

"Listen, Officer Mann, inspectors don't bring you to a coffee shop to chew you out."

Jack laughed. Finished off his Danish. Shirley was there to
fill up the coffee cup. He had something to bring up to the
inspector. "The thing last night, you know, there was something funny about it," said Jack.

Monahan shook his head. "Not ours. It's a Task Force job.
Forget it."

"I hate those guys."

Jack hadn't meant to say it. Monahan's eyebrows shot up.
"Sorry, sir, that just slipped out."

"This a day off?"

"Yes, sir."

Monahan started to fish into his pocket to pay the check.

"Look, Inspector, there was something all wrong about
that scene last night."

"Yeah, a cop got drunk."

Jack blushed. "I'm serious. Will you take a second?"

Monahan settled back, motioned for Shirley to top off his
coffee cup.

Jack bent over, making certain no one was listening. "The
shelves and counters in the market, they were a mess."

"So?"

"Well, first of all, it was a very neat market. A lot of care
went into the display. I was sitting there and with my condition and all, I had my head down and I could notice some

things. There were shelves that were wrecked. But not all
the shelves. Like someone grabbed some of the food. Very
selective."

"Coulda been a struggle."

Jack shook his head. "It was selective. No one went after
cleaning fluid or paper towels. A struggle would have been
random. This was like someone grabbed food."

"Maybe someone did some shopping right before the
homicides."

Again Jack shook his head. "I know the market. I stop
there sometimes. I knew the owner. Fastidious. As soon as
you buy a melon, they're at work, fixing up the display.
They're like the French. Very fussy about the display."

"So what are you trying to imply?"

"Well, from what I heard, this guy who was killed was a
mob stoolie. He's not going in to shoplift a market. I also
hear that he was a very worried man. Called for security."

"The Task Force knows all this," said Monahan, waving
his hand.

"This guy was working for the Task Force. How are they
supposed to investigate the murder?"

Monahan stood up abruptly. He dropped two singles for
Shirley's tip and left the exact amount of the check at the
cash register. Jack followed him outside.

"Listen, Officer Mann, you have undergone a great
shock." Jack started to say something, to object, but Inspector Monahan held up his hand. "Your judgment right now is
not the best. Your observations last night were impaired.
You couldn't even walk a straight line, much less make text-
book observations."

"Sir, there was something else, although right now, I can't
put my finger on it."

"Little green men?" asked Monahan pleasantly.

They were standing on the sidewalk. Detective Toladano
stood at the car door, far enough away so that he couldn't
hear. Monahan continued:

"I hate to burden you with reality, but you are a plainclothes police officer, long overdue for promotion, with an enormous personal crisis. What you saw or what you didn't see, well, who knows. I'm not crazy about the Task Force myself. But it's their case and if you have any pertinent information, give it to them. Call Lieutenant Lukash. Call the Task Force prosecutor, Marvin Sanders. But don't go freelancing. That's an order."

Jack watched him duck into the car and drive off. For some reason he felt a curious fondness for the hard-nosed inspector. He liked it that Monahan had friends like Shirley. He liked it that the inspector had an aversion to the Task Force. And he didn't feel the chilling restraint of higher command. In spite of the direct order, he knew that Monahan almost believed him. And Monahan liked him.

Jack looked for a working phone kiosk to call his partner, Moe.

It was growing dark when Tommy Day aimed the whaler into the waves and stayed far enough offshore so that he couldn't be seen. He then circled in and docked at an abandoned pier at Throgs Neck in the Bronx. There were guards posted on the dock and on the road. Inside the unwarmed house, Tommy knew, was Don Danielo Iennello, the crime boss of a major chunk of Brooklyn, Queens and the Bronx—an area larger than some countries. Iennello—known among his peers as Joey Sharks, an alias that had some connection to the loan sharks in his employ—was a small, thin man who was said to be ailing. But he was only ailing when he had to appear before investigative bodies, or was summoned to face a grand jury, or was called upon to face a judge in the long series of legal actions that went nowhere, only tying up dozens of investigators, attorneys and stenographers. On his own, away from the planted microphones and Harvard-educated lawyers, Joey Sharks was a fierce, ambitious and randy old man. Despite his outspoken devotion to his sainted wife, who had borne him eight children without a word of complaint over some forty years, Joey Sharks always kept under guard a young, creamy blonde in one of the plush, overdecorated apartments in the luxury buildings he owned under dummy corporations.

Before he was admitted to the living room, Tommy Day had to pass through Joey Sharks's personal metal detector: two faithful killers. Tommy handed over his .9-millimeter, his .25-caliber and the .38 he kept in his attache case. "How ya doin'?" said Frankie-the-Fox, an old retainer.

"I'm okay, Frankie. Who's your girl friend?"

The sidekick, who remained stone-faced, wasn't amused.

"That's Stevie. Stevie, say hi." Stevie didn't open his mouth. "Stevie's in a bad mood," said Frankie. "He don't like the ocean."

"No shit? That's surprising. A lot of you guys end up in the ocean. Burials at sea."

"That's pretty funny, Tommy. Listen, he's waiting."

There were four men in the room, their hands hidden inside large overcoats. Tommy was sure each had an automatic rifle under the coat.

Joey Sharks was sitting on a couch, one of the few pieces of furniture without a sheet, sipping whiskey from a large glass. On an end table within reach of the Don was a thick envelope.

He nodded and Frankie-the-Fox, who trailed Tommy into the room, ushered him into a chair across from the couch. Frankie left the sheet on the chair.

"Give my friend a drink and then take a walk," said the old man in a surprisingly strong voice. Then he looked around. "Matter of fact, take all the boys for a hike."

Tommy looked around, wondering if there were microphones and if there were, whose they were.

He and the Don sat quietly while the men filed grudgingly out; they didn't like to leave the boss, even if he wanted to be left. It was not simply the call of duty. It was the aphrodisiac of strength. The Don radiated raw, unpredictable power. He nodded his head and men's lives changed. He smiled or frowned and the sky opened or closed on whomever he devoted his attention. It was fun to watch such rampant authority, if you had nothing at stake.

Tommy thought he recognized some merriment in the Don's face, as if he was amused by the man-made foolishness of the situation. The Don sipped his whiskey.

When they were alone, the Don stared out at the white-caps on the ocean for a while. Tommy knew better than to initiate a conversation. Patience was a test. When you lived as close to the margins as the Don—with mob contacts and legal assassins behind every bush—a certain detached suspicion was essential. The Don could not afford to be careless or predictable or sentimental, although he pretended to be all of these things.

Tommy resisted the temptation to look at his watch, even though he knew that the glass was falling and night fell quickly in winter and he might end up stranded in Throgs Neck.

The Don turned away from the window and smiled at Tommy Day. It wasn't a friendly smile, but neither was it dangerous, not one of the last smiles you'd ever see on the face of the earth, bestowed on dead men. It had its internal reasons, but Tommy felt safe in smiling back.

The Don turned to the end table and lifted the envelope. He offered it and Tommy leaned halfway and took it. If the agreement held, there was $50,000 in the envelope.

"Forty-five," said the Don, looking away.

Tommy understood. The Don had kept five for himself. It was an old habit. He couldn't help himself. The man was a thief.

"You did good," said the Don, gazing out of the window. "You know, in Bari, back in Italy, my family are fishermen." He spoke slowly, although how much truth was contained in what he said was impossible to judge. "Twelve generations, fishermen. A boat handed down to the eldest son and he hands it down to his son—just like royalty. Little dinky boat and my brother stayed behind to get the boat. Now I could buy him a fleet of boats but he won't see me. I come there and he locks his door against me. You know why? Not because of my business interests. He thinks I want to steal his boat."

The Don emptied the glass of whiskey, slapped his knee, then got up and stretched. He held his hand out so that Tommy wouldn't feel compelled to join him.

"I think we shouldn't meet anymore," said the Don.

Tommy took a swallow of his own whiskey.

"I think you are too important. You have a big future. What are you, thirty-two, three, what?"

"I'm twenty-eight, Don Iennello."

"See, I was right. You are young and smart and you have the heart of a snake." It felt like a kiss. "That's not a bad thing," said the Don, turning, looking him in the eye. "To have the heart of a cold-blooded animal is a big advantage to a young man who wants to make his way in today's world. You think these financial geniuses on Wall Street, you think they are not cold-blooded snakes? I wouldn't turn my back on any one of them."

The Don walked over to the table and poured himself some more whiskey. He sipped some more, and took the glass to the window. Tommy saw that the chop was getting worse.

"I have something in mind for you."

"I appreciate how much you've already done, Don Iennello."

The Don waved it away, although he had invented Tommy's career on the Police Department. He had taken an instant liking to Tommy the day his son brought him home. The Don's son, Favio, was a hopeless junkie and Tommy, at loose ends, going from job to job, committing small crimes to keep himself fed and a roof over his ailing mother, recognized an opportunity. He became Favio's friend: the only one who did not shoot drugs. The Don understood—he seemed to grasp situations instantly, it was his genius—took Tommy aside and asked him to keep an eye on Favio, do whatever he could. The Don had shrugged. He didn't expect much; he knew what kind of an assignment he was handing Tommy. Still, he said, do your best, I don't expect miracles. And one night, Tommy, who could not keep his friend clean, turned Favio into the police for possession of dealer-weight heroin. The authorities were amazed at the courage of this 19-year-old youth who informed on the son of a major Mafia leader. They said he wouldn't live through the week.

But the Don was surprisingly grateful. Going to jail was the only thing he hadn't tried to straighten out his son. And it was then that the Don dreamed up the idea of Tommy becoming a cop—"our cop." Using some influence, he got Tommy appointed to the next class at the Police Academy. Tommy became an efficient and obedient Mafia cop. He was given informed tips about major drug buys, he solved baffling murders, he quieted unruly neighborhoods. He became the youngest gold-shield detective in the New York City Police Department. His move up to First Grade was astonishing, unless you knew that a small army of criminals was helping him along, pointing him in the right direction to crack a case, leaning on their own informers, then passing the tips along to Tommy.

No one knew that he was, in fact, working for the Don, although a few perceptive men on the force detected a subtle hand guiding Tommy's career. But their suspicions were never acted upon. For one thing, Tommy was Irish and the Italians did not trust the Irish enough to admit them to the inner sanctums of the mob. For another thing—and this was no small item—Tommy was winningly handsome. The senior members of the police department could not believe that a kid with his movie-star looks, with so much glittering in

front of him, would go bad. They didn't know that he had
started out bad.

For his part, Tommy discreetly assisted the Don. When an
important mobster's child had been running wild, committing crimes and about to be arrested, Tommy had arranged
for the youth to surrender to him. It was a shrewd move.
The kid would surely have cracked under hard questioning,
but the Police Department rule was that the arresting officer
had ultimate control over who questioned his prisoner.
Tommy, as the arresting officer, made certain that the questioning was narrow and safe. The mob made certain that
lawyers and bail were provided. Whatever the youth had to
tell remained untold because while he was out on bail, despite some regrets on the part of his biological family, he was
murdered and dumped in a landfill. The authorities assumed
he had jumped bail and was on the run.

And then there came the time when the Don said that they
needed a big favor. One of the ranking members of the crime
family had committed an unpardonable offense. He had
openly trafficked in heroin, thus bringing disgrace, along
with negative publicity and public condemnation, upon the
mob. The sinner had to be punished. He had to be killed.
He was willing to surrender to a cop, because he wanted to
be safe from mob reprisals. The surrender was arranged on
Staten Island, and Tommy—by then a trusted member of
the Organized Crime Task Force—was to bring him in. Afterward, Tommy's partner, an old sweat named Peter
Bucholz, swore that the mobster drew a gun when they tried
to take him. Bucholz made a statement under oath that only
Tommy's quick reflexes prevented them both from being
killed. Tommy was given a high police medal for his heroic
act. Bucholz retired and went to live in Europe, where he
suffered a fatal car crash a year later.

When Tommy came to the Don and told him that one of
his own trusted lieutenants—a man Tommy had luckily
avoided meeting—was making incriminating tapes for the

Task Force, the Don had ordered him killed immediately. Tommy was given the assignment. He was forced to kill the two Koreans, as well, but that couldn't be helped. Murder was a sloppy business.

"Listen, Tommy, there are good things ahead for you."

"I'm doing fine, Don Iennello."

"Sure. But you can do better. Let me tell you, I was a small captain running a small crew in Brooklyn and one day the Don took me aside and he asked me, do I like the job. Sure, I said, I like the job. I'm happy. So he tells me, the Don, that I should look behind me because there are people in my own crew who would like my job. He shrugs. That's the way it works. Someone wants your job. You want to be the guy ahead of you. If you don't, they'll run over you quick."

"You want me to do something, Don Iennello?"

"I want you to run for Congress," said the Don.

Tommy was shocked. He had no education, beyond high school. He had a secret life. He was a murderer for the mob.

"You could be a senator," said the Don. "Not now. Later. After you're a congressman. People love a hero cop. Isn't that what the newspapers call you, 'Hero cop'?"

Don Iennello touched something. Tommy knew that he had gifts—looks, courage and a deep cynicism that allowed him to do anything. He thought he was making the most of his talents. But now he thought, maybe I could do more. Maybe there are better, cleaner ways. The Don had labor connections. Union leaders were in his pocket. Tommy had seen them when they came to grovel. The Don had social connections. He could travel with celebrities, he could raise money. It was possible, thought Tommy! He could become a politician. Sit in Congress. Exercise raw power. . . .

"Let's take a walk," suggested the Don, rising heavily from the couch. Once they were outside, in the wind where they were safe from microphones, the guards moved into blocking

positions to defend the Don. They stood on the dock and felt
the sting of the water in the air.

"There is something you have to do for me," said the Don,
taking Tommy's hand and squeezing it with surprising
power, looking him in the eye. "This fucking Sanders, he
wants to get me. He wants to be mayor and if he gets me,
he'll be mayor. He has people working day and night to put
me in jail. If he tries hard enough, he'll do it. I'll tell you the
truth, I don't want to go to jail." He smiled at Tommy, as if
he were making a joke.

"You want me to kill him?"

The Don looked out at the sea. His voice was soft, but
clear. "Whatever it takes."

It was a breathtaking order. To kill a United States Attorney would bring down a lot of heat. Unless . . .

"I'll take care of it, Don Iennello," said Tommy finally.

"Good. Good. I knew that I could count on you. Now, we
cannot see each other again. I will get word to you, when it's
safe, how and when we begin the political business. Just
make sure you don't fuck it up, this Sanders business."

Tommy stopped the Don. "What's my party? Am I a Re-
publican or a Democrat?"

The Don shrugged. "Let's see what looks good. You could
even be a Liberal."

6

Bonnie Hudson was reading the latest Associated Press update on what had come to be called the Korean deli murder case when the soundman burst into the Channel 9 wire room and said that she was wanted on the set. "They're looking for you, Bonnie," said Max Gross. He had taken a fatherly interest in the new young weathergirl.

"Who, Max?" she shot back in her mock-interrogative style. "Exactly who are these mysterious people in search of me, and what is their evil intent? Hmmmm?"

"It's the news director. He's starting to turn a slightly different shade of purple because he hasn't found you and the weather segment is coming up in three minutes."

The short, dark-haired woman in the high-fashion gray business suit, which failed to mask a certain ripe undercurrent, gathered up her long wire story, getting ink smudges on her hands and, as she brushed away a strand of hair, on her face as well. It seemed to belong there, for despite the obvious taste of her outfit, this was a woman who had no time or patience for endless grooming. She was too busy to be neat.

"So if I say a storm is brewing, it can be taken as a metaphorical allusion to the nervous state of the crew on the early afternoon news program," she nattered as Max ushered her out of the wire room and onto the set. They arrived during a commercial break.

"Oh, dear!" cried the makeup chief, Lonnie Parks, seeing the ink smudges on what he termed the "on-air talent." "We'll have to do something about that!" If she had been leaking from a breast he couldn't have been more horrified.

A voice from the control booth, barely in control, boomed over the set: "Are we going to have a weather segment for the viewers, Bonnie? I ask that because this station depends on viewers. The sponsors insist on it, and as a matter of fact, so do the station executives."

"You bet!" cried Bonnie, who still didn't know how loud to reply to the offstage voice of the director, being relatively new to television. Until six months ago, she had been a crime reporter on a local newspaper, and she retained a hostile attitude towards the preening stars of television news. She also missed the crime beat, and every interesting homicide made her envious and angry. She should be there. She should be hunting in alleys, finding meaningful clues, tracking down killers, instead of letting some makeup artist wipe ink smudges off her face. The Korean deli murder case set her off like an old firehouse dog.

But the money was good in television—she hadn't missed a rent payment since she began—and management liked her. She was "cute" and "sexy" and viewers seemed taken by the way she delivered the weather—with a touch of impatience and subversion and a complete lack of reverence and enthusiasm, a crosscurrent to the perky weather people on the other stations. "Listen," she said to the viewers at the end of every broadcast, "it's only weather." It had become a signature, a catchy phrase about town. When someone ran into obstinate clerks or bureaucratic gridlock, they defused their anger by remarking, "It's only weather."

The two anchors, indistinguishable apart from gender, were chuckling over what they termed Bonnie's "unprofessional attitude." The sports reporter, Conrad Stone, a lunkhead who thought that his borough accent made him a populist hero, was shaking his head and putting his thumb down. "Listen," he hissed impatiently just before they went back on the air, "we got a game at the stadium tomorrow and lots of plain people would like to know what to wear."

"In your case, I'd say a muzzle," she hissed back, assembling her pointer, reading over the text she had prepared before the program. "Well, stick around, buster, and we'll see who gets what, when, where, and how. Is that the five W's of weathercasting?"

Conrad Stone looked completely ready to go ballistic.

"Five, four, three, two . . ."

"And now, here's Bonnie Hudson with today's forecast."

"Thanks, Chuck. Well, it looks like a lousy day for football tomorrow. The weather should be crisp and cool, in short, perfect football weather, but the Titans are still stuck with Davy Smith at quarterback and everyone knows, he's not so hot. I'd say the Titans are gonna stay out in the cold."

Conrad Stone started bouncing in his seat. Who was this smart ass snip to start doing sports on the weathercast? Did she know a thing about passing patterns or pocket defense? Did she even care that poor Davy had a bad drug problem and all the sports people were doing their best to keep it quiet so maybe he could pull himself together? She'd probably broadcast it, the dumb bitch!

"We have a bunch of highs and a bunch of lows, but essentially we are in the grip of winter, folks, and that usually means outerwear as well as underwear. Tonight 30's and maybe 20's. Tomorrow may go up to the 40's, which I believe is the average age of our Titan ballplayers, isn't that right, Conrad? . . . But, hey! Listen, it's only weather."

The camera switched to Conrad Stone who was sputtering and trying to form a comeback. His fist was clenched and pounding on the desk. "We're gonna kill the damn Lions!" he cried. "Dumb broad!"

Bonnie Hudson was pleased that this last went out over the air. Banter television was now getting a little sizzle.

After the broadcast, the managing editor called her into his office. Harvey Levy was an old newspaper hand—or such was his conceit; in fact he had been kicked off the copy desk of *New York Newsday* for overusing gerunds in headlines after he had been warned—however, he recognized and appreciated the nub of reckless insubordination in Bonnie Hudson. He had hired her to lend spice and a touch of danger to the broadcast, which had been losing points in the ratings. Her flashes of wit were boosting his numbers, but he wanted to keep her under control.

"Coffee?" he asked.

"You think I need the caffeine?" she asked, sitting across from him.

He laughed. "You sure made Stone's sparks fly," he said.

"The guy swaggers," she said. "He manages to swagger sitting down on the air. How does he do that, Harvey? What's his big secret?"

"I got some decaf."

"No, thanks."

Harvey Levy leaned back and closed his eyes. "Are you happy here, Bonnie?"

"Of course not."

Harvey leaned forward and opened his eyes.

Bonnie opened her hands: "Apart from the fact that television is a superficial glide over the surface of events, lacking all substance and meaning, I just happen to hate whomever I work for. It's nothing personal. A quirk. I don't happen to like the people who sign my paycheck. They think it gives them a ruling interest." She shrugged. "If you were not my boss, I'd probably think you were a prince."

"It's a pretty big paycheck. . . ."

"All the more reason."

"Well, let me put it this way, what are you unhappy about?"

"You know what I want. I want a press card. That doesn't seem so tough, Harv. Not for the managing editor of a news program. I feel naked without one. I'm used to a press card. It gives me the sense of having a press card."

"They don't give weather forecasters press cards, Bonnie," he said patiently.

She sat up. "That's just the point. I don't want to stick to the weather." She laid the AP wire update about the Korean deli murder case across his desk. "I want to chase this one."

Harvey shook his head. "C'mon, Bonnie, you know Ernie's covering that one."

"Ernie has the IQ of the ambient temperature. In centigrade. The man believes what cops tell him! Harvey, you're an old news hound. You know what it's like to smell something. This is a major story. Not some bungled stickup. Something. I got an itch about it. Let me backtrack, see who this guy was. Find out about the Koreans. There's something funny here, Harvey, I know it."

Harvey shook his head. "I can't spare a crew and I won't give you a press card, and I want you on the weather. Maybe later we can try out some other things, but let's get the weather right first, okay?"

Bonnie didn't say anything.

Jack spent the rest of the afternoon with Natalie. He sat in the lounger, the light over his head, and read aloud from *The Great Gatsby*. Although Natalie's eyes were closed, Jack thought she could hear.

"She can't hear you," Mrs. Graham had warned when he sent her away for a few hours.

"I think she can hear," Barry had said; he liked the idea of Jack reading to his aunt. Like his uncle, he was a romantic and thought prayers and sentimental gestures counted for something. "I told her she was getting a chocolate milk shake when I changed the glucose and I could swear she smiled."

Mrs. Graham was a pragmatist. She changed bedpans and inserted needles in slippery veins. She had given Barry a withering look. "I'll be back at 4:30," she said. "I'll have some tea and take over again at five. Leave the scones," she said, directing the warning at Barry. "I bought them and I'll want one for my tea."

Several times Barry had eaten Mrs. Graham's "special treats" and each time she had delivered seething rebukes.

Jack had settled in with his book, speaking softly, looking for some sign of a reaction from Natalie. He read for an hour and it was a pleasure, as if he were stroking her with words, the way he would stroke her hair in the mornings when she slept:

"'I believe that on the first night I went to Gatsby's house I was one of the few guests who had actually been invited,'" read Jack, his feet tucked under him, a glass of water on the table beside him, a tissue in his shirt pocket. Long ago, in their early days together, when she had been trying to explain to him her love of books, Natalie had read to him from *Gatsby*. At first, he had resisted, thinking that books were meant to be read in private, almost secretly, but the radiance of her appreciation, the light of her esteem had made him pay closer attention, made him come to that same plateau of open respect. "'People were not invited—they went there,'" he read now. "'They got into automobiles which bore them out to Long Island, and somehow they ended up at Gatsby's door. Once there, they were introduced by somebody who knew Gatsby, and after that, they conducted themselves according to the rules of behavior associated with amusement parks. Sometimes they came and went without having met Gatsby at all, came for the party with a simplicity of heart that was its own ticket of admission.'"

He jumped when Barry shook his arm. "It's for you," said his nephew quietly. "The phone."

He looked over. Natalie was still asleep. Her face was in a neutral state of grace, beyond pain and pleasure, in a gentle repose. For an instant, he thought she might have been reading to him. He glanced at his watch, trying to orient himself, as if the time would explain to him whether Natalie heard, but it was only a watch and it registered ten minutes to five. Soon, he realized, he would have to bear the unbearable and accept the fact that Natalie could no longer hear him, no longer feel him, no longer correct the mistakes he made in his life.

"The phone, Uncle Jack." He followed Barry, dumb with grief, down to the phone in the living room. Mrs. Graham was sipping her tea and eating her scone, scowling at the two of them as if they'd come to grab her snack.

"Jack Mann," he said, and Barry hovered nearby to hear who was calling.

"How is she?" It was Moe, and Jack waved Barry away. "She's the same, Moe."

"I was thinking," began Moe, "come over for dinner."

"No, really, thanks, I was thinking of doing some work."

"On what? We got no open cases. This is our day off. Come, have dinner. We're having pot roast."

"Thanks, Moe, but Barry's been cooped up in the house and I gotta spend some time with him."

Barry had moved away, but he still heard, and his face lit up.

They drove into Manhattan, although Jack didn't realize that he had a destination until he turned the car into a garage on East 79th Street. Barry didn't ask questions: he was happy to get out of Queens. There was a diner near the southwest corner of 82nd Street on First Avenue, a small sliver of a place easily missed called the Acropolis Diner. A sign in the window said it was open for business twenty-four hours a day.

The waiter became impatient at how long they took with the menu. Finally, Jack, who wasn't hungry, put the menu down and said he would have a bowl of chicken soup and maybe something else afterward. The waiter didn't look pleased. Barry tried to make up for it. "I'll have the soup, a hot turkey sandwich, double order of mashed on the side, with peas, a small green salad, a large Coke, and, oh, yeah, some crackers with the soup."

"What kind of dressing?"

"Russian."

The waiter gave Jack a hostile look, as if to say, now that's the way to order dinner! Jack added: "And some coffee for me."

The waiter smiled at Barry and went away muttering about coffee.

"Whatdja have for lunch?" asked Jack, looking around. The counter was filled with singles, people with books, the kind of people who eat alone on lonely weekends. The five tables in the back—where he sat with Barry—were occupied by old married couples eating in exhausted silence.

"Just a hamburger. Nothing else. I feel like I skipped a meal."

The waiter came with the soup. He spilled a few drops, but he remained sullen and unapologetic. "You know we got a seven dollar minimum at dinner," he said to Jack.

"Then put his salad and Coke on my tab."

"No sharing. Seven dollar minimum."

"Then cancel his salad and his coke and I'll have a salad and a large Coke and a bowl of soup and some coffee."

The waiter, a tall, bone-thin man with a dark shadow of a beard, a man in his early 40's growing testier by the day, stood there for a moment, his eyes half-lidded, trying to decide whether or not to push this.

Jack gritted his teeth and changed his tactics. "Bring me a tuna on rye with mayo."

The waiter's expression didn't change. "What about the salad and the Coke?"

"You decide," smiled Jack. "Any way you want to split it up, it's fine with me."

The waiter was unaccustomed to such easy capitulation. He stood there, trying to see the trap. Then, reluctantly, unable to spot the trick, he walked back to the kitchen and flung in the extra order.

They ate quickly for some reason. When he was with Natalie, Jack ate slowly, pausing between bites, speaking about the day's events. On stakeouts, eating was an annoying but necessary function and he swallowed without chewing. Tonight, eating with Barry, who took his meals as if he might be snatched away and better get it in quickly, Jack ate quickly, too. He left half his sandwich and Barry asked if he intended to finish it. "Take it," said Jack.

The waiter came back with the check. Jack asked, before leaving the tip, if the restaurant had been open last night. The waiter pointed to the sign in the window. "Open Twenty-four Hours A Day!" it said.

"Were you here?" Jack asked, trying to sound friendly.

"You lose something?" the waiter asked.

"No. A friend of mine was in here. He said that there was a killing a couple of blocks away."

"Everybody here was working," said the waiter, walking away. Jack stopped him.

"Excuse me, but could I just ask you, did you happen to notice anyone here about that time? It was late. . . ."

"There's always some people come Friday nights, always somebody."

"Did you happen to notice anyone? Anyone in particular?"

"No one. You want something else?"

Bonnie Hudson had been working the west side of the avenue, checking bars and neighbors and people with dogs to see if anyone had seen a killer. At first, she missed the Acropolis Diner, then spotted it as she was about to give up and wait for the late crowd at the singles bars. People gravitated to diners—tugged by regional light and the company of other insomniacs. She understood that recognizable comfort came from the presence over cold coffee of silent watchers, and people found such ports in their stormy nights. Bonnie took a seat at the table in the back of the diner, passing Jack and Barry as they squeezed out. She ordered a plain salad, a yogurt and a diet cola. The waiter liked the look of her, not realizing that he had seen her on television and that familiarity conveyed a kind of friendly aftermath.

"How's the salad?" he asked as she picked at the lettuce.

"Great. Could use some ketchup or mustard. Something."

"You want?"

"No. No. I'm on a diet. That's why I hafta order food I hate. This way I'm not even tempted. You got any fish? I really hate fish."

He grinned.

"Listen, lettuce can't help it," she said with a shrug. "No natural taste. It's like eating paper."

"You're a funny lady."

"You know, I was just gonna say the same thing to you: I'm a funny lady."

"You work in the comedy club? We get a lot of them from the comedy club. Not so funny like you."

"No. Unfortunately I'm an unpaid funny lady. Listen, while we're on the subject, I was at the comedy club last night. And then I was supposed to meet some friends in here. You didn't happen to see any of my friends in here last night?"

"Well, I don't happen to know your friends."

"You tell me who was here at about, say, 10:30, maybe 11," she said, batting her eyelashes.

"Well, we had the usual Friday night people. Mr. Paul, he's an artist, comes in for a late dinner; works all night. Mrs. Timmons, she takes tea after she leaves her lady, the cab picks her up here. A few bums, they come in for coffee, to keep warm. If they have the money. We got our regulars, like everyone. One, he don't seem like a bum. Young, you know. And smart, educated. I hear today that he saw something."

"How do you know?"

"Crazy Edie tells me. She's a bum, too, one of the regulars. She comes in every day for yesterday's rolls. I give her for a quarter maybe five and she gives them to the others in the park. Today she tells me that this educated bum, this Al or something, he sees something in the market. But you know how they are, these people. They make up stories. Makes them feel important."

He shrugged.

"Anyone else? I mean strangers?"

He hesitated, and she could see that he was holding something back. She smiled and took another bite of lettuce.

"One more."

"Stavros!" It was the chef calling the waiter from the kitchen.

"Who, Stavros?"

"A cop."

Then he went to the kitchen and brought some plates out to the other diners.

"How do you know it was a cop?" she asked when he stopped by again.

"I know cops. This one was a cop. Kept looking at the street. Checking his watch. Cops are always checking watches to see how much overtime they got coming. I know cops. Had one in here a minute ago, asking questions. Definitely a cop."

She laughed. "Okay, so what did he look like, this cop?"

"Like a cop," shrugged the waiter. "No, very well dressed. A well-dressed cop. Dressed better than a cop."

"But he was definitely a cop?"

"Like you are definitely a reporter."

7

The Comic Moment club on the east side of Second Avenue near 77th Street had started out its commercial life as a greengrocer, but the vegetable store couldn't support the escalating rent of a bull real estate market. Now the former greengrocer thrived as a comedy club; the owners had no trouble meeting the $12,000-a-month rent, with their high minimums and watered drinks. The snobbish custom of customer exclusion guaranteed success, because there were always those social seekers who wanted to be in the vanguard. The comedy, such as it was, had the ring of a whining, materially-afflicted, narcissistic generation of peevish jellyfish.

The man at the door of the Comic Moment did not recognize Bonnie Hudson—she had a different, more vivid kind of impact in person than she did on television—but he was tickled by some elusive feather of familiarity and opened the velvet rope, letting her skip the line waiting for admission.

"What's her story?" Barry said. He was behind the rope with his Uncle Jack waiting to get in.

"Maybe she's got a reservation," Jack replied, and Barry had to look twice to see if his uncle was joking.

Inside the club, Bonnie staked out a place at the bar and began to study the customers, annoyed that she couldn't just whip out her press card like an honest reporter. "Hi," she said to a tall, blond man in an expensive sports jacket.

"Where have you been all my life?" he said, leering.

"Reading a good book," she muttered, then smiled, and tried her hardest to ask questions that would not arouse suspicion, put him off or, worse, trigger his lust.

"What's your name?" she asked in her best coquette voice.

The blond young man smiled, convinced that his good looks and calculated insouciance had already made the conquest. "Todd," he said. "But you can call me Todd."

"Hi, Todd, my name's Marsha."

"So, Sharon," he said, looking around the room out of habit, seeing if there might be a better opportunity than Sharon, "I haven't seen you in here before, have I?"

"Todd. May I call you Todd?"

"I don't see why not. After all, you won't be the first. That's what my parents called me."

"Are you one of the comedians, Todd? You seem so funny, I'll bet you're one of the acts. Am I gonna see you on stage?"

"No, Sharon, I'm a civilian, like you. Although I have toyed with the idea of getting up there one night. I just don't think, at this point in my life, I'm ready to face any more acceptance."

"You should. You really should." She bit her cheek to prevent herself from adding, "A clown like you should do well here." What she did say, in that sweet, neutral tone, was: "What is it you do do, Todd?"

"Real estate. I turn over apartments, Karen. You looking for a one-bedroom, kitchenette, air, balcony, under three hundred thou?"

"Actually, no. I have a place."

Todd felt a pang of disappointment. The fact was that he

enjoyed his work. Best of all, he enjoyed the unexpected deal. He had a small conversion available and he had been trying to unload it, and even if it cost him a crack at this Laura—was that her name?—it would have been worth it. The bonus. The admiration of the secretaries, the cocky boasts of having unloaded a small albatross, the head-shaking by his peers at his virility in the market—these things mattered to Todd.

Bonnie ordered a wine cooler and he ordered vodka.

The master of ceremonies mounted the stage and an excited shiver ran through the audience. Something was about to begin. The M.C. was one of those aging beach boys, the endless-summer type with a winter tan and the cuffs of his shirt rolled up over the sleeves of his suit jacket. The shirt was open at the collar and worn like cleavage. Bonnie noticed that the M.C. was beginning to develop a paunch. Not much. Not something you'd even notice on someone walking down the street. But up there on the stage, with all that blond, tan effort, she knew that he was aware of it, worried about it, even stayed awake at night regretting his daily calories.

His introductions were intended to be hip, and tinged with enough sarcasm as to be a denial if and when the "act" proved to be bad. "We got a guy here tonight, well, I can't say enough about Jesus Maldenado. Enough said."

The M.C. jumped off the stage, a move that was not as agile as it might have been, and the young comedian, maybe 23, vaulted up. He wore a fixed smile and he was sweating hard. He flipped the microphone from one hand to the other, trying to look cool, managing only to appear frightened.

"How are you all doing tonight?"

They all said it. It was a standard line, a tactic.

"I am Hispanic," said Maldenado. "Which means that I have a close family relationship with roaches. You know what I mean?"

They didn't.

"Lemme tell you, man, Latinos understand roaches. That's because we talk to them in their native language, which is Spanish. At night, when you're asleep, roaches speak Spanish to each other. Check it out. And there are no bilingual roaches, man. You North Americans, you don't even try to get along with them. Kill 'em, that's your attitude. You see these signs they have on the subway for roach killer? This lady—obviously one of the dominant white middle class culture—she says she found a roach on her son's first birthday cake. And she's, like, shocked. What's the big deal? I never even knew that my first birthday cake was supposed to be covered with plain white icing. My parents told me it had raisins on top."

There was, not a gasp, but a shudder that ran through the audience. Then, because they thought that they should be polite to a member of the underclass, slight and scattered applause broke out. "So let me tell you about my BMW," braved Maldenado. "I don't actually own one—they're not allowed to sell them to Hispanic people—but I know about them, which is about the same thing. That's some car, that BMW. You know, I used to think BMW was a designation for a bowel movement by Caucasians. Then I found out it was a car, but man, the way you people carry on about it, I think maybe I was right the first time."

The next comic followed quickly. He was also young, also sweating, but clearly in his element on the Comic Moment stage. His name was David Stein.

"How ya doin' tonight?"

They were doing fine. They were relieved. This guy was gonna kill the roaches. You could just look at the Brooks Brothers jacket and have confidence that there were no insects in his act.

"You know, I spoke to my mom today," he said. "My mom! Lemme tell you about my mom. Any of you folks out there got moms? So you'll appreciate this. My mom mails me food. Not just cans and things, like a CARE package. She mails me home cooking, like pot roast and stuffed turkey. And that's okay, cause she's a good cook, but those envelopes sure do stink!"

The audience was right along with him, on the edge of their chairs, leaning forward, their faces shiny, laughing hard.

"No matter what I say, she mails me food, and you're saying, what's so terrible, lots of moms mail their kids food, right? The thing is, I live at home."

Bonnie didn't want to laugh, but she did. It was hard to resist the mob rule of a comedy club.

"This is not a normal, average, everyday mom. She got mad at Dad and declared her free-agency. She's serious. If she has a good year, she's gone. She's going to the family that offers her a no-cut clause. Going for the big bucks. And you really can't blame her. I mean, here she was batting .320 in the kitchen, and Dad benches her. Takes the whole family out to Friendly's. Well, I took her side in the fight and Dad is really pissed. He's trading me for a kid to be named later."

The sweating comedian named David Stein made his way offstage, trailed by whistles and cheers. His first time out and already the M.C. was jealous, Bonnie noted. A real triumph. The M.C. looked depressed. There was a short break before the next act.

"So, Todd, you didn't say, you come here a lot?"

He gave her a cool look somewhere between a smirk and a smile. "Every now and then, Shari, baby. You?"

"First time."

"A virgin. Really?"

"Be gentle with me, Todd."

The wine cooler tasted of chemical ice.

"So, where is this choice place you have?" Todd asked.

"Fourteenth Street," she replied. "Same building as Bernie Goetz. You remember, the 'Subway Gunman.' Really makes you feel safe. At least on the downtown express."

Todd almost choked. "You are joking," he said. "Fourteenth Street? Is that right? You actually live there!?"

"It's colorful," she said defensively. Fourteenth Street was an open-air market, heavily influenced by drug deals and thieves; female junkies jiggled up and down the block, stopping people for money first thing in the morning, trying to get straight, with terrified infants in their arms, women with babies and eyes as raw as open sores, with men hovering in the background, trying not to queer the pitch, looking shifty and nervous and ready to tear out your heart if begging didn't work.

"Colorful? It is fucking Beirut. You gotta be a graduate kung fu expert, am I right? You into kickboxing? Got your own instructor, teaches you new moves every day? What kind of gun permit you have? Carry? Range? The house? What?"

"All of them, Todd. One for each and every weapon, including the assault rifle."

He laughed.

"Hey, this is not celestial bliss up here, either, pal," she countered. "The fabulous Upper East Side has its downside, am I right? What about those three guys who got snuffed last night on First Avenue?"

"You got a point," he admitted, nodding, holding up his hand for another drink, turning to her, "Want another?" Hers was still three-quarters full. "Still, that was a drug thing or some mob thing or some robbery thing. It wasn't, like, somebody says the wrong thing and people start taking out Uzis and slaughtering innocent people. We don't have suicide bombers and Hezbollah factions. Killings like that do not happen here all the time."

"I'm gonna try to overlook the slur on my native street," she said. "I happen to know that this land of plenty is not perfect. You have, for example, homeless people living up here?"

"Hey! Of course there are homeless people living up here. I wouldn't be in the real estate business if there were no homeless people. What do you think I'm in this for, the lousy commissions? The satisfaction of changing one studio for another with a better view? No, sir! I go to sleep at night knowing that I am providing shelter—one of man's basic, most fundamental needs—to the suffering masses who inhabit the gratings and railroad terminals of our town. I contribute to the solution, my good lady!"

"No, really," she said, "I see a lot of homeless up here, I really do. But I have a question: where do they sleep?"

"There's the park," he said, growing serious despite himself. She was a bummer, this one, he thought. A social conscience, for Christ's sake, on Saturday night! "They live in doorways. There's the shelter on Park Avenue, you know, the Armory. Sixty-seventh. Then there are the private arrangements. Sleeping in alleys behind brownstones. But mostly I'd say the park, by the museum. It's sort of safe because of the police patrols to protect the museum. On the other hand, they get rousted by the cops so it's not perfect."

She was making him depressed; he was here, cruising the club, for someone lighter on her feet. Todd did not like to think about the homeless, whom he regarded as a negative selling point. Whenever he took a client to see an apartment, he detoured around those streets where he knew that the homeless clustered. He never passed the Armory when they were being let out after breakfast. He never passed the softhearted deli owner who cashed in their empty cans and gave them coffee. He kept to the posh Madison Avenue route where the stores had private guards and the streets were always swept clean of eyesores.

"Excuse me," he said, heading for the men's room, heading for open sea.

"You're right about the homeless," said the man on her other flank. "Sorry for eavesdropping."

Bonnie had recognized Todd's intentions, and was glad to expand her investigation.

"How do you know about the homeless, you live up here?"

He was late 30's, she thought, but hard to place otherwise.

Not a businessman. Definitely not an upwardly mobile type. He didn't dress like a seeker of approval; the suit was too thrifty and the shirt was on the verge of being threadbare. He was not a handsome man, not by the classic standards of, say, Todd, but neither was he ugly. The planes of his face were pleasant. He had a nice face, but there was something hard behind the eyes—some knowledge of wisdom or secret.

"I come here," Jack said. He had sent Barry home to look after Natalie—he never entirely trusted Mrs. Graham. "I don't live here. Can't afford it."

Very straightforward, she thought. Very forthright.

"You come to the comedy club?"

He smiled and it broke the ice of his grave expression. "I need a good laugh."

"This is new for you, huh? But you know the area."

"Some things. You?"

She was attractive, he found himself thinking, then was stabbed by the guilt of the observation. He distracted himself by coming back to the case.

She shrugged, held up the glass for another cooler. He held his for another beer. The bartender anticipated them, had the drinks ready, had been watching them. He could read the signs like sailors read the wind: there was something stirring between these two, although like a lot of modern couples, they were twisting away, resisting.

"It's a part of town," she said, lifting her eyebrows.

"There are some derelicts around here," he said.

"More and more," she replied. "If the real estate market is any index, it's gonna get worse." She was thinking of Todd.

"It can't get too much worse," he said, diving through the foam of the beer. He had stashed his wedding ring when he came into the club and felt awful about it. He should be concentrating on the case, the murders, and nothing else.

"Wanna bet?" she said, sipping at her cooler.

They stood together for a while, struck by a wave of awkward silence.

"You know about the murders last night?" she asked.

"I heard about them."

"Did you hear anything about who might have done it? Some rumors? Anything?"

"Have you heard anything?"

"I asked you first."

"What is it that you do?" he asked bluntly. He didn't mean to blurt it out like that, he just did.

"You're a cop!" she said loudly.

He tucked in his head and looked around, embarrassed.

"Why would you say such a thing?"

"Don't bullshit the bullshitter," she said laughing, knowing that she had it right. He was a cop. Local, federal, DA— didn't matter. Underneath that sensitivity and charm, he had the bulldog swagger. Somewhere on his person, she was certain, there was a gun.

"And what are you," he asked, "an insurance agent?"

"What kind of cop are you?" she persisted, lowering her voice.

"I didn't say I was a cop," he hissed at her ear. She had turned her head sideways and was smiling, waiting for his confession. She turned and gave him a scolding look.

"Don't give me that," she said. "Cop. Po-lice. On the job. There's no mistake."

"Why is your voice so familiar?" he said, and she began to blush and try to rearrange the subject.

Just then Todd came back, noticing that the woman he regarded as his date, or at least his conquest, was being pursued by another male. His ego was engaged.

"Hi!" he said, looking at both Jack and Maureen, or whatever it was, insinuating himself back at the bar, making a territorial declaration by planting his elbow on the bar.

"Hello," said Jack, awkwardly.

"You're hitting on my girl," said Todd, grinning.

He was taller than Jack, maybe even a little broader.

"We were just talking," said Jack, his voice low. He knew

enough not to embarrass the man, force him into a physical confrontation. It wasn't Jack's style and it wasn't necessary.

"Oh, you were minding my place," Todd said.

Jack started to speak, but Bonnie pulled Todd around to face her. "Listen, Todd," she said, trying to match Jack's diplomatic tone but failing, "piss off!"

He laughed. "Let me get this straight. You are telling me to piss off? Is that right?"

"Close enough!"

She was sputtering. The people at the bar were all listening. Even the bartender had positioned himself so that he could hear while serving his customers.

"Look," began Jack, putting a hand gently on Todd's shoulder, trying to defuse things.

Todd put a forefinger in Jack's face and spoke boldly. "Listen, asshole, if this cunt prefers you instead of me, if that is the extent of her mental illness, I don't give a . . . Uhhhhhh!"

Jack reached up and snatched the finger. It was a quick move, discreet almost, and no one except Bonnie and the bartender saw the expression on Todd's face change from arrogance to anguish.

"Don't say anything else," said Jack quietly. "Not one more word."

Todd nodded obediently, bending down towards his finger, trying to prevent Jack from breaking it.

"I'm gonna leave now and you are gonna stay here at the bar. If you follow me outside, I promise you'll wake up in an emergency ward. Do I make myself clear?"

Todd grunted. "Yes," he said.

"Would you like to join me for coffee?" he asked Bonnie, and she smiled and said that she would.

The bartender waved off Bonnie's attempt to pay. "On the house," he said, cheerfully.

As they were leaving, as Todd tried to rub some circulation back into his finger, Bonnie turned and said over her shoulder:

"Nice meeting you, Todd."

"I am a cop," he said, nodding, smiling, almost grinning, feeling a little silly.

"Of course you are. I could see that. It was obvious the way you handled yourself."

They were bent over coffee, leaning towards each other across the table at the Acropolis Diner on First at 82nd Street.

"I am also married."

"So?" she said, oddly annoyed. "Why should you tell me that? Lots of cops are married."

She was angry because she was disappointed that he was married and because it was humiliating that he declared his unavailability. That meant he detected her interest.

"And how cold will it be tomorrow?" he asked.

It took her a moment to catch on; he knew that she was a weathergirl.

"We could have an informal agreement," she suggested.

"Like what?" he asked skeptically.

"A pooling of information. Like for instance, I know a few things that maybe could help."

Stavros stood behind them, in the back of the diner, and wondered if they had arranged that he would come in first and make him vulnerable to the girl. Could they be that devious? Americans were not so simple. He refilled the coffee cups and she smiled at him, acknowledging him, and it made him feel peculiarly disarmed.

When they were alone again, she told Jack about the cop who had been at the diner. Stavros had told her, she said, indicating the waiter behind them.

"Did he say what the cop looked like?"

"Handsome," she said. Then smiled. "Lets you off the hook."

"There are some descriptions you don't mind fitting."

Then she told him about the derelict. That seemed to interest him. It struck something. There were two leads to pursue. The derelict was interesting. The derelicts would know some things, some good rumors, even if they didn't know the identity of the killer. It was a place to start. The cop business sounded wrong. Off. Maybe a cop stopping in after work, between jobs. Maybe not. A cop would come forward if he had seen or heard anything. No work to be done there. It was the derelict that had to be found.

"Why is the Channel Nine weathergirl chasing a murder story?" he asked, finally.

She rolled her eyes and threw back her head. "I used to be a police reporter," she said. "On *Newsday*. You know *Newsday*?"

"The Long Island newspaper."

She was always surprised when anyone knew *Newsday*. It was such a local, suburban newspaper. It had no impact in the city. By intent. The editors and managers were suburban types, men who had moved to the suburbs to escape the urban melodrama. The fact that they had to come hat in hand to Manhattan to increase circulation—there was no more expansion possible on Long Island—was a constant source of irritation.

"I loved chasing police stories," she said. "I love newspapers, they're so gritty and unkempt. Crime stories have a beautiful symmetry. Beginning, middle, end. Morality, evil. Everything that goes to make up life."

She blushed.

"So why television? Why the weather?"

"Because newspapers pay badly, and they don't like spunky women who tell them that they're full of shit."

He nodded. Not so different from the Police Department.

They drank coffee, then he said, almost casually, as if it had not been on his mind: "My wife is dying."

He was sorry the minute he said it. He hadn't meant it the

way it came out; it sounded cold. It was just that she seemed
so sympathetic.

"I'm sorry," she said.

He got up, fumbled in his pocket, then dropped two dollars, his share of the check, on the table. He said he would
call her tomorrow, today actually, or later, when he had a
chance to think about things. She wasn't sure what things he
had to think about—whether it was her or the murders.

8

Tommy Day could hear the faraway peal of church bells as he left his car outside of the old factory on Lower Broadway. Once, this district on the tip of lower Manhattan had been crowded with warehouses and garment factories. Now it was government offices, courts, holding pens—a kind of bureaucratic factory mall. The state and federal courthouses, in their Greek revival majesty, marched down Centre Street like some stretch of Athens. The straight, strict towers of the federal and state office buildings standing on Broadway—modern glass and limestone sentinels housing passport offices and senatorial headquarters—left a sour aesthetic aftertaste. Tucked between parking lots was the decaying, peeling old beaux arts factory in which the Organized Crime Task Force occupied one floor.

It was breathlessly quiet in this section of town on Sunday without the heavy chatter of government employees and the weepy denials of indignant family members as their kin were

being swept into court. And Tommy Day could hear the
church bells clearly all the way from Greenwich Village,
summoning parishoners to early Mass. It sounded like a summons from the moon, down here in the canyons of Sunday
silence. Nearby the sick addicts were being plucked from
their weekend holding pens and shovelled like so much trouble through metal, barred doors by tired policemen. Only
the click of shoes, a nervous cough and the endless rattle of
metal handcuffs echoed in the streets. And the wind whis-
tling off of the East River. And the dying, distant call of the
bells.

Tommy snapped open his small leather case with the gold
shield and showed it to the guards on the front desk of the
old factory. He signed in and took the wheezy elevator to the
fifth floor. When the door opened, it was as if an air lock
broke. The whoosh of panic almost drove him back into the
elevator. The bay was packed with more than forty cops.
Men and women were walking briskly with hands full of
urgent reports. Detectives barked impatiently into tele-
phones, trying to force out useful information like someone
squeezing the last bit of toothpaste out of a tube. The squad
room had the look of chaos, but it was deceptive; there was a
rough form of order and discipline amid the turmoil. Assignments were being carried out. Details were being checked.
There were cries across the room. "Lieutenant Korman on
line five!" "Someone get coffee for the sergeant!"

This was the investigation into the murders at the Korean
market. Squads were forming to canvass the neighborhood,
other teams were being organized to investigate the back-
grounds of the victims. Parking tickets were being checked to
see who was there that night. Snitches were being pressured
for rumors. Students of the crime families were asking themselves who stood to benefit from Mario Barone's death.
Could the target have been the Kus? Was it a robbery gone
sour? Was it a coincidence that a Task Force informer was
killed? What were the rumors floating through the back-
waters of the mob?

In the center of the huge bay, where machines once cut out dress patterns, encased in the glass office where the garment manufacturing boss once sat, stood the strike team leader Lieutenant Bill Lukash, a thick man who looked hairy despite the fact that he was balding. Lukash was studying some papers, a cigar stuck in his face like a punctuation mark. Assembled around him, looking worried, were the five senior sergeants assigned to the command, as well as a member of the state police team and two federal agents.

As if he had a sixth sense, Lukash looked up and saw Tommy. He blinked, then motioned him inside.

"I thought you were still on vacation?" Lukash said. The others in the room all looked at Tommy, waiting for an explanation. The organizational chart of the Iennello Crime Family was laid out on Lukash's desk. For an instant, Tommy thought that he had been discovered. But then he knew better. He swallowed his fear, pushed it, as he had taught himself to do, to some far, inactive part of his brain.

"I heard about Highway," he said using Mario Barone's cover name. "I thought maybe I could help."

"Good man," Lukash said, and the others all softened, seeing the reaction of the leader. "Wait outside, I'll give you something to do."

As they bent back into the family chart, with the photograph of the Don at the head and the capos spread out underneath him like corps commanders, and the pictures of the soldiers clustered together and glaring back at the Corrections Department cameras with the same, uniform expression of open contempt, Tommy went back to the coffee machine and took a container of a black mud-like substance.

"Aren't you on vacation?"

Nancy McDaniels was a plainclothes officer, young and deceptively small and uncommonly pretty. She had been in the Task Force for three months and had asked Tommy to dinner twice.

He had been tempted because she was attractive and had an appealing glint in her eye, but the life he led was already pledged. Like liquor, women were dangerous. A man could get careless and sloppy and divulge secrets that shouldn't be told. Tommy found it safer and altogether more relaxing to confine himself to one-night stands with empty-headed bimbos. He had long since accepted a permanent state of loneliness.

"I am," he smiled. "I always come here for vacations. The food is good." He held up the coffee container. "And the company is even better."

"Well, imagine all those silly people who go to Mexico or the Bahamas in the winter," she said.

"A big waste of money," he agreed.

She took a cup of coffee, gagged and shook her head. "So," she said, "how was the vacation?"

He looked up at the ceiling, noticing the dust accumulated into stalactites, then smiled at Nancy. "It was restful," he said.

She nodded and sipped at her coffee. "I got some time coming," she said. "If I don't take it, I lose it. Trouble is, I have no money to go anyplace. I'd rather be working than stay home."

"I could let you have some. . . ."

She held up her hand. "No, no. If I wanted to borrow some money I could always go to the union. I hate being in debt. Can't stand it. No, next year I'm going to Europe. Gonna take some time now and work in Macy's. They always need Christmas help."

"Really? You're gonna do that?"

"Yeah. What's wrong with that? This way I can go to Europe in maybe March or April."

"Listen," said Tommy impulsively, "you wanna have dinner tonight?"

Her eyes widened. "You need a cover?" she asked.

"I need a date," he said, regretting instantly the invitation, seeing four or five arguments against it.

"Oh," she said, her voice dropping miserably, "I can't."

He was surprised, wounded. He wasn't accustomed to rejection. Especially by someone who had already invited him out twice. Maybe she had a boyfriend by now.

"I have to have dinner at my parents' house," she explained, a little embarrassed, as if she were confessing that she was still a baby.

"It's okay," he said, "we all have family obligations."

"I'm sorry," she said. "We do it every Sunday and my uncle Pat is in from California and everybody's gonna be there. I'd invite you to come along but it's really very hard to take. I can hardly take it myself and I'm one of them."

"It's okay, really. . . ."

"Maybe we can do it another time," she said.

"Right. Excuse me."

He turned away and headed to the men's room, a grimy, sticky institutional row of urinals and bare seats. The sinks were filthy and the water dribbled out and there were never enough paper towels. But she couldn't follow him there and he needed to end the discussion. If he let her continue, she would talk herself out of her parents' dinner and he remembered why he had come in early. He didn't need to clutter up his mission by having a woman along.

She was waiting for him when he came out of the bathroom.

"I fixed it," she said, following him into the bay of the squad room. He turned and looked at her quizzically. She nodded. "I called my mom and told her that I'd have to work."

"Nance, call her back," he said. "That was stupid. It's no big deal. We can always have dinner."

"I was just looking for an excuse, Tommy. You don't wanna have dinner, fine. I can manage." She was getting angry, a flare of something in her cheeks.

"Tommy!" yelled one of the sergeants, then threw his head back, indicating the glass office.

"Gotta go," he said and she glared after him.

Lieutenant Lukash was chewing on the cigar, his face still unhappy. He was staring at the first detective reports. "You know how many fucking cases this costs us?" Lukash didn't look up.

"A lot," Tommy said.

"A lot," Lukash said. He hadn't been listening. Then he looked up, saw Tommy's handsome, worried face and smiled. Tommy's looks had a soothing effect in times of turmoil; nothing could go too wrong with a man like that on your side, a man with such obvious fine bones and serious mien. You would think him incapable of an ignoble act, to look at him.

"Tommy, thanks for coming in."

Tommy smiled.

"Listen, kid, we are in a fucking crisis. Someone had a wire in here and knew this guy was ours. I have no idea who. I was more than careful with Barone. Never met him in public. Never brought him in here. Nobody here except a few honchos and Sanders knew he was ours. He was babied like . . . only Sanders was his contact. Did you know that? Fucking Sanders. Barone had a direct line."

Tommy shook his head.

"You never met him, right? You didn't even know him, right?"

"I never met him. He was only a rumor as far as face-to-face," said Tommy.

Lukash slapped the desk.

"See what I mean? It's a fucking sieve." He looked out of the glass walls into the bay, condemning everyone with a smoldering look. "Listen, I want you should go out and tap some of your people. Just put your ear to the rail and listen for a train. Somebody has to know something. Somebody has to hear something. Guys talk. Especially mob guys who sit around with nothing better to do than bullshit each other. So go take a listen, okay? We got troops all over the fucking place and I don't wanna waste you pounding on doors."

Lukash knew that Tommy had grown up on the fringes of crime. He knew that Tommy had rough edges and a crude beginning. He knew that Tommy had some connection with the Iennello Family, but he didn't know the full extent of Tommy's corruption. He didn't want to know the details. The only significant fact to Lukash was that these contacts added to Tommy's value in the task force. Tommy could go places and do things that no one else in the squad could dream of doing.

"How's Sanders taking this?" asked Tommy, standing at the door.

"He's going bonkers. Gonna arrest every Mustache Pete he can lay his hands on. I'm doing my best to calm him down, but the man is having serious problems holding his fucking water. He wants to bring down all the trees in the forest."

Lukash rolled his eyes and Tommy laughed.

"Get outta here."

Jack Mann was sitting on a bench waiting to see Lieutenant Lukash. He'd been waiting for two hours, watching the frenzy of the squad room, waiting for an opening. He saw one cop arrive and his head turned. He thought, well, he's a striking man. Good-looking. But something else bothered him, although he couldn't say what it was. Then Jack saw the gold shield and felt a small twinge of resentment at the youth of the detective. Here he was, forty-two years old, and still a plainclothes officer who could be bounced back to uniform at the whim of any senior commander.

An ungenerous thought, he decided. He sat there and waited, watching Tommy Day come and go, watching the other purposeful members of the force come and go in pairs.

"Officer!" said the sergeant who was acting as Lieutenant Lukash's secretary. Jack leaped up and followed him to the glass office. Lukash had put away all the charts and the reports and was sitting with his hands folded. He stared hard at Jack. Two sergeants stood on his flanks, as if they were bodyguards, exuding an air of menace.

"You were among the first officers to arrive on the scene, is that right?" Lukash's tone had the hostility of an old, impatient interrogator.

Jack told the lieutenant what he had seen, and the lieutenant's head was bent over a notepad. Jack finished by telling him about the rifled shelves and his suspicions.

"Is that it?" asked the lieutenant. "That's the important evidence?"

"Well, there was someone who saw a derelict in the vicinity," Jack said.

"You gotta be kidding! For Christ's sake, somebody saw a derelict? That's news? This city's crawling with derelicts. I got 'em sleeping out front when I come to work in the morning. What are you, fucking blind?"

Jack gave him Stavros's name anyway. The lieutenant wrote it down, handed it to one of the sergeants.

"Listen, I don't wanna hear another word outta you," Lukash said, smiling. "I don't mean to sound unpleasant, but this is a big fucking case. This is a Task Force investigation and it gets a little tricky. I don't want our people bumping into an anticrime cop. You understand what I'm telling you?"

Jack nodded.

"No, no, no," Lukash said, pulling the cigar out of his mouth, as if it was a plug. "No fucking nod. Do you understand what I'm saying, Officer? Is it one thousand percent clear?"

Jack was furious. "Perfectly."

"I hope so," Lukash said, plugging his cigar back in place. "This is serious fucking work. We got trained personnel here and you could be standing on someone's dick. I'm giving you a direct fucking order."

Jack's face grew red. He knew what he was being told. The help he was offering was spurned. His observations, his evaluations were worthless.

"You stay outta that fucking area," continued Lukash, who saw a dangerous flame of insubordination in Jack's eyes. "This is for the fucking grown-ups."

Jack didn't hear the last little bit. He stormed out of the office, slamming the door, marched to the exit, and stood there waiting for the elevator while everyone in the room took a turn sneaking a look at his humiliation.

But he knew that he was right. He had seen something in that Korean deli. It had significance, although he wasn't certain what that was. He was not going to be sent away like a child. No matter what the fucking lieutenant said.

9

Tommy left his car in the garage near his apartment, then walked south along Broadway, past the closed theater where bare wooden planks, like pennies, covered the dead eyes of the box-office. The sidewalks were busy, but on a Sunday the pedestrians lacked the usual emphatic, headlong weekday purpose. You could stop in your tracks and not feel that you were about to be swamped. No one was rushing back from lunch or to catch the bank before it closed. Mothers walked easily with baby carriages while fathers kept pace like Indian scouts, studying the flanks for sudden threats. Elderly couples, who still followed old habits of decorum, were outfitted carefully for an appearance on the street, as if there were still such a thing as society to be considered.

If there was a live, active Sunday society on the Upper West Side, it was the young professional class who loved to go to Sunday brunch; where they ate and what they ate defined their subclass, gave them status. There were the macro dieters and the vegetarians and the red-meat eaters. There were the pasta believers, the joggers, and the calorie counters who baked their own bread. There were the wine lovers, and there was the eclectic mob that followed the latest trend. But almost all of them went out for Sunday brunch.

They had come to expect as their God-given due a complimentary screwdriver. And they depended on the sight of the other half-lidded Manhattan boulevardiers at the neighboring tables. No one talked about politics or art or late twentieth century spiritual fundamentalism versus rampant materialism. They didn't compare the high-tech, computer-chip revolution and its impact on the world of Marx and Freud to the industrial revolution and its impact on the world of agrarian culture. They didn't debate the moral relativity of Nietzsche and Hitler or the foul collapse of hope that trailed after them. They spoke instead about the relative merits of the french fries—praising restaurants which made them fresh and crisp, denouncing those that ran out of energy and served bogus, frozen fries; they spoke of this sadly, tragically, as one might refer to a friend lost to cocaine. Tommy lived in this world, ate there, and appreciated the finer points of french fries, but the obsession, the localized intensity of the concern escaped him.

As always on a Sunday, the Upper West Side of Manhattan was freckled with stumbling junkies and sour winos in their layered winter wardrobes; they were always there, in their glazed stupor, Sundays, Labor Day, it didn't matter—holidays only made them more visible. Christmas, with its implied bounty and insistent undercurrent of generosity, only made them more intolerable. Once they had been a source of righteous pity, a Dickensian example of civic need. You could give away your spare change and feel virtuous. Now there were too many for that. Too many unsteady hands reached out for money, too many unsteady voices made cynical pleas for help. The men were all Vietnam veterans down on their luck, the women were all victims of male abuse who had children to feed. But what they had to feed was all too apparent to Tommy Day, who brushed by their outstretched hands unmoved.

As he walked, he tried to put off thinking about a plan for the murder of Sanders. He needed a plan, but the good plans came out of the blue, when he wasn't trying to think of them. He could manage to get the United States Attorney alone and just blast him, but that was wild with risk. They would investigate officially and unofficially and he would inevitably fall under suspicion. Everyone nearby would become a suspect. The cloud would prevent him from ever rising to Congress.

He didn't yet have a plan for Sanders. He turned and retraced his steps, heading back to his apartment. He daydreamed about his future in politics. At first, when the Don suggested it, political office seemed such an unlikely thing, a movie-star promise to get him to do the Don's work. But the more he turned it over, the more possible it seemed. He knew about men with all sorts of skeletons in their pasts who became congressmen. Scoundrels, screwballs, and crooks—they made up a large part of Congress. He even knew some who were "connected" to the mob. Although, when he thought about it, he only knew rumors. Nothing for certain. And that's all they would know about him. No one knew for certain about his other life. No one could prove it. At worst, it might come out as a whisper of scandal and that would not entirely hurt. There were citizens of the land who preferred a hint of the rogue in their elected officials; it made them feel that the officials had power and thus gave them a vicarious edge. As far as anyone knew for certain, Tommy Day was a cop—the best cop—who, for sound professional reasons, kept close contacts with unsavory characters. It was essential in his job to remain familiar with the criminal element. You don't catch fish by casting your net in a bathtub. So rubbing elbows with the mob wouldn't necessarily work against him. Besides, no one except the Don himself knew it

all. There was no proof that he was anything but an enter-
prising detective who had a single-minded devotion to his
job. No one had seen him kill the snitch at the Korean deli.

The line of homeless people at the soup kitchen began to
move as the doors of the church opened. Tommy Day didn't
notice. He was preoccupied, and he had developed a tactical
blindness to the eyesore across from his apartment.

Tommy began to drift off into thinking about the pleasures
and perks of occupying a congressional office in Washington.
Tall women dangling from his arm. Money pouring in from
all sources. Oh, the money would flow like water. He knew
how it worked. You wanted a project in the district, you
paid. They were like the Mafia, these public officials, skim-
ming off a piece of whatever action took place in the district.
Not to mention the trips and free dinners and speaking
engagements. Of course he wouldn't be stupid enough to
get caught, not like those idiots in the Iranscam. No one
would catch him on a videotape taking an incriminating envelope. He would not personally meet with the indictable
bribers. He would have a cutout, an intermediary of de-
niability between him and the contractor. The trouble with
these other public officials, the ones who got caught, was
that they were not paranoid enough. You had to assume that
you were surrounded by enemies. You had to assume that
microphones and cameras were always turned on. Paranoia
was the only way to stay alive. That was the way to protect
yourself. If he was careful, he estimated, he would be able to
retire by the time he was forty.

Come right down to it, he wouldn't be such a bad congressman. He would campaign on a promise to clear the
streets of these homeless pests. And he would do it, too. If
they couldn't work, he'd put them away someplace. He'd
think of a place. But the important thing was to put the able-
bodied men to work. They could clean up the streets or wash
down subway cars or clean up the parks. There was plenty
of useful work around. All you had to do was walk down

littered, smelly Broadway and you could see all the jobs that had to be done.

A small swell of pride bloomed in Tommy's chest as he began to glimpse the visionary beauty—the sheer grandeur—of public office. He could, for want of a better expression, make a difference in the corroding and dying world in which he found himself.

And then, as he felt the uplifting moment upon him, it came to him: the beginning of a plan to murder Special Assistant United States Attorney Marvin Sanders.

Less than a mile away, Marvin Sanders was closeted in the den of his East Side duplex with his friend and advisor, Jerry Casolaro, working on his own political future. Sanders's wife had been sent to her mother's house on Long Island, along with the children. Sanders was an unannounced candidate for mayor and Casolaro was trying to inch him closer to a declared status. Sanders was reluctant to surrender the moral high ground of his status as an assistant United States Attorney engaged in the people's business. You're not on a mission from God, was the way Casolaro put it when he urged Sanders to begin hiring a campaign staff. Sanders shook his head.

"The minute I hire staff one, I am fair game," Sanders had said quietly.

"I understand that," nodded Casolaro.

"Do you know what's gonna happen?"

"I got a pretty good idea."

"Every single one of those sharks in the press room is gonna come after me. Even my friends. Friends! Ha! Even the ones who have my private number and drop my name. Even the ones who have been to my home and eaten Marilyn's food—especially Kovacs who got the burnt pot roast—every swinging dick is gonna write, 'Well, that's what he was after all along.' They're gonna say that I only wanna be mayor."

"But, Marv, you do wanna be mayor. Sooner or later you're gonna hafta say so."

This was true—irrefutably true—which was why it made Sanders so mad. He had an edge now, he was employed in the name of the people of the United States. He spoke for them, even in court, appearing "for the people." It bestowed on him a mantle of virtue and altruism that even he sometimes believed. Hiring a campaign manager would render him naked, his ambition exposed. People would reassess all his acts in the light of this new, raw self-seeking factor.

"You don't understand, Jerry. I'm gonna put Iennello away first. This scumbag has got to go. He just nailed one of my people. He's got judges and councilmen and state senators in his pocket. The man is dirty with drug operations and numbers and hookers. I don't want any misunderstanding about my motives. I don't want people saying this is a cheap media exploit to become mayor. I'd sooner give up a chance to be mayor than walk away from locking this guy up."

Casolaro listened to Sanders, let him finish his grand speech, then uttered one word: "Bullshit!"

The word cut so deeply into the crust of Sanders's piety that he slammed down his drink and began circling the room, clearly furious with his friend. Casolaro circled in the opposite direction, both men racing to work up an argument, or to refrain from saying things that would be unforgivable.

Casolaro realized that he had gone too far. "Listen, Marvin," he said, collapsing on the couch, grabbing his glass of whiskey and melting ice, "you want Iennello, I know that. The people know that. But they also know that you wanna be mayor. You think they don't know? What, you think people are dumb? They think you show up at every B'nai Brith dinner because you like the food? You march in the Columbus Day Parade because you like Italians? You're fucking running for mayor. They know that. You're the only one who doesn't know."

Sanders sat and listened for the tone of an apology.

"I'm not criticizing," continued Casolaro, a short, thick man, puffing from the exertion of chasing around the room. "No one gets elected mayor of this town by shrinking away

from attention. There hasn't been a shy mayor since Bob
Wagner, and he got in on his father's coattails. Nobody gives
a shit if you are Saint Francis of Assisi and Albert Schweit-
zer rolled up in one. The only fucking thing that they care
about is, is this guy a schmuck? People don't want a schmuck
for mayor. And only a schmuck leaves it to amateurs. Go,
attend the breakfasts. Go to cop funerals. But spend a few
fucking dollars and hire some professionals."

"Nobody on this earth can talk to me like that and get
away with it," Sanders said, standing up again.

"Bullshit, what are you gonna do, arrest me?"

Marvin Sanders was not certain when he had been struck
by political ambition, or when, exactly, he decided that his
deeply held beliefs were standing in his way. He had gone to
college and then law school with the intention of defending
people wrongfully accused of crime. After all, his father was
an old liberal, a labor organizer for the city's clerical workers;
his mother was a school teacher when that meant unions and
passion and real education. In the middle-class home in
which Marvin Sanders was raised, there was no sympathy
for the ruling class, no love lost between politicians and the
working class. Marvin, the youngest son, was expected to take
his place in the family by using his professional skills to defend the oppressed and brutalized victims of management
depredations. The fact that he had chosen to join the Republi-
can Party and work for the government—the same government and the same type of people that staged raids against
aliens in World War I and that hounded innocent, soft-hearted
liberals, presenting them to the world as dedicated Commu-
nist revolutionaries—the fact that Marvin was now one of
them was a wound to the Democratic heart of his family.
They could understand the fact that he married a blonde god-
dess of another religion and that his children were being raised
as spiritual neutrals, these things they could understand, rec-
oncile, explain away. But to turn your back on the liturgical

belief in the devil McCarthy, this was too much for the ex-
tended Sanders clan, who included a few apostate Jews, a
Catholic convert and a right-wing Zionist lunatic.

No one clipped the newspapers with Marvin's picture in
them. No one kept track of his television triumphs, or even
the whispers about the possibility that he might become a big
shot politician. He came to the holiday dinners. He brought
his wife. The grandchildren were fussed over and spoiled.
But nothing was uttered about his work. It was a deep unspoken shame.

Imagine, thought Marvin to himself, I could be elected
mayor and they wouldn't mention it at the Passover dinner.
Not even, "What's new?"

And so they circled some more, Marvin and Jerry, stopping
every now and then to rest and sip a drink, and then they
resumed wearing out the carpet. Finally, Sanders broke out of
his orbit and went to the window, with its view of Central
Park. It was dark already and he always felt a slight tremor,
gazing into the black patches of the park. You couldn't even
imagine what was taking place down there, not from this
height, not from this distance. Sex, crime, murder—all the
sins man was capable of committing, right under his window.

"You think I'm a schmuck, Jerry?" he asked plaintively.

Casolaro was sprawled now in an uncomfortable re-
cliner—Mrs. Sanders's taste in furniture did not include
comfort. "No," replied Casolaro carefully. "I don't think
you're a schmuck. But let me tell you something. I have seen
other men—good, sensible men who would have made fine
public servants—written off as schmucks because of indecision."

Sanders nodded, still facing deep into the park. In the
black, empty socket of the night, he thought he saw the beck-
oning temptations and pitfalls of irresistible opportunity.

"What will my mother tell the women in the cousins' club?"

10

M oe and Jack were fighting their way into Manhattan through the painful crawl of families making up the bulk of homeward-bound Sunday traffic. The faces of the drivers in the other cars had that blank, bewildered look of losing linemen late in the fourth quarter. The children were smack up against the rear window, staring angrily at the backed-up traffic behind, as if they'd like a shot at them, having worn out the occupants of their own car. The mothers, with their hands in their hair and their eyes wide with fatigue, looked like prisoners of war.

Moe was concentrating on the driving, and Jack was concentrating on the case. "What case?" Moe cried when Jack brought it up. "There's no case. Didn't the lieutenant tell you—didn't he order you to lay off?!"

"Since when do we listen to lieutenants?" Jack replied.

Yes, well, not always. They listened, selectively, when it suited them.

"I'm not working on any case," Moe declared, still heading across the Triborough Bridge, plunging into the Christmas-tree glitter of the Manhattan holiday skyline.

Technically, they were still off duty; they weren't scheduled to report back to their anticrime unit until Monday at noon, when they would once again go after seasonal criminals—pickpockets in the department stores, purse snatchers on the street, bogus Santa Clauses. But that was Monday and this was Sunday, and the doctor said that Natalie needed to sleep, that Jack was a hindrance and had to stay away from her so that she could truly rest. Mrs. Graham had given him her stingy smile. Barry was out dodging his gambling debts.

So Jack called Moe, who said definitely, absolutely, under no circumstances was he going to poke his nose into a case against a commander's direct orders. Positively. Don't even suggest it. Only there was a powerful history between Jack and Moe, and "no" was not something that Moe could say to his friend with conviction. Not to Jack.

In 1967, when Moses Berger, a captain in a United States Army Reserve Armored Division, took a leave of absence from the NYPD and joined an Israeli tank unit during the Six Day War and got himself shot up on the Golan Heights, Jack had arranged for his return to New York and his admission to NYU Medical Center. He had also managed sick leave for "injuries suffered during a car accident." The Police Department chief physician, a man named O'Leary, kept Moe from being examined too closely by a disability board. He later told Jack that it was the first case he had ever seen of shrapnel wounds from a car accident. Then, because he was an old soldier in the IRA and understood men swept up by grand political passion, the police physician had winked and approved leave until Moe was fit to return to duty.

The debt lay unmentioned between Moe and Jack, but never forgotten. There were also the usual binding memories of police partners. The dependability of their backup. Nei-

ther Moe nor Jack ever had to look around to know the other
would be there when danger began. When Jack woke up
after being knocked silly by a mental case, Moe's was the
first face he saw. When Moe found himself confronting two
armed stickup-men in a grocery store, Jack was beside him,
facing them down. It went beyond money or favors to life
itself.

There was another thing, also unacknowledged, also impossible to ignore, and, in the end, maybe the thing that
most closely fused the two partners together: Moe Berger
had a crush on Natalie. Not that he didn't love his own wife,
Christine, and, no mistake, he was happy with her and their
life together. But Natalie was someone rare and fine and
smart and dignified—a member of a high, natural aristoc-
racy—someone he admired beyond his own understanding.
Of course the yearnings of his secret heart were never so
crass as to be carnal, and, for that matter, he would never
betray Jack—but he did appreciate the fact that the unap-
proachable Natalie of his dreams remained a small, remote
part of his life. And now that she was dying, he grieved for
her. Of course Jack knew about the tender feelings Moe felt
for his wife. He respected the chaste delicacy with which
Moe dealt with his problem. And it was a comfort that they
grieved together, in spite of the fact that they could never
mention it to each other.

"I think we chase the derelict," Jack said. He flashed his
badge to the toll collector on the bridge as Moe kept the car
rolling through the toll gate.

"No, no, I say we go after the woman who hangs at the
Acropolis," Moe said. "She's the key."

"You mean that reporter?"

Moe gave Jack a twisted look, a reproach. "No, not the
reporter, you dumb shit. Besides, she's not a reporter; she's a
weathergirl who wants to be a reporter. Like you want to be
a cop. I mean the other one, the one who saw the bum."

"Oh, you mean Crazy Edie. Yeah, well, first we find her,
then she leads us to the bum, then we crack the case."

"What case? How many times do I have to tell you, I'm not working on any fucking case. Especially one in which a chief witness is named Crazy Somebody. I'd have to be Crazy Somebody Else to work on a case which we have been officially warned to avoid."

"The diner?" Jack asked.

Moe shrugged and headed south along the FDR Drive. "I could go for a hamburger, but remember: no case!"

Jack smiled.

"That's your trouble, my friend," Moe continued. "You have trouble following orders. Me? I'm told to stay away, I stay away. An order is issued, and I obey like it was one of the commandments on the sacred tablets. The man says no case, I say, Okay, no case. . . ."

"What case?" Jack said, staring out of the window as the city flickered past.

Gene Harman, station manager of Channel 9, leaned forward in the leather chair and punched the sound button on the remote control switch. Harvey Levy, managing editor of the news program, was on the verge of saying something, but Harman held up his hand like a traffic cop. "I want to get this, Harvey," he said.

On the seventeen-inch screen, Bonnie Hudson was waving the weather pointer, an electronic gizmo with a light at the end which had set the station back $250. It was supposed to pinpoint the highs and lows, but more important, to impress the viewers with high-tech razzledazzle. At the moment, Bonnie wasn't performing weather tricks with the state-of-the-art pointer, she was waving it recklessly at the Sunday anchor, a worn-out old veteran named Tony Canasto, dumped by all the larger local stations because age and liquor had rendered him mentally slow and his confusion was seeping onto the air. Every Sunday during the 9:00 news, he said he didn't know a high from a low and what's more, he bet most people didn't give a fig. He said it again and again, whenever he was filling in during the week, too, until something had to be done to put a stop to it. He didn't give one single fig for Bonnie's high. Bonnie, who didn't give any more of a fig, took the matter in hand.

"Tony, this high pressure system is going to be a good thing," Bonnie said earnestly. "Oh, maybe not now, but soon. This is not just another weather front. This high-pressure system is going to bring us clean air so that our children can breathe. It's going to help the farmers clean up this business of acid rain and it's going to deal with toxic waste. We'll be talking about this high-pressure system well into the twenty-first century." Then Bonnie dropped her mock serious tone and brightened. "On the other hand, it's only weather."

The camera came back on Tony, whose face was frozen in horror. His mouth was open and he even forgot to tighten the age lines on his face, a thing he never neglected on camera. It took a long four seconds for him to recover, look down at the papers on his desk, shuffle them, spill one, and then smile idiotically. He couldn't help muttering, "Something frightening about that girl." Then he began reading a story about renewed shelling in Beirut.

Gene Harman, the station manager, shook his head, punched down the sound, and turned to Harvey. "Tony's right about her; there is something frightening about that weathergirl."

"But spunky," said Harvey defensively.

"I know how you feel about her, Harvey, but she is very unstable."

"She's influencing ratings, Gene. The focus groups all love her."

"They loved McShane."

No one at the station could forget the short, terrible lifespan of shock television's Morton McShane, who finally had to be tossed off the air for yelling at his audience when they disagreed. Oh, sure, at first his blue-collar outbursts were a novelty and attracted viewers with his aggressive and offensive style. But eventually, the man spun out of control.

Gene Harman picked a small piece of lint from his knee, careful not to disturb the crease on his Paul Stuart suit. This weathergirl—it was true that she had a certain flair—even he couldn't deny that. There was something very appealing about the way she teased the old anchor. It was funny, but more important, it lacked cruelty.

"She has to be watched," he said to Harvey Levy, who let out his breath. Harvey had been afraid that he was going to have to fire her, just when she was starting to move the viewers away from Channel 11.

They sat in the bright office and watched the anchor stumble through the rest of the news without any hope of regaining his composure. Harman sipped at a club soda while Harvey drank a beer.

"What's her story?" Harman asked, his eyes still glued to the set.

"What do you mean?"

"What's she trying to prove? Is this her idea of style? Does she think this is going to get her a call from the networks?"

"She's not interested in the networks," said Harvey, who couldn't help chuckling. "In fact, she hates television."

Harman gave him a very severe look, but Harvey smiled and shrugged.

Harman's belief was that he didn't want flashy reporters, he didn't want outstanding reporters, he didn't want ambitious reporters working for the news department of his little station. If they were flashy or ambitious or too smart they'd demand raises or be gobbled up by the big stations. Better, he'd decided long ago, to have a nice stable pack of grateful mediocrities. No network raiders, no huge expenses. The trouble with that fine theory was that it cost them rating points. The news department was stable, but it was boring.

Bonnie Hudson was not boring. And it disturbed Harman's fine balance. She was smart and bursting with something. "What's she after?" Harman asked.

"She wants to be a reporter," said Harvey.

Harman turned away from the set and looked at his news

manager to see if he was serious. "What are you talking
about? She is a reporter."

Harvey shook his head and swallowed the last of the single
beer that he allowed himself in the evening. "No, a real reporter. She wants a press card."

"Do they give weathergirls press cards?"

Harvey shrugged. "She wants to go out and cover murders," he said. "She wants to investigate Watergate and expose the mayor and rattle everybody's cage." He smiled.
"You remember how it was."

Harman had been a wire service man twenty-eight years
earlier. A good one, too, he thought. Sat on stories for days.
Felt the bulletins like short jolts of electricity. Hanging
around the fringes, getting to know the principals, understanding the nuances and background so that when something happened, you grasped it right away. You were
prepared to cut loose with informed stories. This was before
camera crews changed the atmosphere. This was before television stole the patience of the reporters. The television reporters now . . . well, they couldn't help it. They walked
into a story like movie stars and the people in the story became fans. Spectators at their own spectacle. Shooting victims went gaga over seeing a face familiar from the 6:00
news. People with fresh blood on their shirts, people with
fresh deaths in the family—they couldn't help it either.
They waved to the cameras and grinned at the reporters.

To his credit, Harman saw it early. He recognized almost
at once that something important was about to happen to
journalism. Television would overwhelm it. It would no
longer be journalism. It would be television. But even now,
three decades later, Harman still held a deep, unspoiled
memory of what it was like when he sat up close at the birth
of the civil rights movement, when you could sit among politicians and they wouldn't notice you, or would at least dis-
count you, when the dead flesh and burnt aftermath of urban
riots was authentic rage, not a media event, when he roamed

the fringes and saw the way things worked, and he couldn't honestly blame this weathergirl for wanting a taste. Not that she could ever have it.

He got up slowly, checking the cut of his suit, and slipped into his overcoat. "Keep an eye on her," said Harman.

"I'll do my best, but she's a pistol."

"Hey," Harman said smiling, "it's only weather."

Stavros wasn't on duty at the Acropolis Diner. The man working the register, who said his name was Nicky, told them that Stavros had the night off. Jack nodded, showed his badge. Nicky wasn't impressed. He knew the difference between a plainclothes's tin shield and a detective's gold. Moe kept his distance. It was half empty in the diner, just the usual Sunday evening people, bent without appetite over their meals. One reading Hemingway. Another gazing out of the window. All looking lonely.

"Let me ask you something," Jack said. He could see Nicky's unfriendly look as his head turned grudgingly in Jack's direction.

"You people have been in here ten times already," Nicky said. "You know something, you drive away the customers."

"I'm sorry, Nicky, but sometimes it's necessary," said Jack.

Moe closed in from the other side, boxing the cashier between them. "Hey," Moe said with a little show of anger, "three people were murdered Friday night. Capish?"

The cashier nodded. "Okay, okay," he said. "But every time you come in here, after, the customers want to know if it's roaches. They don't think you're cops; they think you're the health department."

"Don't they know about the murders?" Moe asked.

"Sure, they know about murders. Murders they're not afraid of. Roaches in the kitchen they're afraid of."

"You want us to yell roaches?" said Moe. "Because I could

stand here and start screaming about the vermin in the kitchen."

"No!" said the horrified cashier. "Please!" The wrong word could spread through the neighborhood quickly. Did you hear about the Acropolis? On the rat list. By morning there would be no breakfast trade. If they found a dead body in the kitchen, his breakfast trade would double. But a roach had the power to put him out of business overnight.

"You know Crazy Edie?" asked Jack.

"Crazy Edie? What does she look like?"

Jack rolled his eyes. "She's a bum, a regular, she comes in for coffee. Uses a lot of change."

"Oh, the crazy lady. Yes, sure, I know her."

"Good. When's the last time you saw her?"

"The crazy lady? I see her a week ago."

"The other guy . . ."

"Stavros."

"Stavros said she was in here yesterday."

"Could be. I didn't see her."

"Where does she hang out?"

Nicky paused, baffled by the question. He worked on the translation, then figured out what they meant and laughed.

"Oh, these people, they're in the park. You know the park? They go to the park and they live by the Museum of Art. It's warm and they stay there."

"Has she been in for coffee today?"

"The crazy lady? I told you, I don't see her."

They went around the same circle a few more times, then Jack left a five-dollar bill and they went out, uncertain where to take the investigation.

Bonnie Hudson was waiting for them on the sidewalk. She smiled at Jack and shook hands with Moe. "Moe Berger; it's only weather," Moe said, smiling, although he felt some twinge of resentment. "I'm not working on this case," he told Bonnie.

"What case?" Jack said.

The three of them walked south on First Avenue, then turned west along 79th Street, Bonnie between the two cops. "Did you find Crazy Edie?" she asked.

"No," Jack said firmly, "and I doubt that there even is such a person."

"Maybe you don't know how to look," she said.

Jack gave her what he thought would be a hostile glare, but it wasn't entirely successful. She looked so small and enthusiastic in her red nose and blue bubble coat that he found himself smiling in spite of himself. At Park Avenue, Jack excused himself. "I'm gonna check a doorman," he said. "You two stay here around the corner."

When he was gone, Bonnie asked Moe about Jack's wife. "He told you about Natalie?"

"He told me she was sick," said Bonnie defensively. She knew enough about cops to appreciate that she had to tread carefully through certain areas of high emotion. Cops could be like teenagers in matters of sentiment.

"Yeah, well, she's no better," said Moe, looking away.

"I'm sorry," said Bonnie.

She sounded so miserable that Moe turned back to her and smiled and patted her arm.

Jack came around the corner, half running. "The doorman told me where to find her," he said.

11

It took the homeless man two days to cross Central Park. On the first day, Saturday, he became disoriented, lost in delirium, and circled the Great Meadow until, exhausted, he fell into a bush and nursed a small bottle of wine through the night. That was the 20th of December. He had wanted to put as much distance as possible between himself and the Korean deli and he thought he had come a great distance, but in fact he had travelled less than a mile. His plan was to reach the West Side of Manhattan. He had an idea that it was a safe station. They wouldn't be looking for him on the West Side of Manhattan. They would be searching for the gun, and of course, him, on the East Side. He knew of some soup kitchens across town—crowded and more dangerous than the churches on the East Side—but he felt that he had no choice now but to uproot. It was a trek that grew in proportion in his mind.

Funny, it used to be easier to make his way across town, or even uptown or downtown, but it was getting harder and harder to move anywhere. Maybe it was age, he thought. Maybe I'm getting old. He had lost track of the fact that he was only twenty-seven. He thought that he had lived a long time, maybe too long. Sometimes he was ready to die and like an Indian would go and search out a good spot to lie down and spill out his last breath. He had read about the tribal habits of the Apache, or maybe he saw it on television.

So much of what he knew was blurred. First it was the liquor that clouded his mind, causing the small storms in his head. But then he began to lose track of almost everything. He didn't even know that he was not a ravaged alcoholic. He drank wine when he could, but he was not driven by the need. He thought he was a victim of the disease simply because that was the explanation society offered. But the homeless man was not an alcoholic; he was simply lost and confused and mentally unhinged. He thought he had a mother, but maybe not. He dimly remembered attending school, but maybe that was a television program he saw in a shelter. Still, there were times when he had an absolute clear recollection of receiving his college diploma, of moving the tassel from the left to the right—or was it from the right to the left? He knew words and facts that he thought he had no business knowing. Some plays from Shakespeare floated in and out of his mind. Sometimes he thought that he was Bill Cosby, but then he wasn't sure if he was black or white. He knew where to get a bottle of wine and how to beg for food and where, when things got truly desperate, to find shelter. But the details of the world, and his own life, slipped away, one by one, like leaves in the winter of his shrinking sanity.

Deep in the pockets of his ragged coat he still had a few apples and a crushed banana that he had taken from the deli. He ate his dinner. Then he was afraid to change his location, because maybe the predators would fall on him. Maybe he'd been followed from the Korean deli and people were waiting to grab his gun and charge him with stealing the fruit. He shivered at the thought of the dead bodies, and, they too, were fragments now, maybe real, maybe not, lost in his fog.

He lay down to sleep, but it was not restful. His dreams were fitful, but vivid and filled with blood and death and so terrifying that they kept waking him up. Once, he thought he saw someone standing over him, and he pulled the gun from his belt and leaped to his feet, ready to defend himself. But by the time he got the gun free and ready to use, the person was gone and then he wasn't certain that anyone had been there after all. Maybe it was the shadow of the tree. Maybe it was one of the packs of figures he saw moving past, the steam coming out of them like engine smoke, like anger, like vengeance.

For some reason, he got it into his head during the night that he had travelled far out of the city and had reached some northern forest. Maybe in Canada. He thought that he had better be careful of bears. He had heard about them coming down to campsites and clawing the campers to death. He put the gun under his plastic pack, which was filled with shapeless cloth and cans which could be used for a cup and a plate. He kept his hand around the barrel.

In the morning, he saw a bench with someone sleeping on it and thought, they must have homeless living in all the forests. He saw a man walking a cluster of dogs. When the man saw him, he pulled the several chains and moved his herd to another bush. He saw a mother and a child, and the child pulled the mother away like the man pulled the dogs. His heart sank as he realized that he was unfit for children or dogs.

Then he thought, maybe they saw the gun. Maybe they knew he was armed and dangerous. He quickly hid it under his coat and sweaters and shirts. He saw a cop on a motor scooter riding in the distance and then he looked up and saw the towers of the skyscrapers above the trees and he knew that he hadn't escaped the city. He was still in New York, still in Central Park. His mouth ached with a sour aftertaste.

The wine was gone and so was the food. He reached deep
into the pocket of his coat, and through a hole in the pocket,
down in the lining of the coat, he retrieved a crumpled,
dirty, and half-empty pack of mints. He picked out two and
put the rest back. His mouth felt better at once. He had to
empty his bladder and he made certain that the cop had
driven out of sight before peeing behind the bush.

He was hungry now and thought, maybe I could live off
the land. He looked for roots. Then he saw a trash can and
found a half-eaten bar of candy and made that his breakfast.
He washed it down with water from a fountain. He was a
tall man but had no idea that the sight of him coming down
the park path—with his bulky coat and cotton cap and torn
gloves and his beard and smoky breath—was frightening.
When he tried to approach a jogger to ask for some spare
change, the jogger broke into a sprint. There were some
workmen checking the trees. He asked one of them for some
money, and the man began yelling at him to get lost. The
workman was fat and smelled of garlic. The homeless man
thought of shooting him, now that he had a gun. But the gun
might not work and then he would be set upon and killed.
He would use it only as a last, desperate resort.

As he stumbled south into the Brambles, he saw a dead
squirrel and he thought of cooking it. He would skin it and
build a spit and make a fire. But then he found a subway
token and he forgot about the squirrel. He began to cry, and
a woman walking past gave him five dollars. She looked very
frightened and he tried to thank her, but she practically ran
out of the park. She would have run, if not for the high heels
on her boots and the fact that she was sixty. I wonder if she
knows me, he thought.

He spent the money on hot chocolate and sweet rolls from
a vendor. He thought of shooting the vendor, hiding his
body in the bushes, taking over his business and starting a
new life. He wondered if the vendor had a wife. Children. A
home. He wondered how he would find out where he lived,

how he would learn the business and insinuate himself into the family. Would they notice? If he kept his head down and covered his mouth when he talked, maybe he could win them over before they told anyone. Would they finally accept him, as he had come to accept the things that came swiftly and overwhelmed his own life? Then he saw the heavy wooden club that the vendor kept in the storage compartment of the wagon and he changed his mind about shooting him.

As he finished off the last of the sweet rolls, he began to feel somber. The gun was losing its power. He didn't know if it worked. He might never know. The first exhilarating sense of freedom that had come when he lifted it in the deli was ebbing away.

They were lined up outside the soup kitchen door, cold and blowing into their hands. Jack, Moe, and Bonnie each experienced some pang of guilt as they broke through the long line of hungry people and entered the church on 79th Street off Madison Avenue.

The entryway of the church was brightly lit. Elderly church women waited at tables to greet the homeless with exaggerated cheer. They ushered Jack and Moe into a small anteroom while they went to fetch Father Bob. Bonnie stayed outside chatting with the churchwomen, thickening women of middle age who giggled when they recognized her. The priest was a young man who looked as if he were swimming inside his clerical collar. He held out a soft, weak hand. On a closer look, Jack could see that he was not young, but simply frail. He had shrunk out of his collar and now had the pale, drawn face of illness. The smile was an effort.

"Can I help you?" the priest asked.

Jack showed him his badge. "We're checking into some things about the murders on Friday night," he said. "On First Avenue. You've heard about them?"

"Yes," he said. "Terrible thing."

They dropped into seats, and one of the churchwomen brought tea in styrofoam cups on a tray. The priest pulled out a cigarette. "Anyone mind?" he asked, then he lit up before opposition could develop. Jack saw nicotine stains on the unsteady fingers.

"Terrible thing!" the priest said again, sipping the tea and sucking on the cigarette. "Some of your colleagues have been here already," he said to Jack.

"Yes," Jack said, "terrible thing."

The priest was lost for a moment in whatever reverie carried him away—his own mortal reminders, no doubt—then smiled and turned back. "Of course we are having a lot of murders these days. A lot of violent deaths. They say that it's the drugs. This new thing now. Crack."

"You don't think so," Jack said.

The priest shook his head.

Moe poured sugar in his tea and stirred it, seeming to pay little attention to the conversation.

"Don't you think that there is something far larger going on?" the priest said, directing his question at Moe. "Don't you think the drugs and the crime and the hunger are all connected to some larger sense of despair?" The priest took a large pull on the cigarette—his own act of despair.

"I think that there are always times when we are tested," Jack said. "Some of us measure up, some of us don't."

The priest nodded; a fellow Catholic, he thought. He had spent his whole life delivering such comforting explanations for life's cruel blows. Your child is dead, but he's baptized, thank God, and safe in heaven. You have to be grateful for the years you had with your husband, even if they were cut short! The priest had come to believe that his whole church was constructed on that kind of false optimistic sand. Life follows death, spring follows winter, hope lives eternal. But now that he was suffering a spiritual crisis of some depth, now that he had begun to doubt the assumption of good triumphant, he began to see life as tragic, not as a careful balance between good and evil. Moral relativity seemed a thin reed by which to pull himself out of his despair.

"Some of us," the priest said in a flat voice drained of all hope, "think that the test is bullshit."

Moe and Jack exchanged looks. Even the priest looked surprised. "I'm sorry," Father Bob said quickly, smiling with embarrassment. "It's the soup kitchen. You see, every night the lines get longer and longer. More and more mouths to feed. You see the same people and then there are just more of them. And younger." He laughed. "I'm really sorry. It's nothing theological. I swear. Just, well, I haven't been holding up . . ."

He drew on the cigarette and began to weep. Not great, gulping sobs. Just a few tears trickling down his cheek. Moe drew himself up. He'd seen this kind of emotional turmoil before. Some people break under stress, wind up on the floor, crying and screaming to deaf heaven. Bitterness and rage. All mangled together, usually in the aftermath of some vast tragedy. He didn't expect it from a priest. Father Bob punched out the cigarette, got up and walked over to the picture of Christ in his agony. He spoke quietly to the picture.

"Three people murdered. Yes, I heard about it. Lord, you hear everything in this church. Everything. I come from Ohio and let me tell you, I never dreamed . . . The confessional is the worst. That's when they tell you things that make you want to run into the street. But this is what Christ meant, of course. Go into the marketplace, he said. Sometimes I look down at my hands to see if the stigmata have opened up." He turned away from the wall, smiling gamely.

They all sat in silence for a moment, reassembling their composure. They sipped tea and Father Bob lit up another cigarette. Jack decided that this had gone on long enough. He handed the priest his card.

"Do you know a woman named Edie?" he asked.

"Edie?"

Moe and Jack looked at each other.

"Well, they call her 'Crazy Edie' on the street," said Moe.

The priest nodded. "Oh, Crazy Edie. Of course. Do you know why they call her Crazy Edie?"

Both policemen shook their heads.

"She puts the garbage back in the bags," said the priest, grinning. Jack and Moe didn't get it. "You see, the cans are an industry for the homeless. When begging or stealing doesn't work—and forgive me, gentlemen, but they do all steal—rounding up used soft drink cans keeps them going. They go down the street and they attack the garbage waiting to get picked up. You know, they can get twenty or thirty dollars in cans from a large building. Edie was one of the first to go out canning. She was bothered by the fact that the other people would leave the garbage all over the street. They'd rip open the plastic bags, take the cans, then leave the garbage spread out all over the street. Bothered her. Imagine that? So she went to some merchants and she presented her idea. She said that she needed the extra-ply bags to put the garbage back neatly."

"No kidding," Moe said.

The priest nodded. "The first few merchants started calling her Crazy Edie. But they gave her the bags, and she repacked the garbage. Even in front of buildings she didn't work. She put someone else's garbage away."

"And they called her crazy!" Jack said, shaking his head.

"Saved a whole industry around here. The doormen stopped complaining. The police, if you'll excuse me, stopped hassling people going through the garbage—as long as they had bags on them. It gave everyone a sense of neighborhood pride."

"What happened to her?" Moe asked.

"What do you mean?"

"Do you know where she is?"

"Of course. She's right outside."

Both Moe and Jack turned to look at the door. Was one of those smiling, saintly elderly churchwomen Crazy Edie?

"She lives here now, runs the small shelter we have for twelve women. She's good at that sort of thing."

"Does she have any kind of substance abuse problem?" asked Jack.

"She smokes," the priest said, looking at his own cigarette. "But she doesn't drink and she doesn't use drugs."

"Forgive me, Father, but how did she wind up here then?"

The priest sighed and took a deeper draught of the cigarette. "She lost her apartment, and then she lost her job and she ran out of possibilities," he shrugged. "It happens a lot. More than you think. There are a lot of normal people out there. A lot of talented people. It's just that they've changed the rules of social engagement, and so a lot of people can't cope. Crazy Edie is fine. She's helping cook dinner now."

When they went into the dining room, they found Bonnie interviewing Crazy Edie.

"It's okay," Jack said when he saw the expression on Father Bob's face. "She's with us."

Crazy Edie was a lot younger than they had expected. Mid-thirties. She had the clear-eyed look of someone who knows what's going on.

They all sat down at the table she had just set for dinner. "We hafta hurry," she said in a rough Brooklyn accent. "Those guys'll tear down the doors if they don't get their dinner."

"We're looking for a guy," Jack said.

She held up her hand. "Yeah, I know all about it. Miss weatherlady here told me all about it. You're looking for Jimmy Coffee."

"Jimmy Coffee?" asked the priest.

"That's not his real name. That's what we call him 'cause he's always trying to hustle some coffee. He's a regular, Father. Comes from a good family. College kid. Had a breakdown. Belongs in a home or something. Never make it on the street. His real name is Charles Benson. Call him Coffee though."

"Oh, I think I know him. He talked about Aquinas with me once. Very smart. Very well-educated."

"Very screwed up," said Edie. "Anyway, he came tearing in here Friday night and said that he saw some dead people and that I should hide him. Said he saw some guy running out of the deli right after the killings, thought maybe the guy was the killer. I didn't believe him, naturally. But he was really scared. And now that I think about it, he had some fruit and stuff on him. I thought he was having one of his spells and told him to head for the men's shelter."

"How do you know he wasn't just making it up?" asked Jack.

"I told her." Edie pointed to Bonnie, "I only heard about the murders later, after he ran outta here. A lot of these guys come in here with wild stories—whatever shit they're on causes some lulu nightmares. You should hear. But this was too early. When he came in here, all scared and sweating, no one knew about it yet. You could still hear the first sirens. I think he saw something."

"Where is this Jimmy Coffee now?" asked Moe.

She shrugged. "Nobody knows. Not in his usual spot behind the museum. None of the regulars have seen him. He's gone, in the wind. Probably scared shitless, excuse me, Father."

"What's he look like?"

She rolled her eyes. "Who knows? They all look like scabs with oily rags on. He's tall. And skinny."

"An aristocratic nose," the priest said.

"What the hell does that mean?" Moe asked.

"Impressive."

"What's he wearing?" Jack asked.

"Like most of them; everything he can get his hands on."

Jimmy Coffee was very frightened. It was pitch black and the only light came from a quarter moon. He had been watching the figure lurking in the bush ahead of him for ten minutes. It was a man, he was certain. The man was waiting to ambush someone. He had a knife and it was held like a dagger. The homeless man couldn't decide what to do. Should he run and summon help? The man might overtake him and cut him. Should he wave the gun and try to scare him away?

A well-dressed man came hurrying down the path. The man in the bushes began to move, creeping up behind the walker. Jimmy Coffee stood up. "Stop!" he cried.

The victim turned and saw the two men behind him and began to run. The man with the knife turned and came towards Jimmy Coffee, his weapon gripped tighter in his fist. Jimmy Coffee began to back up, but he stumbled over his own bundles. Then he reached under his coat and pulled out the .9-millimeter gun. The mugger was coming fast and the homeless man held the pistol in a combat stance, the one he remembered from watching television, and pulled the trigger. He felt a little jolt from the gun and saw the mugger's jacket pucker. The mugger cried and fell back in the mud and ice. A large cloud of steam emerged from the mugger's mouth, and then all breathing stopped.

Jimmy Coffee didn't wait to look around. He stuck the pistol back in his pants and began to run out of the park. He saw the lights from the West Side exit and headed for them. At least he knew that the gun worked, he told himself.

12

It was 7:30 Monday morning, and the nerve center of the Organized Crime Task Force was almost empty. A few weary detectives were making calls, but there was a flat, desultory atmosphere in the bay. Shifts were waiting to change. Only the strong coffee kept the last crew going. But inside the commander's glass cage, a bolt of lightning had just been tossed into the investigation.

"Are you sure?" Lieutenant Lukash asked, fingering the photographs.

"Listen, Loo, I been on the job for twenty-seven years, twenty-five in Forensics, and I looked at more bullets than you got hair—when you had hair. I just gave you an expert opinion." Bob Kovaks tolerated no back talk, and no challenge to his own carefully defined island of authority.

Lukash could be just as nasty. "Listen, you miserable fucking hairbag, this is important: you better be totally fucking right about this. Anybody can make a mistake. I don't wanna hear later that some labels got mixed up."

"Lieutenant, I don't make no mistakes when it comes to bullets. I am right, and by the way, you can go fuck yourself, sir. Do I make myself clear enough?"

Lukash wasn't listening. He knew that Kovaks didn't issue soft opinions when it came to ballistics. Lukash was staring at the report and the pictures, chomping on the dead cigar. Trying to read the meaning of the report, trying to see down deep into the implications waiting at the bottom of the murky facts. "Same damn gun," he said.

"I'll leave the pictures," said Sergeant Kovaks. "I got dupes." The lieutenant couldn't take his eyes off of the blow-ups of photographs of several bullets taken from several angles and a duplicate of the report, which stated unequivocally that the bullet plucked from the heart of the unidentified male found in Central Park on Sunday night matched in caliber, weight and markings the bullets recovered from the bodies of Mario Barone and Mr. and Mrs. Ku on Saturday morning. Kovak's conclusion was that all the bullets were fired from the same gun. No possibility of error.

"How do you like that?" said Lukash, after Kovaks had gone.

Out in the squad room, Lieutenant Lukash sat on a desk, the habitual cigar poking out of his unshaved face. It had taken an hour and a half to round everyone up, but now, at 9 A.M., there were fifteen detectives, two prosecutors and one federal agent clustered around the desk in various stages of curiosity and indifference. The Special Assistant United States Attorney sat in the desk chair behind Lukash, like a shadow.

"I don't have to remind you people," Lukash began, removing the wet cigar from his face, "that what is said here stays here."

There was a low grumble, like a shuffling of chairs, at the vaguely insulting implication. These were professionals. Yet Lukash continually reminded them about the basic rules of security. Like he didn't trust them.

"Does that mean I can't tell anybody at all?" joked a solid detective who had lost all normal fear of authority chasing drug killers in the Bronx.

"No, Walters, you can tell any-fucking-body you want. You wanna know why, Walters?"

"No, Loo, I really don't."

"The reason why you are exempt from the rules that govern the rest of us is that if you tell anyone, first they won't believe you, and two, they won't understand you. You could go on "Live At Five" and "Eyewitless News" and spill everything you know and still not blow investigation one."

"Could you run that by me again, Loo? I didn't understand that."

The laughter disturbed the lone federal agent. These New York cops were slack, thought Agent Hugo Barnes. Sloppy. Every one a wise guy. Every one had some sideways way of talking so you never knew if they were serious or pulling your leg. No discipline. No fire in the belly. No, not every one. There was that kid, Tommy Day. Too good-looking for his own good, but a crackerjack when it came to hard work. Even came in on his vacation. Always neat as a pin. Always alert. Didn't drip sarcasm. He wanted the kid for a partner. But that's not what he got.

Agent Barnes was partnered up with a detective who gave spare change to addicts. He tried to explain to the detective that the money would go for dope, and the officer agreed, and then Barnes said, trying to make his point, that giving an addict money was like being a supplier, and the detective shrugged and said lighten up. He said that the addict was in obvious pain and that giving him some spare change was the human thing to do. Agent Barnes shook his head. He couldn't see it. It might have been the human thing to do, he told the detective, but it was not the right thing to do. Lighten up, suggested the detective again. Barnes couldn't stomach it. They were all like that. All except the kid, Tommy.

Agent Barnes sat in the back of the circle, West Point

straight in his chair, and listened for the next command. Lord, he would be grateful when his assignment to this Task Force was up and he could return to his regular duty station in Phoenix. They didn't give money to junkies in Phoenix, and they sure as hell didn't make fun of the commander.

In back of Lukash, Special Assistant United States Attorney Marvin Sanders held up his hand for silence. He, too, was smiling, and it confirmed Agent Barnes's opinion that Sanders was not a serious man. First of all, he was running for mayor. Everyone knew that. Political ambition was a poison. It made them all greedy for publicity, which was the enemy of solid law enforcement.

A few more detectives drifted in, took chairs. "We're not supposed to talk about this," said Sergeant Jake Cummings, one of the squad leaders, bringing the late arrivals up to date. "We're supposed to stay off "Live At Five." Everybody but Walters."

"Loo, what about "Sixty Minutes," can we do that if they electronically disguise our face?" asked one of the late arrivals, emptying five sugar containers into his coffee.

"Your face is already electronically disguised," said Sergeant Cummings.

"Settle down, settle down," said Lukash good-naturedly. Then, growing serious, "Let's take some notes." The leather books came out, along with the ballpoint pens. "The bullets recovered from our guys in the Korean deli match a bullet recovered from an unidentified black male shot in Central Park last night. Nine millimeter. Same gun markings. The Central Park thing matches in other respects. One bullet, in the heart—in other words, a pro. Gentlemen, and ladies, we are looking for a bad-assed professional killer. We have not ID'd our Central Park victim but chances are he's mob-connected and our hit man took him down because he was an accessory or could make him. The big thing is that we have a definite link and connection. Now we just put some pieces together, and we got ourselves a case.

"Anyway, our first job is to ID the victim. We'll put a squad on that—Cummings, you got five guys. Next we are still chasing the Korean hit full tilt. I want you to tap the precinct squads for manpower. Let's really go door-to-door. Maybe we'll get lucky. This kind of neighborhood, somebody left for the weekend on Friday night. Maybe they're out loading the car and they saw something—a stranger, a strange car. Something. Maybe they saw our guy Highway being tailed, being grabbed."

Lukash passed out pictures of Highway and the Central Park victim. "The computers are down in Albany, so we can't get a print check right away. We're trying to make connections here."

"I'd like to know when the computers in Albany are up," muttered one of the old timers. "I spend more fucking time waiting for the fucking Albany computers than I do waiting for my wife."

"Yeah, and she don't come across either," someone in the back quipped.

"Okay, okay," said Lukash, cutting off the remarks. "I know a lot of you guys worked over the weekend and your asses are dragging. But this is important. We'll catch up with your time off later. Detective Day, you come with me."

Tommy Day followed Lukash and Sanders into the glass cage. Nancy McDaniels was right behind them.

"Nancy, you know Detective Day, I believe," Lukash said. Officer McDaniels, certain that everyone could read her open affection for Tommy Day, blushed and nodded her head.

"I personally think this is bullshit," Sanders said.

"Sir, we cannot afford to take chances," said Lukash, then turned to Tommy and Officer McDaniels. "We've had a tip that someone is going to make an attempt to assassinate the United States Attorney."

"That's me," interjected Sanders.

"We have city coverage: he's got a blue-and-white outside

his house and a uniformed man outside his door. But I want to put some Task Force backup on the case for a while. Just in case. The city's on it around the clock. But you never know. You two are pretty much free and I'm assigning you full-time. Wake him up and put him to bed."

"Sure, Loo," Tommy said. "Could we get copies of your schedule?"

Sanders reached into his brief case and broke out three copies of his daily schedule and handed one to each person in the room. Like he's on a campaign swing, thought Tommy. What would he say if he knew that I'm gonna kill him?

Bonnie Hudson was tapping her foot, waiting to go on-air with the 12:30 weather update. Harvey Levy was standing just off-camera biting a nail. He could still see the spark in her eyes after the morning battle. "Listen, I'm just trying to be your friend," Levy had told her a few minutes earlier when she plopped down in the chair to submit to "makeup." "You can't go around telling everyone to go fuck themselves."

She swivelled her head, causing the makeup artist to groan. "Not everybody. Just the deserving few. Harvey, I'm trying to get my makeup put on."

He tried to be stern. "It's not nice," he said. "Why do you have to tell poor Tony Canasto to go fuck himself? He's too old for that. He's afraid of you. He thinks you'll do it on the air. Why do you have to scare him?"

"I'll tell you why," she said, turning again, causing the makeup man to throw up his hands. "Because this morning he tried to tell me that I'm not taking my work seriously. Because he said that we should all have a little reverence for the tube. Even a weathergirl. His exact words. 'Even a weathergirl.' Because he made his noble speech about duty and loyalty while his hand was glued to my ass!"

"Okay, okay, but the guy can't help it. . . ."

"Harvey, gimme a break! He's a lech and a fucking

lounge-act anchorman. He reads the news like he's doing a Gershwin medley. He smiles like a dead fish. Go away and let this poor man finish my makeup."

"Bonnie, I'm just trying to help you. . . ."

"Harvey, I hope you don't take this personally, but go fuck yourself."

And now Harvey stood off-camera watching Bonnie tick the seconds away with her foot, hoping that she wouldn't go ballistic on the air.

The director gave her a cue and Tony Canasto tried to lead into her smoothly. A lounge-act segue. "So, Bonnie, are you going to give us a good week to get that last-minute Christmas shopping done?"

"How do I know, Tony?"

Bonnie Hudson was smiling when the camera turned to her. She lifted her shoulders in a great, cosmic shrug. "Let's face it, folks, we're only guessing when it comes to clouds. We don't really know what a cloud is gonna do. It could rain, it could snow, it could just sit up there and make faces at us. That's why weather is such fun—always a little surprise."

She turned to the map and pointed at a large letter "H" floating over Canada. "Uh, oh! This looks like trouble," she said. "It could bring some more cold weather. At least that's what the National Weather Service says." She ran down temperatures and humidity and barometric readings and then smiled at the camera: "My advice is to dress warm and stay indoors. But, hey! It's only weather."

Tony was still agape when the camera turned back to him. Harvey chased Bonnie back to the dressing room where she washed off the makeup. He sat down in a chair, trying to think of some way to impress on her that she was fast rolling off the end of the envelope.

"You know, Harve, I know that I upset you. I know that I make Tony crazy and Gene nervous, but it's the only way I can get through this." She was scrubbing her face clean, then took a fresh towel to dry herself. She looked at Harvey squarely. "You want me to take the work seriously, give me a press card, get me NYP plates and let me chase murders. If I have to get fondled by Tony Canasto I'm gonna be a little weird."

Harvey got up heavily and sighed. "A little weird is fine. You're fine. Just try not to give our viewers the idea that we have employed some outpatient weatherperson."

Bonnie glanced at her watch, ran a comb through her hair and ran to catch a cab for her appointment with Jack and Moe.

The Anti-Crime unit was under the overall command of Chief Inspector Marty Nolan, who was away on a Christmas vacation. During his absence, his duties fell to Deputy Inspector Ray Monahan.

Inspector Monahan didn't want to know what Jack Mann was doing about the Korean deli killings. He knew that he was doing something; he sensed that when they talked the day after the murders. And so they met like spies at the Museum of Modern Art on 53rd Street. They walked around the exhibits, looking at the scrawls and blotches held in such esteem by the critics.

"My God, you'd think someone would be liable for fraud," muttered the inspector.

"Some of it's not bad," said Jack.

"Really? Yeah, well, I liked *Guernica*. But we gave it back to Spain."

"I think we are supposed to surrender to the sweep of the lines and the mood of the colors," said Jack. "At least, that's what my wife says."

Monahan turned from the Jackson Pollock sprinkle of paint on canvas and faced Jack. "How is she?"

Jack did not take his eyes off the vivid colors. "She's in a coma. They put her in the hospital this morning. Booth Memorial. Can't take care of her at home."

"Christ!"

Jack shrugged. "She can't feel the pain, I'm told. The doctors tell me that. They tell me that she can't feel the pain and she is comfortable. I am supposed to be consoled by the fact that they think she's comfortable. In a fucking coma!" The anger was contained, but there, unmistakable, like the mood of the art.

They inched sideways down the corridor.

"I know you ordered me not to, but I've been asking some questions on the Korean deli case," continued Jack, recovering his composure.

"Look, Jack, I really don't want to know about it."

"I really didn't violate any regulations. I went to the Task Force."

"You went to the Task Force?"

"They didn't want to hear about it. They told me to mind my own business."

"You think that that's bad advice?"

"I think some of those people are very touchy, Inspector."

"And you intend to continue to go against my specific order to stay out of the case?"

"I'm not doing much. Just asking some questions. I'm not a rogue cop."

Monahan shook his head. "Leave it alone. Those guys can handle it."

"Sir, if you saw someone walking off a cliff, wouldn't you try to stop him?"

"You know, Jack, this may be some way of compensating. For the helplessness over your wife. Have you thought of that?" The inspector spoke softly, without being patronizing. In his own grief, he had gone over the line between police work and suffering. The arrests he made were more brutal. The attitude he had was less forgiving. He knew about the seepage between a policeman's personal life and his work.

"I've considered it," said Jack. "But, look, Inspector, I got a hot witness who saw something. I know that I saw something. . . ."

"You were half-bagged."

"But I saw something! I know that I saw something. There were the shelves. And a homeless derelict told someone he saw someone come out of the deli. Shouldn't we be looking for that derelict?"

"The Task Force, Jack. I'm sure they're looking."

"They're not looking in the right places. They're looking for the mob or some scapegoat. I don't mean to be insubordinate, but those guys are not like cops."

Then Jack told him that he had a fuzzy memory of seeing something. He and Moe were parked on First Avenue and he saw something.

"What is it that you saw?"

Jack shook his head. "I can't remember."

"Maybe we should get our hypnotist."

"Maybe. I think it'll come to me. It's like something on the tip of my tongue."

Monahan was standing in front of a canvas that seemed at first glance to be blank. A closer examination revealed two lines extending to infinity. It was, the longer you looked, breathtaking. The lines going on forever, down into the heart of the canvas. Forever. The inspector felt as if he was being sucked into the lines of infinity on the canvas.

Monahan did not like the Task Force. He didn't trust Sanders and his exploding ambitions. He was convinced that the Special Assistant United States Attorney was using valuable members of the New York City Police Department to advance his own career. He was also playing with fire, as the shootings at the Korean deli demonstrated.

Monahan knew that police work was not all science and technology. There were great leaps of intuition and luck. It was, often enough, a gift, and Jack Mann seemed to the inspector to be in the throes of a powerful hunch.

"What is it you want?"

"A few days," said Jack. "A week."

"What are you working on? Or, what are you supposed to be working on?"

"Midtown anticrime patrol. Pickpockets and lifters."

Monahan sidestepped down to the next canvas. "You want off the duty roster, okay, you're off the regular duty roster. But day to day. Not a week. And you are not investigating this case. I don't want my ass in a sling. Jack, be discreet. And call me Wednesday."

"Yes, sir."

"At noon."

"Yes, sir," and Jack was off, leaving the inspector to gaze at the opening of a tic-tac-toe game, which, according to the critic for the *New York Times*, was supposed to be high art.

13

The two uniformed officers in the cruiser outside of Sanders's apartment building on Fifth Avenue near 81st Street recognized Tommy Day and nodded. Tommy left the U.S. Attorney in the lobby— "Could you wait here just a second, Mister Sanders? I just want a word with the security people in the squad car"—and came back outside.

"How ya doin'?" he said casually, leaning into the window of the squad car, which was dirty with McDonald coffee cups and old lunch containers. There was a stale odor of smoke and sweat.

"Good, how are you?" replied the senior man in the passenger seat.

"Listen," Tommy said, showing his gold shield, "I'm Detective Tom Day."

"Yeah, we know you're on the job," the driver said. "We seen you before."

Tommy became unfriendly. "I don't give a fuck if we're

married, you guys are on post. You check the fucking ID and you check to see who's who and you stay alert."

The passenger cop bristled. "Hey, that gold shield don't make you God. We been on duty since eight and my partner and I know you—if you were a fucking stranger, you'd be chewing cement by now. So ease up on the cowboy shit."

Tommy spoke very quietly.

"Okay, asshole, lemme make it real clear: I am in field control of the security for the United States Attorney, Officer Simone," he said reading the man's name tag. "As far as you're concerned, that makes me God. We got an active death threat and since we already have some fresh stiffs in this case, it's very credible. Do I get through? Now pass it along to the next shift that this is a live post and anybody who fucks off is gonna be walking tours in Staten Island."

Both uniformed men began shovelling the debris accumlated during their shift into a white McDonald's bag.

"We didn't know about the threat," said the driver.

Tommy nodded. "I'm not trying to bust your balls, but four people have been hit this weekend."

"Four?" said Simone.

"At least four. This guy stays alive."

Then, after tucking Sanders into his apartment and making sure that Nancy McDaniels had arrived after packing an overnight bag, Tommy Day, as senior security man in the field, made a complete inspection of the building. He began in the basement and found all the hidden rooms. He checked the entrances and exits and crawled around the dark spaces. He found an old hatch once used as a coal chute. It was sealed. The metal chute was rusted and was still there in the basement, standing in the corner, leaning up against the old brick wall.

Someone had parked it, maybe even before Tommy Day was born, when the building converted to oil heat, and left it there. It smelled wet in the basement, like the hold of a sailing ship. He sat there on a wobbly chair and stared at the

coal chute and the hatch. Big enough for the chute. Big
enough for a man. Sealed with something that was flaking
down into the basement. Tommy could see a pinprick of
daylight here and there. It slanted down from the wall, nine
feet above the ground. He could stand on a few cinderblocks
and work on the hatch. It wouldn't take him long, now that
he had his plan to kill Special Assistant United States Attorney Sanders.

Tommy came out of the basement bristling with energy
and fire. He was the model of caution and efficiency, running makes on the doormen. He alerted the superintendent
that there would be uniformed officers in and out of the
building and obtained a listing of the tenants and the people
who worked in the building. The list would be run through
police computers at One Police Plaza. Lives would be examined. Tenants disturbed. Leads followed. It would all be a
great diversion since the person they were looking for was
leading the pack.

Lieutenant Lukash didn't know that the "snitch" who
phoned in the death threat was in fact diligent and careful
First Grade Detective Tommy Day himself who wanted to
throw a possibility of violence into the cocktail. He wanted
Lukash to react. Being assigned as security had come as a
surprise, though, and Tommy had had to improvise a plan.
This was perfect.

Moe had fallen asleep. The unmarked car was locked and
parked in front of the Plaza Hotel, near the Victory Fountain. Jack tapped on the window, but Moe could sleep
through anything. On the Golan Heights, they said that he
even slept through a battle. An out-of-town visitor suggested
that Jack call a policeman. A traffic enforcement agent, new
on the job, began writing a ticket. Jack showed the traffic
agent his badge, but being new and eager and jealous of the
small wallop of power he possessed, the agent continued to
write the ticket and called the truck to tow the unmarked
cruiser to the piers.

"I'm a cop," Jack hissed, trying not to cause a scene.

A crowd, however, inevitably began to assemble. Crowds always form when a car is towed in Manhattan. There's always some chance of fireworks, and New Yorkers believe that witnessing public fights and confrontations is part of their inherent tenant rights.

"Don't matter to me if you're a cop," replied the traffic agent in a musical island accent. "The car is badly parked and have to go. Now stand out of me way and let me do my duty, mon."

People in the crowd heard the remark about being a cop, saw the badge and began to switch sides. At first their sympathies were with the towing victim—albeit flavored with some small perverse portion of glee at the poor devil's helpless humiliation. But the rumble—a cop was going to get towed!—left room on both sides of the issue.

"Wait a minute!" said Jack, getting a little annoyed. Two uniformed men assigned to midtown traffic for the holidays came out of their blue-and-white and took charge. They grabbed Jack firmly under the arms and walked him out of range. One on each side. They were accustomed to motorists irate at getting towed.

"This your car, pal?" asked one of the uniformed officers.

"Fellas, fellas, I'm on the job!" cried Jack.

"No shit?" said the uniformed man on his left.

"Then you should know better than to leave your car in front of the Plaza," said the cop on the right. "What are you, plainclothes?"

"Yeah," said Jack annoyed, flashing his badge. "It's a fucking unmarked car." The two uniformed cops looked at each other and smiled. "My partner is asleep in the fucking car!"

The tow truck, waiting up the avenue, arrived and began hooking up to the fender of the cruiser. The two uniformed cops and Jack turned to look at the cruiser just as the tow truck began to lift the car. Moe woke up and hit the horn, but the noise was lost in the racket of the hoist.

As the cruiser hit a thirty-degree angle, the driver's door opened and Moe leaned out.

"Hey, there's a guy in that car!" cried someone in the crowd.

"Lookit this, they're towing cars with drivers now!" cried someone else.

The uniformed cops went over to the tow-truck driver, whispered something, but he shook his head. "Once it's on the hoist, it goes," the tow-truck driver said.

Moe climbed down, then pulled himself back up and reached inside and grabbed the newspaper.

The traffic enforcement agent, smiling, slapped the ticket under the windshield wipers. "Just doing my job, mon," he said happily.

Jack and Moe stood there on 59th Street, watching their cruiser being towed to the West Side piers. The crowd lost their confusion and unleashed a lusty cheer. Somewhere in all that mess, they sensed that they had witnessed a nice bit of holiday justice.

Bonnie stepped out of the crowd, unable to hide the big grin on her face.

"Don't say anything," said Jack.

"I was just gonna offer you guys a ride in my cab."

"Yeah," said Moe, "thanks. You going over near the piers?"

At the piers they had to wait for the tow truck, which got stuck in traffic on 34th Street. Jack paid the $75 towing fee, borrowing $20 from Bonnie, then snarled at the attendant who wished him a Merry Christmas. "Hey, Mac, at least we didn't lock you up for Christmas!" cried the attendant as they drove off in the cruiser.

The attendant and the tow-truck operator exchanged high-fives.

The woman from the Health and Human Resources Agency was in the midst of a crisis. It was Tuesday, De-

cember 23rd, two days until Christmas, and the usual wave
of seasonal sorrow had fallen like a heavy frost on the homeless of the city. She was trying to arrange turkey dinners and
donations of warm clothing and small gifts to counteract the
holiday despair. She had just gotten off the phone with a
supplier of Christmas tree ornaments, after finally managing
to convince him to decorate the trees in the shelters and
kitchens—trees she didn't have yet. Her name was Mae
Geller and she had been swimming upstream in this agency
(renamed four times), eking out benefits for the poor from
grudging supervisors, for twenty-five years. In a quarter of a
century, she had become a tough old bird who retained the
heart of an angry angel.

"Yeah, yeah," she said, looking at Jack's shield. "Put that
thing away."

"We're trying to track down a guy," said Jack. She gave
him a look as if he were a brain-damaged child. "I know, I
know, you've probably got more than one guy to find," continued Jack. "We've only got one."

"Look, Inspector, I know you're busy, but I don't have
time to play games. This is New York City and it's Christmas. That's the superbowl of suffering. Tell me what you
want."

"A homeless guy named Jimmy Coffee," Moe said.

"That's not a name," Mae said.

"I know," Jack said patiently. "That's his street name. But
he hangs on the Upper East Side and you operate some shelters and some kitchens up there. He's tall and thin and not
too old and he's educated."

They didn't tell her the name, Charles Benson. Let's see if
it checks, let's see if she comes up with it on her own. An old
cop trick.

"Educated?"

"As in school. Somebody has to know him. He's been
around for a while."

She wrote down the name: Jimmy Coffee. "When I get a chance, I'll make some calls," she said.

"How about giving me a list of the shelters and pantries, and we'll make the calls," suggested Jack with the hard edge of his trade.

She looked at him, trying to decide whether or not he was just taking up time. He was serious. "Sit down," she said, and they all took chairs near her desk: Jack, Moe, Bonnie. "I'll call our East Side coordinator. If anybody knows, she'll know. Or at least she'll know where to look."

He only heard Mae's end of the conversation, but Jack could tell that he was in the hands of a professional. "Alice, look, I'm trying to track down one of our clients. All I got is a street name. Jimmy Coffee. He's tall, thin, not too old and educated. . . . You do? . . . He does? . . . I'll send some people up to see you. Try not to give them coffee, they can afford to buy their own. Later, Alley."

She hung up and held up her thumb. "Your guy reads poetry," said Mae Geller. "We get a few poets. We tend to remember them. They stick out at the shelters. At least Alice remembered him."

Mae Geller wrote down the name of Alice Vitale and an address on the back of a used envelope. "The city doesn't give us much in the way of supplies," she explained. "I like to save the letterhead paper for begging letters." She smiled and handed Jack the envelope.

Alice Vitale had a closet-sized office in a public school on East 57th Street. The coordinator was one of those upper-class women dedicated to good works. She was thin and agile and didn't mind the squeeze. "I'm out in the field most of the time anyway," she said. "The people in the Armory on 67th Street know him. I used to find him in the alleys and send him up there. Sometimes he'd sleep in the shelter, sometimes he wouldn't."

"They remember him?" asked Bonnie.

"He brought books," Alice said. "They'd steal his shoes,

but not his books. You're the weatherperson, aren't you? I watch you now and then."

"That's me."

"You make that newsman, that Tony person, very nervous."

A few minutes later they were riding up Madison Avenue, Jack driving and Moe beside him. The two women were in the back.

"His name isn't Jimmy Coffee, you know," said Alice. "It isn't even Jimmy. His name is Charles Benson. A sad case, really. Bright, bright student. Four-point average."

"Where at?" asked Moe leaning back in the seat, happy at the confirmation.

"Columbia, from what I understand. One of the counselors at the Armory was always trying to rehabilitate him. Make him go home. Go back to school."

"What happened?" asked Bonnie.

Alice stared out of the window. "He had a breakdown," she said sadly. "Too much pressure. Some cannot bear up under such pressure. Good family. Has a sister. Father owns a bunch of hardware stores. They tried everything. Homes. Private care. But he seemed to prefer being homeless. Sad, isn't it?"

"Sad," agreed Jack.

Marilyn Sanders was a little taller than her husband and, as a result, spent a lot of her time sitting down. Standing next to him was a political liability, she had been told by his advisers. But now she was nervous and she paced. Officer McDaniels tried to make herself inconspicuous and read a magazine. The children were still with their grandparents on Long Island and Marilyn had a lot of time to fret. Marvin was eating his lunch—a plate of tuna salad and some lettuce—ignoring his wife's march of nerves.

Jerry Casolaro was banging on the push-button phones, reading numbers out of his black book.

"This is not something to worry about," said Marvin to his wife.

"Not something to worry about?! Then why are the kids with my parents? Why are there cops in my living room?"

Officer McDaniels kept reading the magazine, which was one of those sneering New York trendsetting slick publications that made everyone who read it feel ill-informed and out-of-date.

"It's a precaution, hon. C'mon. Be reasonable. You know that this sort of thing is part of the territory."

The article that Officer McDaniels was reading was a profile of Special Assistant United States Attorney Marvin Sanders. The thrust of the piece was that Sanders was the hot candidate—a fearless crime fighter who put Mafia killers in jail and went after corruption wherever and whenever he could find it.

There were glossy pictures of Sanders and his family, and Officer McDaniels made a noise as she realized that the picture she was looking at had been taken right here in the living room. She was sitting on the couch where the family had posed. It was a strange feeling. She read newspapers and watched television, but the stories and the pictures had very little to do with everyday reality. Seeing something in print, and at the same time in person, was a shock.

Marvin and Marilyn looked over at the policewoman, who grinned idiotically. She held up the magazine. "It's the picture," she said. "It was a surprise."

Sanders got up, came over and took away the magazine. "I hate that piece," he said. "Dumb fucking reporter got everything wrong. What's this doing in the house?"

"I thought the children looked nice in the picture," Marilyn said. "It's a nice picture."

"Nice picture?! The guy murdered me. He hated me. He wrote down every fucking thing that I ate, and it happens that I was hungry when we went out for lunch."

"Where'd you go?" asked Marilyn.

"What difference does it make? The guy wrote it down and then I picked up the check. I hate reporters. I hate all fucking reporters."

Nancy McDaniels eased out of the living room. She and Tommy Day were using the children's room while the kids were away. Tommy was resting on the boy's bed and she tiptoed into the room and lay down on the second bed.

"They fighting again?" Tommy asked.

"Quibbling," she replied.

They lay there, listening for each other's breathing. Then she heard his bed creak. He walked over and gently lay next to her and she backed away, uncertain about his intentions. She could smell him next to her and he could smell her. They swallowed each other's odors and their breath became quicker. He reached a hand out in the darkened room and touched her hair and she winced. He pulled her head to him and she almost said something, but there was nothing to say. Their mouths were open and they drank like thirsty lovers.

They held each other and he stroked her hair and moved closer. He could feel her through her blouse and she could feel him through his pants. Then he got up slowly and went back to his own bed.

"Tommy?"

"Yes?"

"Was it my breath?"

"Yes."

He heard her move. She crawled in next to him. "I'll brush my teeth," she said.

"I like your breath."

She worked on the zipper of his pants.

"We're on duty," he said.

"I know," she said, then slid down the bed and took him in her mouth.

And as he stroked the back of her head and bit his knuckles stifling the noises in his throat, he thought: It's all going according to plan.

14

Bonnie ordered coffee and a slice of chocolate cake. To hell with television's ten-pounds-less and the damned diet. She needed sugar. The stout young woman sitting across the table asked for half a grapefruit and some cold water.

"I have to be careful," said Jenny Benson, who was not fat, but had dangerous inclinations in that direction. She looked at Bonnie's cake wistfully, then turned away. It ruined Bonnie's appetite.

Bonnie said, "When I was a little girl, my parents would load up the refrigerator with cake and ice cream. Very disciplined people, my parents. They could take a sliver of cake and put the rest back. I never had that kind of control. Once I got started, the cake was gone. One time, when I was about fifteen, I snuck downstairs in the middle of the night and started in on a container of ice cream. Chocolate ripple. I'll never forget. I was putting it away. All of a sudden, a light went on upstairs and I could hear my mother coming down. She must have heard me open the freezer door. She had ears like a hunter. I didn't want to open the freezer door again and give myself away so I hid the ice cream container in the pocket of my bathrobe. The next day, my mother was doing the laundry, and she took the bathrobe out of the dryer. When she pulled the washed and dried flattened ice cream container out of the pocket, she just looked at me. I was a big disappointment to my parents."

Jenny laughed. "But you're so thin."

"It is a war that never ends."

And so they became friends.

"You still use your maiden name?" Bonnie asked, nodding at the wedding ring on Jenny's finger.

Jenny nodded and blushed.

"What's your husband do?" Bonnie asked.

They were in a coffee shop on 72nd Street off Broadway. The investigative team had split up at the 67th Street Armory on the East Side; Jack and Moe, led there by Alice Vitale, had gone off to find a social worker who remembered Jimmy Coffee. Bonnie had gotten Charles Benson's old address from the Human Resources Agency. She had rung the bell cold and Jenny had asked her to wait outside. Her mother and father, she had explained, couldn't bear to talk about Charles.

"My husband is a musician," said Jenny.

She was not as old as she looked, thought Bonnie. Maybe it was the strain of fighting off the weight that made her seem so high-strung. Then she decided that Jenny had a long agenda of worries.

"I met Howard through Chuck."

"Chuck?"

"Chuck plays the piano. When he was in college he played in some clubs in the village, and that's how I met Howard. My husband. Howard plays guitar. Not now. It's hard to find a gig so he has to work with my father, but that's just temporary."

She spoke fast, but Bonnie understood the rhythms of nervous people. They either clammed up or poured out their souls. Misfortune always seemed to change the speed of the automatic denials, the hard justifications. She had learned the rhythms when she was working as a street reporter, standing by the screen, listening to the families. Not my son. Not my husband. Not my brother.

"Chuck was always very sensitive." Jenny smiled with a kind of apologetic pride. "He wrote poetry, but I suppose you know that."

She spoke of him, Bonnie noticed, in the past tense. And she'd accepted Bonnie's explanation without question. "We're doing a special about the homeless," Bonnie had lied.

"The people in the Armory were quite taken with your brother."

"You know, he's four years older than I am so we weren't that close. Matter of fact, there were the usual sibling resentments and jealousies."

"How old is Chuck?"

"Twenty-seven."

Bonnie was surprised. For some reason, she had placed him in his mid-thirties. It had to take at least that long to fall so completely between the social cracks, she thought. But maybe now it was different. Maybe now it could happen overnight. You wake up one day and skip the rent and offend the boss and you're gone. Most people were one paycheck away from disaster; she'd read that someplace. Maybe it was that quick and that absolute.

"Chuck was the reason I started to study English. He'd read these great big books when I was a kid and I wanted to be just like him, so I started reading the Russians and Dickens and everything else I could get my hands on. The trouble with great literature is that it doesn't prepare you for reality. It's full of parables and metaphors and significant insights. What's that got to do with the rent?"

The coffee was strong and hot and Bonnie's hands hadn't

warmed up yet from the cold. "It doesn't feel like Christmas, does it?" Jenny said.

"No."

"Chuck used to love Christmas. He'd be up all night, listening for Santa Claus."

She had sad, moist eyes.

"What do you suppose happened?" she asked Jenny.

The sister leaned across the table and took a forkful of chocolate cake. She shook her head. "That's so good. Can't tell you how long it's been since I had a piece of chocolate cake." Bonnie pushed the plate towards her and Jennie broke off a few more pieces of the icing.

"He cracked," Jenny shrugged. "Plain and simple. Why he cracked I have no idea. But there was a definite crack-up. One day he was intact and the next day I looked at his face and it was like a piece of porcelain had shattered and been glued back together. I could actually see the cracks. Or, I thought I could. My poor brother."

"I hear the same story a lot," said Bonnie, taking nips of the chocolate cake. "I blame the Republicans. And my parents."

Jenny ordered a cup of hot chocolate to go with the chocolate cake.

"We're all disappointed," said Bonnie.

"Not you. Such a glamorous job."

"C'mon! You know better than that. It used to be fun. On newspapers. I was a newspaper reporter and that was great. You hang around the fringe and listen to stories and sometimes you are able to convince someone to do the right thing."

"Well, isn't that what you're doing now? I mean, bringing the problems of the homeless to the attention of the public. Isn't that socially useful, a community service? Aren't you helping someone?"

Bonnie felt a pang of guilt and tried to change the subject, but Jenny was determined.

"I, myself, am no stranger to disappointment," said·Jenny. She nodded. "I wanted to dance. I suppose life is always wanting what you're least likely to get. Fat girls want to dance. Guys with poetic hearts want to live soulfully. Some people handle disappointment better than others."

"Why didn't Chuck accept help?"

Jenny leaned across the table. "Because he's schizophrenic. Clinically diagnosed." She straightened up. "He can't help himself. He has delusions. My father thinks it's a matter of willpower. If the boy would just make up his mind, he'd be fine. I have a strong, forceful father who is so afraid that he might be nuts that he'll never admit that there are some people who cannot help themselves." In a deep voice, she said, "'When he's ready, he'll come home!' That's my father."

"But can't he be treated?"

"Not against his will and not without my father's permission. Not unless he harms himself or someone else. So far he hasn't harmed anyone. I don't think he could ever harm anyone but himself. So many of these people who are living on the street, they're very frightened, very alone. Most people are afraid of them, but they're more afraid of us."

Alice Vitale introduced Jack and Moe to the housing coordinator of the Armory, then had to rush to a board meeting of the Museum of Modern Art. The basement of the Armory smelled foul. A hundred men had slept in the room and the odors of sweat and urine and cheap whiskey hung in the air. Danny Jackson was supervising the changing of the linen and the cleanup. "You find everything in here in the morning," he said. He was a huge man who looked to be about forty-five. He looked as if he had seen it all.

"Empty bottles?" asked Jack.

"Empty syringes," Danny said not taking his eyes from the floor. The men cleaning up and changing the linen for minimum wage were city employees, but they were former clients, and some would be clients again. They wore rubber gloves and had raw eyes. "Empty crack vials. Sometimes dead bodies. We get one or two a week. Not always violent shit, either. You'd be surprised. Sometimes it's some young dude who just stops breathing. Like he give up. Can't hassle it no more. Especially now. They sit in front of the TV and they watch Christmas shows and some of these guys come out of that room crying. Thinking about the families they don't have."

Moe was standing on Danny Jackson's other side. He was struck at the slow, underwater pace of the cleanup. Danny saw the expression on Moe's face and understood it.

"You gotta be half cop and half priest," Danny Jackson said. Jack saw a lot of hard time in his face.

"Tell me about Jimmy Coffee," said Jack.

The supervisor turned and looked at him. "A busted case," he said. "Looked like a fucking abominable snowman, know what I mean? Big guy, but could not take care of himself. Didn't know how to use the soap. See, they have to take a shower when they check in. I remember when he first came in, one of the guards said you better check this guy out. He's standing in the shower and he's chewing on the fucking bar of soap. You hear what I'm telling you? The man was eating the fucking soap!"

"Whatdja do?" asked Moe.

"I told one of the guys in the shower to show him, but, hey, man, they're afraid of this guy. I mean, he's big and they don't wanna be taken down for a fag. So I just let him get wet and dry himself off."

"What'd he do with the soap?" asked Jack.

"Ate it, man."

One of the clients brought them coffee and they stood in the bay and sipped at the undrinkable liquid. "This tastes like soap," said Moe.

"He never became what we call a regular, you follow? He was erratic. He preferred the park. People leave you alone in the park. You come in here and you gotta take a shower and you gotta stand in line and you gotta go to bed at a certain time. And them's just our rules. The people down there in the bay, the bad asses who run the place like gangs, they got their own rules. You gotta give them half your cigarettes, you gotta hand them your dessert, you gotta give them some money. You give it up or they cut you. You understand what I'm saying?" He shook his head. "Guy like Jimmy, he's very confused, know what I mean? I mean, he understands that he has to take some shit from the bad asses, but he don't like it. He likes to sit in a corner and read his poetry. Once a month, he'll get up on the table and start shouting and they hafta pull him down. He's all right, though."

"When's the last time you saw him?" asked Moe.

"Me? Oh, that be about a week. But some of the others, they seen him in the park on Friday night. He was carrying on about the dead people. Sayin' he saw brains and guts all over the floor."

"Did they believe him?" asked Jack.

"They believed him. Jimmy doesn't lie. He sometimes has his wild dreams, but he was loaded down with food and he had blood on him."

"Did you report this?"

"No, sir, I surely did not."

"Why not?"

Jackson yelled at one of the workers on the floor: "Get off your ass and sweep the damn floor." Jack thought he was stalling for time.

"Guy comes in and flips me a badge," said Jackson. "Got a mile-wide attitude, this guy. Like I smell bad. So he asks me do I know something. Not polite like you guys. Not with respect. Like he dissed me, you understand?"

Jack nodded. Moe nodded.

"So, I told him there's this junkie who knows a guy named Jimmy who maybe knows something. It was the truth. I'm being honest. That's where I got it from—the junkie. Don't know no name. Just another junkie. I know it's true 'cause I got a good ear and I know the truth when I hear it. But this guy with the badge, he ain't even listening. Him and his partner just wanna get outta here. Can't take the stink. Fuck 'em."

Jack thanked the supervisor and pulled Moe after him. As they were walking out, Jack said. "So, Jimmy Coffee was a witness."

"Sounds like it," said Moe.

"And those dinks in the Task Force, they are chasing their fucking ass."

Sergeant Jake Cummings, who headed one wing of the Task Force investigative unit, had set up a blackboard in the conference room of the Task Force. Only the senior commanders were allowed into this meeting. Federal Agent Hugo Barnes took his usual place in the skeptical rear. On the blackboard Sergeant Cummings had written the name: "MARVIN JAMES."

He brushed the chalk from his fingers and glanced around the room. He had a grin on his face as if he had broken the case. Cummings had a theory: It wasn't a mob hit on an informer, he decided. The murders were the random act of a nameless, homeless beggar.

"We finally got a make on the prints on the dead man in the park," said Sergeant Cummings, pointing to the chalked name on the blackboard. "This victim-slash-suspect was a career criminal; a junkie with a long string of convictions for assault. Just come out of upstate himself. Had to be a falling out with his partner when they tried to nail this other guy."

"Excuse me, Sarge, but I read this man's record and from what I have seen of his M.O., he worked alone." said Lieutenant Lukash, Cummings's commander.

Sergeant Cummings shrugged. "It is well-known that criminals often change their M.O. Especially when they start to get a little older and the legs go. Figure they need help. This guy was running on a bad leg. Maybe he wanted a partner. Maybe the partner thought he was greedy. Who knows. The Korean thing, this makes a lot of sense."

"How?" asked Sanders.

"A crazy junkie murder," said Sergeant Cummings, turning from Lukash to Sanders and Detective Tommy Day.

"You are telling me that they hit our guy by accident?" said Lukash, getting out of his chair, mashing the cigar in the ashtray—despite the fact that it wasn't lit—and throwing his arms in the air. "I'm supposed to buy some wild theory that this is one big fucking coincidence?"

Officer McDaniels pushed open the conference room door, carrying a tray of coffee. They all ignored her.

"This is amazing," Sanders muttered, pacing back and forth in front of the room. "Fucking amazing. But, hey, listen, strange coincidences happen. Stranger things have happened."

"Our guys are now running down the shelters and soup kitchens," said Cummings.

"Okay, lemme ask you something, where did this homeless beggar get an expensive, sophisticated .9-millimeter automatic? Huh?"

"I dunno," replied Cummings. "Maybe he found it. Maybe he took it off the Koreans."

Sanders stopped. "You mean to say that this guy Barone calls me because he is afraid that someone is after him and then he accidentally walks into a murder? Isn't that a little hard to swallow?"

"This is New York City, sir," said Sergeant Cummings.

Lukash paused, held up his hand. "We had a cop in here yesterday. He said something that makes some sense now. He said that the shelves in the deli were screwed up. But not just screwed up: like they were looted. Like someone was grabbing food."

The lieutenant's words sank in.

"Okay, I've ordered a full-scale redeployment of the men. They will track down the armed beggar. They will bring him in and they will question him and they will get to the bottom of what happened Friday night at the Korean deli.

"Let's not take any chances," he added. "Somebody's done a lot of killing. Let's try to take him alive, but let's get him."

Sanders was disturbed. Cummings had not convinced him, even though he wanted to be convinced. He would much rather believe that it was a random act of violence than think that evil forces were at work. The fact that Barone called him right before he was murdered, the fact that Barone sensed that he was being stalked, seemed to rule out a coincidental robbery and murder. Barone was too careful to place himself in that kind of danger. However, he had no power to overrule Lukash and his men. They were the investigative arm.

Federal Agent Hugo Barnes decided to phone Washington and ask for a transfer. Nothing could be as bad as being forced to follow the inept wanderings of this investigation, this wild scramble for a derelict. He could not believe that these so-called professionals were serious. As the late Tuesday meeting began to break up, he decided not to make the call from his home phone; there could be a tap on it.

"You know, Tommy," Sanders said to his bodyguard, "something else bothers me."

"What's that?"

"If this was a guy killed during a stickup, if this was just some maniac killer who happened to murder our snitch, how do you explain the death threat against me? Does that connect at all?"

"Don't worry, sir, I'm still gonna stick with you."

15

They were heading back to the apartment building on West End Avenue, strolling along 72nd Street, pausing every few feet to look at shop windows or simply slow the pace, when Jenny stopped abruptly, told Bonnie, "Wait here!", then bolted across to the north side of the street.

Bonnie looked and saw him backed up against the wall, as if he could blend into the bricks of the building itself. He was tall and had long hair and an old man's stoop. Of course she knew who he was. Jimmy Coffee. It occurred to her that she could have passed him easily, writing him off as one more doomed derelict. Had she bothered to look at all. But now that she knew him, knew something about him, she recoiled at something almost dangerous. Even from a distance, she could detect a smoldering look in his eyes. The kind of signal you get on a subway when someone begins to run out of medication.

Even so, she considered crossing over, just to check.

Maybe she was imagining it. Maybe she was inventing threats. But she decided it would be a mistake to break into the conversation.

Jenny and her brother were talking in deepest concentration, leaning towards each other, in motion—he moving one way, she moving closer to hear. It was a tango of siblings who know the rhythms of each other's arguments.

Bonnie stopped at a vendor's cart and bought a pretzel. She ducked behind the umbrella and watched. She could see Jenny glancing over every now and then, making certain that she was still there. Her brother inched back, drawing Jenny into the building shadow, talking and waving his left arm. His other arm was jammed inside his coat pocket. Holding something. At least that's how it looked from the way he kept his arm rigid. His plastic garbage bag of possessions was behind him, tucked into a crevice, defended.

It was almost as if Bonnie could hear the conversation. At least she could see it growing in intensity. First Jenny would implore, and Jimmy Coffee would turn into stone. Then he would bend down from his angry height and say something vehement. Jenny would back up before it.

Finally, Jenny opened her purse and passed him some money, and he began to half-walk, half-run away. He was heading west and he was moving fast. Bonnie thought Jenny would have to run to catch up. But Jenny was coming back across the street and she looked angry. Bonnie hid behind her pretzel, and felt foolish.

Jenny took her arm, pinching some skin, and Bonnie cried out. "That hurts," she said.

Jennie walked east. "Did you know that he was in trouble?"

Bonnie didn't answer.

"Of course you knew."

She dropped Bonnie's arm. Jimmy Coffee was out of sight. She had protected his retreat.

"Look . . ."

"Don't give me 'look!' You knew!"

Bonnie hurried to catch up as Jenny hurried away. She didn't say anything—she just quick-walked alongside the furious sister. "Boy, you people!" Jenny said, and there were tears in her eyes. She stopped and spun on Bonnie. "Isn't there anything, anything at all that's sacred?" She shook her head. "No, not sacred. Isn't there anything you won't profane?" Then she picked up speed again.

Bonnie shuddered. Didn't Jenny see his face? Didn't she notice the wild split between the eyes and reality? As if the motor functions were going off in all different directions. No, she was his sister and only saw her big brother.

"Do you wanna hear my side?"

"No, I don't."

Bonnie hurried to keep pace and spoke breathlessly. "Yes, I knew that he was in trouble, or, at least, I knew that he was a witness to something. I didn't know the extent. I didn't know how much you knew. It's very tricky when you are feeling your way . . ."

"Tricky, there's the right word."

They stopped at the benches on the strip dividing Broadway. Jenny collapsed in an empty spot—a kind of surrender. Bonnie sat alongside her.

"How could you do that? I thought you came to do something good, I thought we liked each other. How could you deceive me?"

"I don't know," Bonnie said, defeated. "It's a bad habit. You can't be in this business and not develop bad habits."

"Don't be so kind to yourself. It's not like substance abuse; it was very conscious and it was, well, dishonorable."

"You're right. There's something very ugly about what I did. It doesn't seem ugly when you're out to fool cops and congressmen. It becomes a habit. You wind up tricking everyone. You don't trust anybody."

"What an awful thing. What an awful, awful thing."

They sat on the bench and watched the policemen watch-

ing the drug dealers; they watched the elderly strollers moving cautiously down the street like a night patrol in enemy
territory, and they were overcome, each in her own way and
for her own reasons, by the complexity and enormity of the
things that people had to do to survive day to day.

Bonnie was shocked by the realization of the lengths to
which she would go to get a story. Reporting was always a
shock. The first time she covered a car crash on the Turn-
pike, back when she was a wire service reporter working out
of Albany, a state trooper had taken her to the wreck and
said, "Take a look at this gal's face." There was no face.
There was no head. Just a torso. The driver had been decapi-
tated in the crash. It was a cop joke. She realized, in her own
way, that she had become as callous and cold-blooded as that
state trooper.

"Let me explain," she began.

Jenny turned away, but Bonnie persisted. "I started to do
a piece about the killing at the Korean deli on Friday night.
I'm sure you read about that. Three people shot."

"I know."

"Well, it turns out that there was a witness to the killings.
This is a big case. Very big. One of the victims may have
been an important mob informer. If there was a witness—
and the word was pretty good that there was—that witness
could be very important, as well as in big danger. It turns
out that the witness is a street guy who goes by the name of
Jimmy Coffee. And Jimmy Coffee is . . ."

"My brother."

Bonnie nodded.

"He wasn't a witness," Jenny said. "He happened to go
into the deli after it was over. He didn't see anything. He
stole some food because he was hungry. That's what he told
me. He was hungry and now people are after him. Oh, God,
how could he be a witness? He's got a mental history! He
can't testify."

"He could still tell them things they want to know. The

cops are still gonna be looking for him, Jenny. They're a few steps behind me, but they're coming. And that's not the worst. Whoever committed the killings is gonna think that he might be a witness. There aren't too many places for a man like your brother to hide. What else did he tell you?"

She nodded and then shook her head. "Nothing. It was incoherent. He's afraid. I can't talk to him. I told him to come with me and we'd go to the police and he got very frightened. He started screaming—did you see? He started calling me names and threatened to kill me. Of course he doesn't mean it, he's just very scared. I don't know what to do. I can't tell my father—he'd kill me. Him I'm afraid of."

Bonnie laughed, then, after a moment, so did Jenny.

It did not escape Bonnie that she had just maneuvered Jenny into further, deeper revelations. It was an old habit, hard to break.

They'd arranged to meet at Jay's on First Avenue near 80th Street. Tuesday nights the fish was supposed to be fresh. Moe was drinking beer and Jack was drinking ginger ale. "Cannot deal with my head," said Jack. Bonnie ordered a bluefish platter. The fish was cold, but the french fries were decent and the bread was fresh. Bonnie's story, as much as she told, leaving out her humiliation and abject apology, made Jack decide that he would go to Monahan. The inspector would drop it in the lap of the Task Force and they would pull in Jimmy Coffee. Maybe the homeless man was the killer. It wouldn't be the first time that some harmless-looking derelict had gone berserk and slaughtered everyone in sight.

Still, Jack was bothered. There was some piece of this case that didn't quite match up. Somewhere, he had the key to something and he didn't know what it was. He took the name of the sister and went to the phone to call the inspector. It was too noisy in Jay's to talk so he left to look for a quiet phone. The closest phone he could find was the one inside the Acropolis Diner. The waiter, Stavros, was on duty, wearing a crooked smile, as if he had bested Jack at whatever game they were playing.

"How are you tonight, officer?"

"Fine. Fine."

"I hear you talk to Crazy Edie."

"Where did you hear that?"

"We hear. If something happens, we hear. Everything comes in and out of the Acropolis."

"You pass along everything you hear?"

"Not everything. If I tell you everything, you don't have a job. I wouldn't like to see you wind up sleeping in the Armory, begging me for food scraps."

"Listen, if you're holding anything back, you can get into big trouble, pal."

"Oh, really? Big trouble! Ship me back to Athens? Go ahead. This country stinks."

Then Stavros said something, tossed it out, almost carelessly, that stopped Jack cold: "You find the handsome cop yet?" asked Stavros.

"What?"

"The cop, you find the handsome cop?"

"What handsome cop?"

"I told the girl. Your friend. There was a cop in here Friday night. Sure, a cop. Very good-looking. You find a good-looking cop yet?"

The hairs on the back of Jack's head tingled. His gut instinct as a policeman was aroused. It was not always possible for him to say, precisely, what it was that set off the alarms. He had the intuitive eye of a born policeman. He studied the world for small disturbances—a night light that burned during the day, a coat that didn't match the rest of the outfit because it was hiding a gun—tiny signals that implied a glitch in the universe.

Jack had forgotten about the cop. Bonnie had mentioned him, but he had been more interested in Crazy Edie. The fact that a cop had been in the diner on Friday night had not seemed important on Saturday. But as time passed, as it became clear that this was a major case, why hadn't that cop come forward? Why hadn't he identified himself and offered to assist? That's what cops do. They look for excuses to insinuate themselves in big cases. Some cop was having coffee a few blocks away, he'd automatically come down to the Task Force and spill everything that he could remember. Who came into the diner? Who looked out of place?

And then he remembered something else. Something that had slipped out of his mind, falling into his hangover. He had been drunk, but now he remembered: Friday night when he was in the midst of his drunken vomiting, half out of the window of the unmarked car, another car passed by, going up First Avenue. The driver had looked at him, made eye contact, then Jack had gone back to his dry heaving. He remembered now that it was a police car. An unmarked cruiser. He was positive. And the driver was a cop. A good-looking cop.

"No," he told Stavros calmly, "we didn't find the handsome cop yet. I'm not sure there are any."

"Sure. He come back. I don't say anything, but he come back. With some other cops. They have a hamburger."

"Describe him a little better for me, would you, Stavros? We could put him in the Adonis contest."

The waiter got a little nervous, but he cooperated. "Like I say, good-looking and not too tall. Maybe even a little short. Very nicely dressed. Expensive suit. And he has a cashmere coat, lays it very carefully on the back of the booth. Doesn't want it to get dirty."

Jack listened, his face betraying nothing. The handsome cop was crucial. Of that he was certain. But he wasn't ready to bring Monahan in on the hunch. It was, as yet, too flimsy. He would firm it up first.

The phone was in the back. Jack called his nephew, Barry.

"How is she?" he asked. Barry had been planning to go to the hospital that morning.

"The same," said Barry in a flat, emotionless voice. "In a coma. Uncle Jack, Aunt Natalie's not gonna come home."

"I know, kid. I was at the hospital last night. I'll meet you there again tonight. Later. I'm still working. I'm not sure what time I can get off."

Barry didn't understand. He thought Jack should keep a vigil at the bedside. He thought he should be there to assist in whatever ways bystanders assist. He didn't understand that Jack was not a bystander, not in his wife's death. Natalie had understood. She had tried to guard and protect Jack against the long sorrow that awaited. Not that there was much she could do. On Monday night, when they spoke, when she finally opened her eyes and pulled him a little closer to him as he lay on her sickbed, she whispered that she loved him. And when he began to cry, she shook her head. We've been lucky, she said. We've had each other and we have nothing to regret. Not many people can say such a thing.

"I've loved you every single day I've known you," he said.

She couldn't even move her head to nod. But he felt her agree. "I know," she said in that fluttery, vanishing voice. "I know. And I've loved you and I've been grateful for that. But we have to let go now. Jack, sweetheart, we have to let go. I can't stand the pain and I can't stand the guilt. I know that you don't want me to die. . . ." She held up her withered hand against his protest. "But you must let me die. I need some peace. I need some rest. I'm so tired. So very, very tired . . ."

And then the medicine kicked in and she drifted off to sleep, then finally, blessedly, into a coma. Jack felt her sigh as she left the pain behind.

He didn't think that he could cope with the vast combination of guilt and relief. Jack could not bear the deathwatch. He could handle an emergency, he could deal with pain. But not witnessing Natalie's death. And he would not sit at the bedside, with her in her coma, not for the sake of appearances. Natalie wouldn't allow it. She wouldn't want it. They had had the best of it and he would be left to grieve in his own fashion.

He would now live alone in the house in Queens. He would sleep in the bed alone. He would wander the rooms and feel her absence as he paced like a prisoner in a cell. Sentenced to life without her. The strong coffee she liked—the French roast that he remembered to pick up in the city—he would have to forget to buy it now. The notes under his pillow when he worked late and she left early for work, he wouldn't find them there anymore. No more sweet missives: "Please remember to pick me up and take me to dinner and then later I'll show you some new tricks I learned in the sack."

Long ago, when he was a young cop and she was a young bride, they had made a pact. She would not grieve for him. She would not wait, every night he was on patrol, for the phone or the doorbell. She would go on with her life and assume that he was all right. If not, she would deal with that when the time came. Not that she didn't care for him. That was the trouble. She cared too much to bear the loss easily. They had their pact. He went about his dangerous duty, and she didn't think about the worst. And now the worst had struck her instead of him.

"Barry, I know she's not comin' home."

A deep sob emerged from Barry's heart, for if they did not have children, Barry was her next best thing. She'd pampered and fussed and forgiven Barry's faults and made Jack swear to care for her nephew. She hadn't said, "When I am gone," but she might as well have said it.

He could not watch her die, not in that cold hospital room. Not lost in a coma, stitched to tubes and monitors, gone already, the burden of pain put down.

"Uncle Jack?!" Barry said, like a bewildered child.

"I'll meet you at the hospital," Jack said.

Jack told Bonnie he had to check on some things down at headquarters. "Did you guys shoot some pictures of the Task Force up at the scene Friday night?"

Bonnie said almost certainly. He was walking her to her car on 58th Street. He said it would be valuable to get as many pictures of the Task Force as possible. He didn't tell her why.

"I have to go home and change first," she said. "I need a shower and I have to feed the cats."

"You have cats?"

"If they haven't eaten each other."

"You like cats."

"No, not particularly. They were there when I sublet the apartment. I was gonna dump them, you know, load them in a carrier and lose them in Coney Island, but I couldn't do it. Now I go home and feed them. I'm their keeper. I don't like them much—they're much too smug—but I'm all they have. It's strange. You sublet an apartment and you find yourself leading somebody else's life. When I moved in, I started using her makeup. I drank her tea, and I hate tea. Now, I don't mind it so much. I even think I'm starting to look like this woman I've never met."

Jack looked at her. "I didn't think of you as a cat lover."

"Well, don't. Think of me as a lover of fine art."

She got in the car and drove off. She wondered why Jack wanted the pictures; well, she'd find out later.

At the station on 33rd Street, Bonnie picked up the news tapes, then, in the parking lot, grabbed Ernie Winters, the police reporter, coming in from an assignment with his crew. Ernie Winters cultivated a windblown, fifty-mission look. He thought of himself as a combat pilot, coming back from a flight over Berlin where the flak was so thick you could walk on it. He wanted to look haggard and triumphant and brave, like the pilots he had seen in those old newsreels.

In reality, he took police handouts and ran police errands and managed to make his voice soft and husky at every police funeral. The cops loved him. They invited him to their dinners, they fed him innocuous tips on stories that made them look good. The other police reporters fed him lies.

He and Bonnie had gotten off on the wrong foot her first

week on the job. She'd called him a wuss for defending a corrupt sergeant, and he'd countered by calling her a man-hating cunt.

"Ernie! How the hell are you?"

He flinched. The sound man and the cameraman smiled and stood back to watch, maybe even grab some film, because if these two ever went at it, they wanted a record of it. They had worked with Ernie Winters long enough to cherish the thought of him lying bloody in a parking lot, the victim of a weathergirl wilding.

"What do you want?" he asked angrily.

She smiled up sweetly. "I wanna be friends."

He turned away. "Okay, we're friends."

She blocked his escape again.

"C'mon, Ernie, you're still mad 'cause I put itching powder in your makeup?"

"You did that?"

"No, no, not me. I just heard about it."

He stopped, turned and faced her, a true glint in his eye. "I thought I had an allergy. Stay away from me, Bonnie. I don't like you. I don't trust you. I think you're a lousy broadcaster and I don't even find you attractive."

"This sounds like the start of something beautiful," said the sound man.

"I was just gonna say the same thing," said the cameraman. "This is how they hit it off in *It Happened One Night*. Next thing you know, they're on a honeymoon."

"No honeymoon," bellowed Ernie, brushing past, entering the station, showing his pass to security. (He was the only on-air talent that they made show a pass every time.) He reported to makeup. Bonnie was hot on his heels.

"I wanna talk about the Korean deli thing," she said.

"Watch the broadcast," he said over his shoulder. "That is, if you can bear to watch professionals."

"I know you're mad and you have every right to be. I behaved badly. I am very sorry."

He turned to see if she was serious. He couldn't be certain.

"I think I have a lead," she said.

"I'm not interested."

She was starting to get angry and had to control her temper. "Listen, I have to go out there in a few minutes and face that camera and tell the public that we're in for some bad slush. You know, rain mixed with snow. It's not all sunshine and the pretty changing of the leaves, being a weather reporter."

He didn't understand this. Was she really sorry? "What's the tip?"

"I heard they're looking for someone in the Korean deli case. I heard they got a prime suspect."

"Nah. Lukash would have told me."

"You guys are that tight?"

"Hey, the man calls me when he's ready to go public."

"So he might be chasing a suspect?"

He shrugged.

"Would you call him and just ask him?"

"Hey! I do not bother him when he's in the middle of an investigation. We respect each other's professionalism."

"Listen, listen, okay, forget the call. But you did a profile on the Task Force, I remember. Great piece. Now the library can't find a copy and I know that you keep your stuff. Would you mind if I looked at it?"

He thought for a moment, then turned and went through his file. He kept his locked files in the makeup room—his theory was that there they would be safe. "Sure," he said, unlocking the cabinet. "No harm."

She took the cassette, put it in her bag, started to leave, then turned and looked at Ernie and smiled. "You are such an asshole."

16

"Coffee?"

Frankie-the-Fox didn't answer. He was a hardhead. One of the old breed. The kind who turned everything, even a container of coffee, into a life-and-death matter of honor. The kind who didn't take anything from cops. Not coffee. Not shit. Not anything. This was one of the reasons Don Danielo Iennello tolerated Frankie as one of his bodyguards. Frankie said something, he meant it. You could take it to the bank, as the Don liked to say. You couldn't threaten him, you couldn't bribe him, you couldn't tempt him. You had to kill him. He was as tough as a snake.

But he was also as stupid as stone. He once robbed a bank and wrote the stickup note on one of his own deposit slips. His specialty was knocking off grocery stores near police station houses. He did three years in Elmira for breaking into Gracie Mansion. He had the mayor's stereo set in his hands when he walked into the arms of SWAT teams, special response units, and the normal uniformed contingent of guards. Fifty guns were levelled at Frankie when he came out of the mayor's house. The judge sent him away as much for his own protection as society's sake. Which is how he came to be called Frankie-the-Fox.

Sergeant Jake Cummings emptied five packets of sugar into his mug of black coffee. It was one of those official mugs with a Police Department shield on the face, as if even coffee mugs had to have a badge to get past the Task Force guards. He stirred the coffee with the back end of his cigar. Leaning back in a chair behind Lieutenant Bob Lukash's desk in the Task Force headquarters, Cummings let Frankie stew. Not that it would make any difference. Cummings was trying to figure out what it would take to loosen Frankie's cement. Gonna be hard to crack this nut, he thought grimly.

Detective Larry Cohen stood guard behind Frankie-the-Fox, whose real name was Francis Catalbo. Earlier that night, Lukash and Cohen, along with six backups, had grabbed Frankie when he came out of a movie theater showing *Rocky II*. Frankie had taken in the situation with uncharacteristic speed and surrendered without a fight. He could take one or two down with him—of that he was certain—but in the end he'd be dead. They'd grabbed his gun, taken his automatic out of his shoulder holster and put the handcuffs on tight. Frankie went quietly, if not meekly, expecting nothing, asking nothing, showing nothing. He'd bide his time. Wait for his moment.

Frankie didn't know why they grabbed him and he didn't care. One thing or another. He had committed enough outstanding crimes to qualify for a bust. You couldn't believe what they told you. Cop says he wants to know about a heist on Park Avenue, means he wants to know about a shakedown in the Bronx. Or the dealers in Queens. The last thing they want to know about is the heist on Park Avenue. If that's what they ask. Frankie always had to concentrate hard to know how to fool the cops. They were always trying to trick things outta you. Better to stay mum. Say nothin'. Spit in their eye.

"The Fox don't want no coffee," Detective Larry Cohen said in a kind of sideways street slur. He didn't care how it sounded. Cohen was six-six and all muscle. He had spent two years working decoys and the word was that he enjoyed getting hit and then hitting back. They said the fight had left him a little goofy, but he started out that way. Cohen lifted cars in the street to let off steam. He went out of his way to make collars. He hung out in waterfront bars listening for an insult, waiting for the bottles to fly, then put his head down and dove in like a running back. For fun, he asked big cops in the squad room to hit him. Punch me, he pleaded. They always came away with hurt hands, and there was King Kong Cohen, grinning, with a trickle of blood running down from his lips. He was all action.

"The handcuffs too tight, Frankie?" Sergeant Cummings asked, eyes on the piece of paper on Lukash's desk. The paper was the warrant allowing them to grab Frankie as a possible material witness in the death threats against Special Assistant United States Attorney Marvin Sanders. Frankie didn't answer. "Loosen the cuffs," said Cummings.

"You got a real friend here, Frankie." Cohen opened the cuffs with his key, then pressed them even tighter. "In a minute, you shouldn't feel a thing." He winked.

The blood was cut off, but Frankie didn't show any pain.

"He likes this much better, sarge."

Frankie and Cohen were both big men, both savage types, and there was a jungle recognition between them: it didn't matter if one was a cop and one was a mob hitter, they were both born killers. And they were both a little dim. They regarded each other with a curious sympathy, like doomed soldiers on opposite sides of a disputed trench.

Still, Frankie felt he had the edge. He had balls. He went in without a badge or a pension plan.

"Too much pasta," Cohen said, pushing at the bulge in

Frankie's belly. It wasn't a big bulge, not even a spare tire, but Frankie had noticed it, been bothered by it, and knew that someone would notice it. Some thick-witted rat kid like this Jew cop, he thought. Some other stonehead with a cold eye for weakness. "You eat too much pasta, hey Frankie boy?"

"Leave him alone," Cummings said. "Frankie's gonna help us. He don't think so, but he's gonna be a big help in our investigation. Don't worry about it. Frankie's on our side."

"That right, Frankie? You on our side?"

Frankie had been through police interrogations. He'd been questioned gently and he'd been beaten. He'd been through the mind games when they fucked with you. Told you that your mother was outside ratting you out. He didn't believe any of them. Just sit here and keep your mouth shut, he told himself.

Outside, Lieutenant Lukash watched from a distance. Agent Hugo Barnes was cracking gum. Like everyone else in the squad bay they were pretending to be busy, but the real business was the interrogation of Francis Catalbo. "I think a guy like that has to be encouraged to cooperate," said Detective Jimmy Paolo.

Lukash gave him a sour look.

They shuffled papers and snuck peeks at Frankie sitting there like the soldier he was, taking what he had to take.

"Fucking guy's not gonna give us spit," Lukash said with admiration. He looked around. He hadn't meant to speak out loud. He turned to the others. "Listen, fellas, I want this done carefully. Cummings'll soften him up and when we go in, we treat him like gold. Only I talk to him. No insults. No pushing. Let him feel the power, not hear it."

The detectives and agents nodded. They understood the psychology. They didn't necessarily agree with it. Not with an old bone like Frankie. But they understood.

There was a fuss at the door and they turned to see Marvin Sanders arriving. Everyone said hello and made room for him to pass. He was flanked by Tommy Day and the media advisor, Jerry Casolaro. It was unseemly for a candidate for mayor to duck behind his bodyguard, Casolaro warned. Get out. Show you aren't afraid. People do not admire cautious politicians.

Sanders marched into the bay, surveyed the scene, then held up his hand and beckoned to Lukash. They moved off to a corner of the room, chasing a typing detective away so they could speak in private. Casolaro hovered nearby.

"What gives?" asked Sanders, indicating the prisoner.

Lukash shrugged. "This is one of Iennello's main guys. A real head case. He's dumb enough to tell us something. This is Frankie-the-Fox. A real joke."

Sanders jutted his jaw in the direction of the exposed office. "So you put him in a fucking glass cage like Eichmann? You think Frankie-the-fucking-Fox is gonna break in a fucking glass cage?"

Lukash shook his head. "I think I want the Don to know that we are taking this threat very seriously. We grab one of his pistols, he'll think twice before he makes a move. If nothing else, he knows we know. And maybe Frankie gives us something to go on."

Sanders shook his head, took off his hat and fell into a metal chair that began to skid. He fought to recover his balance, then pushed himself back in closer to Lukash. "You know, tell you the truth, I don't think our problem is with the Don."

"You don't?"

Sanders shook his head.

"He's the guy you swore that you'd put away."

"I know. I know what I said. Now I say it's bullshit. I figure the derelict did the hit. I figure that it had nothing to do with the mob and that our guy was there by accident."

"What about the threat?"

"It's bullshit. Someone calling in bomb threats on planes.

Someone taking credit for someone else's work. Bullshit. Besides, I really don't need a babysitter." Sanders nodded at Tommy Day who was standing nearby, listening, facing away.

"Humor me," said Lukash.

"No." Sanders sounded firm. "It's wrecking my life. It makes me look like a coward. You remember de Gaulle after Paris fell?"

"What?"

"Paris. World War II. You heard about it? It was in all the papers?"

"Before my time."

"De Gaulle walked into Notre Dame with snipers shooting at him. Everybody ducked, but not de Gaulle. Stood straight and kept walking. And he was a big target. Big as fucking Cohen."

"You are not de Gaulle and we are not ducking snipers. We don't even know who we're ducking. You gotta have security."

"Why?"

"Let me put it this way. Don't get mad, Mister Special Assistant United States Attorney. Nothing personal. Let's assume someone takes you out. Okay? Nothing personal. Business. If you get killed, there will be an investigation. Not some piddling little hearing. Major investigation."

"So?"

"So, someone will leak the fact to the *Washington Post* that before you were killed, you were threatened. The Attorney General of the United States will be hauled before a hostile congressional committee and made to explain why he didn't provide adequate security for a high civil servant in peril. The Attorney General cannot say that you didn't want protection because Charles de Gaulle wasn't afraid, so how can we show less courage than some frog. . . ."

"Be careful!"

"Be realistic! The Attorney General insists that we provide
security. The mayor insists that we provide security. . . ."

"The mayor?"

"Well, how would it look if you got whacked and he got
elected? They'd say he rode to office on your hearse."

"Pretty cynical."

Lukash shrugged.

"He say anything?"

"That's Frankie-the-Fox. But we'll take him in the back
room and let him know that if anything happens to you we'll
bring down the sky."

Sanders was silent. Casolaro came over and put a mug of
tea on the desk. Tommy Day had vanished. Lukash assumed
that he had gone to the john.

The men's room was near Tommy's locker. He made certain that there was no one around, then went to the locker
and got out his "drop-piece," the untraceable gun that he
carried to leave behind if he ever had to kill an unarmed
civilian.

He jammed it into his winter coat, then slipped into the
windowless "back room" where they would soon bring Frankie-the-Fox. He made certain that the gun was loaded, then
planted it in the bottom drawer of the desk, under an expense form.

He came back to the squad bay and when Frankie went to
the john, he trailed along behind him. "I got him," he told
Cohen, who went to get a sandwich from the stack of food in
the rear of the bay.

"Listen," said Tommy standing alongside the urinal while
Frankie peed, "these guys, you know what they want?"

Frankie didn't say anything. He knew. Frankie knew that
they wanted Tommy. He wasn't going to give him up.

Tommy went to work on Frankie. "They're gonna take
you in a back room and get nasty," he said.

Frankie shrugged.

"It can get painful," said Tommy.

"I guess I'll have to give you up," said Frankie. He smiled, then looked around. "This place wired?"

Tommy shook his head. Frankie was washing his hands.

Frankie was a real threat. He shouldn't have said that. Tommy couldn't trust him.

Tommy looked at Frankie in the bathroom mirror and felt some twinge of emotion. The thing that he liked about Frankie was that Frankie didn't like Tommy. A real perverse excuse to like a guy.

Frankie wasn't young, thought Tommy, noticing for the first time the sags and signs of age in Frankie's face. Like seeing cracks on Mount Rushmore, he thought. Tommy had never associated him with time or age; he wasn't the sort of man you placed in any particular generation. He spoke of women, and you didn't question whether or not it was appropriate. He spoke of fights and strength, and it never crossed Tommy's mind whether or not he was still capable. He called Tommy a "punk," and Tommy liked that. It showed judgment.

It was a clear moment. Tommy did not hesitate. "Okay, listen, Frankie, they're gonna take you in the back room. There's a desk and some chairs. They put guys in back of the desk when they talk to them. That's because there's more room for the others if they wanna crowd in. There's probably gonna be a crowd."

Frankie wiped his hands on the filthy roll of towel.

"I put a piece in the bottom right-hand drawer. It's under an expense form. I'll make sure the door's open. Nobody'll be expecting anything. Pull the piece, get the drop on us and get the fuck outta there. The staircase to the right, it leads right outta the building."

Frankie looked sharply at Tommy, who shrugged. "Hey, we don't have a choice. You got a better plan?"

"Maybe I should take a workout and just go to court. They got nothing on me."

"The Don wants you in the wind."

That ended the argument.

"You know what this is about?" began Lukash. The room was small and crowded with cops. Sanders stood in the back of the room and watched.

"We found three kilos of cocaine in your apartment," said Lieutenant Lukash. "Pure. That's sale weight, that's life plus forever since you are a habitual offender. And don't look for deals. You are going away for time and a day."

"Shithead dope dealers don't get deals," said Agent Barnes. "Even your mob colleagues will blow you away."

Frankie asked for a glass of water. The request startled Lieutenant Lukash. He didn't think that Frankie had any physical needs. But maybe the threats had worked. Maybe mentioning the planted dope had dried out his mouth. He nodded to Detective Cohen, who brought Frankie water in a plastic cup. Frankie spilled it and when he bent down, as if in a kind of reflex, he went into the bottom drawer, dug under the expense form and came out with the drop-piece.

"Watch it!" yelled Cohen, diving for cover.

"He's got a gun!" cried Lukash.

Frankie aimed for Tommy, grasping in that final instant that he had been betrayed, but his hands were sore and unsteady from the handcuffs and his aim was off. The bullet he fired hit Detective Cohen in the eye—a fatal wound.

Tommy had his own gun ready. The instant that Frankie showed his weapon, he began squeezing off rounds. They made perfect bull's-eyes in Frankie's chest.

As Paolo and Lukash and Agent Barnes bent over Cohen and then Frankie, making certain that they were dead, Sanders took Tommy's hand and pumped it. "You saved my life!" he said with heartfelt gratitude.

"It's my job," Tommy replied.

17

J ack couldn't breathe. Hospitals had that effect on him. Especially at 11:00 at night with the Christmas tinsel hanging on the tile like an empty promise. The heat was suffocating. They kept the temperature at a tropical pitch because Booth Memorial Hospital in Queens was old and wheezed and leaked and it took a lot of heat to defeat the draughts. The heat. And the guilt. Walking through a hospital, listening to the sighs and moans of the patients in pain, was like walking on broken glass. His own healthy swallows of air seemed indecent.

The nurses didn't tiptoe after the visitors went home. They produced loud, professional noises. They jiggled their trays and made their remarks with the confidence of their art. It was soothing to hear them ordering medication, recording temperatures, uttering opinions. The nurses looked automatically into the glass-enclosed waiting room where Jack sat with Barry. The staff was accustomed to the ordeal of the families. Sometimes the relatives sat for days, as if they were in the depths of their own comas. The nurses kept a respectful distance, regarding the death watch as a state of holy grace.

Jack felt exposed and vaguely resentful, sitting in the glass-enclosed waiting room. He sipped at a coffee and put his hand, every now and then, on his nephew's knee. There, there. Barry would look over with calf eyes, also silent. A late night languor had settled over the hospital. The corridors were dark. The cleaning shifts had finished and the streets were quiet, as if the city itself was one more patient gone to sleep.

Still, it was private. Jack could tolerate the professionals. Barry didn't bother him. He preferred Barry or the nurses to the calf-eyed civilians who oozed such moist sympathy. This thing, he believed, was between Natalie and himself. At night, he could sit in the waiting room unmolested. Only the nurses going about their rounds in clicking efficiency disturbed the holy silence.

Every once in a while they'd hear a sound coming from some bed or another—impossible to tell which—and the nurses would prick up their ears. They didn't move in with the needles or the pills unless they had to. They could tell the real thing. Like being a cop. You could tell, when you were out on the street, who was going to throw a punch and who was just cocking an arm. You learned to distinguish the real threats from the bluster. When they had to, the nurses moved with no-nonsense grace. Like the nuns in parochial school coming down the aisles to smack your wrist. Once, when Jack described the ferocious nuns, Natalie said that they reminded her of the Jewish sisterhoods. The rabbis could be strict, but the sisterhoods were ferocious. Jewish nuns. He liked the way he told her things, and she explained them to him and he understood life better.

He shook his head and found it impossible to imagine her dead. Who would explain such things as Jewish nuns? When they met and he ventured an opinion about the way it should be between men and women, one speaking and one listening, one going out to work and the other staying home, she cut him off like a blade. "Would you like to stay home and wash dishes and clean floors?" she asked.

No, of course not. That quickly she got to the heart of it. And a whole sand castle of false starts and lame assumptions came down. She opened his eyes to the pigheaded opinions he spouted like truth. Don't be silly, she would say, and after he flinched from her meat-axe method, he saw that she was right. He relied upon her to identify and name the slick perversions, the public fools, the error of Vietnam, the cruelty of power, the pity of life itself. He counted on her to keep him honest and correct the gyroscopic mistakes of false logic and cheap sentiment.

At 11:15 the rabbi stopped by. He had heard that Natalie was a Jew. "Yes," said Jack. "Not practicing."

The rabbi shrugged. "So? Nobody practices anymore. Even the ones who practice don't practice. We have a lot of wholesale members of the congregation, you know that? They come to hedge a bet. Sure, they'll discuss ethical relevance, situational this, moral that. But God? Don't mention God. Don't even talk theology because who—outside of Yeshiva University for credits—talks theology? Nobody pays the full retail price of being a Jew."

"Well, it's not easy."

"Not easy? Let me tell you, it's hard. To be a full-scale Jew is to believe in spite of the fact that it's fashionable to have opinions, but not beliefs. It's okay to have skepticism, but not faith. Listen, I understand. Being a Jew you have to believe without having any definite promises for the future. That's blind faith! That's buying a pig in a poke, if you'll excuse the metaphor."

"Sounds about right. Catholics pay lip service to a hereafter. But they don't believe it. Not the Jesuits. Not strictly speaking."

The rabbi looked at Jack carefully. He smiled his thrifty

smile—he wasn't a man to give up his emotions cheaply. "You could be a Jew," he said. "You know that?"

Jack nodded. "I could. But then, I'd know why I was oppressed, and I prefer confusion."

The rabbi laughed softly, because he didn't forget that he was in a hospital late at night and maybe somebody—possibly God—was listening.

He seemed like a nice old man, in his threadbare suit and hand-stitched yarmulke, the best garment he wore. His beard was half white and half gray and his eyes looked worn out by whatever it was that they had seen over the years. Not one of the modern rabbis, thought Jack. Not an American rabbi with a temple congregation in a secular suburb. His fingers were stained with nicotine and his breath smelled of neglect. It was his manner that impressed Jack. Something solid and unbroken, in spite of the shadows around his eyes. "Is there anything I can do?" the rabbi asked.

Jack looked at Barry, whose head was bent over, who didn't want to make eye contact with the rabbi.

"I just ask," the rabbi said, "but what can I do? I can say a few prayers, which I'm sure you are saying yourself, in your own faith."

"I have very little faith left. She's my faith."

The rabbi nodded. He had heard such expressions of despair before. They didn't mean much when a man was waiting for his wife to die. An old man wandering the wards of the hospital in the middle of the night—Jack wondered. "Are you visiting someone, rabbi?"

"Someone," he said.

"I'm sorry."

"It's not your fault. It's nothing." The rabbi shrugged. "It's my father." He looked over his shoulder, indicating the coronary care unit. "Another old rabbi. Two old rabbis holding hands." The rabbi looked toward Natalie's room. "If you don't mind I'll mention her anyway," the rabbi said kindly.

Jack reached into his pocket and took out a bill.

"Not necessary," said the rabbi, waving his money away. "Say something in your own faith. That would be nice."

"I can't promise."

"Who can? I didn't ask for a promise. Just, if you can, say something. If you can't . . ."

The rabbi shuffled away, stooped over by his burdens and his heavy load of shifting faith.

The doctor arrived a few moments later and buried himself in the charts. Jack followed him into Natalie's room, started to say something, but was stopped by the sight of his wife's arms. The nurse had just switched one of the intravenous tubes and Natalie's arms were all bruised. They were thin, with the flesh wrinkled and baggy, with empty pockets, little circles of empty skin, like broken blisters.

"She's not in any pain," said the doctor, pulling Jack away from the bed and out into the hall.

Jack nodded. How could the doctor know? How could anyone know? They said things—anything—to soften the blow. Or to deflect attention from the fact that they were helpless. They couldn't defeat the great enemy, death. It must be an awful thing, Jack thought. To dedicate yourself to a profession so completely futile. There is no other final outcome for a patient but death. None. Not ever. It must be a melancholy thing to be a doctor, he thought.

"We'll keep her as comfortable as possible."

The nurses had a suppressed look of underdog rage. Women left to clean up the mess, to tend as gently as possible, as their gender always was left. The doctors maintained their parched distance and babbled in medical tongues, like professors lost in theory. "We are running some cultures and some blood tests," this doctor said, and Jack nodded as if the tests and the attention would make any difference at all.

The doctor left quickly, his jacket whispering behind him, walking fast in the dead of night, as if he were hurrying to some other urgent rendezvous.

Barry was weeping softly while eating his second hero

sandwich. He kept a bag of sandwiches handy whenever he had to deal with reality. The stench of salami worked against the knowledge of an impending tragedy. Natalie would have laughed, thought Jack. Laughed and hugged her soft nephew who had a heart of gold and no willpower at all. She would comfort him on her own deathbed because she could cope better. So now it was left to Jack and he was not sure that he could cope at all. He had limited gifts when it came to being graceful. He could touch Barry on the knee. But Natalie was the one who had the wisdom and the gift of solace. Jack had a barroom talent, Irish wit. He saw life through the bittersweet punch line of a cosmic joke.

"Barry, listen, this one is going around. This guy is on the beach and finds a magic lamp." Barry looked bewildered. The food was stuffed into his mouth, but he was so taken by surprise that he did something he almost never did: he stopped chewing. A joke! His uncle was telling a joke. To break the tension, no doubt, but still, a joke! "The guy rubs the lamp and a genie comes out to do his bidding. . . ."

"Uncle Jack?!"

Jack held up his hand.

"So the genie says, 'You have three wishes,' and the guy says, 'Great.' 'There's only one catch,' says the genie. 'Anything you wish for, your mother-in-law gets double.' 'Okay,' says the guy, who really hates his mother-in-law.

"'What is your first wish, master? and remember that your mother-in-law gets double.'"

"'I wish for one hundred million dollars,' says the guy. 'Fine,' says the genie, 'but remember, your mother-in-law gets two hundred million. Now what is your second wish?'"

"'My second wish is for a huge mansion on a lake and five hundred acres of land.'"

"'Okay,' says the genie, 'you have your mansion on the lake and the five hundred acres; your mother-in-law, of course, has two mansions and a thousand acres of land. Now what is your third wish?'

"'Give me a minute,' says the guy, who thinks and thinks and thinks and finally says, 'I got it!'

"'Fine,' says the genie, 'now tell me your third wish.'

"'My third wish is that you beat me half to death.'"

Barry smiled.

"Okay, okay," said Jack, nodding, plunging ahead. "What's an Irish sex manual?"

"I give up."

"In, out, repeat if necessary."

"Uncle Jack!"

"Okay, okay, what's Jewish foreplay? Give up? Twenty minutes of pleading."

A passing floor nurse shook her head. But she understood. The wait for death was intolerable and telling jokes was the same as hard liquor. If the families dwelled on the pain too long they, too, began to die. The nurse paused to hear what came next.

"What's Irish foreplay?"

"I give up."

"Brace yourself, Bridget.'"

"Okay, I've got one," said Barry. "This guy comes over from Ireland . . ."

"You're getting back at me for the Jewish joke."

"Damn right. So, this guy comes over from Ireland and he can't meet girls. He's a country boy and he tells his friend, who's been here a little longer, that he has a problem with the American girls. 'So,' says the friend, 'what seems to be the problem?' 'Well,' says the country boy, 'every time I meet one and I tell her how great I am in bed, she walks away from me.' His friend shakes his head. 'No, no,' he says. 'You've got to be subtle. You can't tell a girl that you're a great lover. Here's what you do. You go to the beach and you wear one of those tight bathing suits and you put a tennis ball in it. That'll make the girls think you're a great lover.' So, the Irish lad tries it out and a few days later he sees his friend and he's sad and depressed because the trick

with the tennis ball didn't work at all. 'I know,' says the
friend, 'I saw you at the beach. But let me give you a piece of
advice. The next time, put the tennis ball in the front of the
bathing suit.'"

The nurse laughed, then walked away.

They fell asleep on the stiff false-leather couches of the
waiting room with the prints of flowers hung there, as if to
remind the public that there were other seasons coming. The
nurses tiptoed around them, cleaning up the garbage from
the sandwiches. And Jack dreamed that Natalie was home
and he was a detective with a gold shield. He forgot about
the murders and the pursuit of Jimmy Coffee.

In the five months since she had seen Greg Lowrey, Bonnie had thought about him often. Not in the yearning-long-
ing way, but in the what-did-I-ever-see-in-him style. He had
been a date, a colleague—nothing serious. But now she
needed protection and she summoned him out in the middle
of the night for a drink. She wore her best outfit, the one
that clung and moved with her body. A silk thing that made
its own soft, seductive sound. She had to wait for him, but
she didn't mind. The bartender at the Lion's Head smiled at
Bonnie and poured a screwdriver.

He'll swagger in and smile, look at his watch, and ask inso-
lently: "Am I late?

"You look marvellous," he said when he arrived.

"You look . . . the same," she said grudgingly.

It was noisy and smoky at the bar. The long drinkers were
starting to feel the effects of the liquor, staggering more and
more often to the men's room. The women were pulling at
the men, eager to go home.

Greg ordered a whiskey sour and indicated a refill for Bonnie, who felt the full lead weight of complete uninterest in
Greg Lowrey. Her only plan now was to end this night
alone.

"I watch you on the news and I listen and I dress accordingly the next day," he said. "You know, you're very good on television. A natural."

"I stopped reading that shit you write," she said, smiling.

"I'm being truthful," he said, smiling back.

"I know. And I know what you think of television. A trivial art form that has no real connection to intellect."

He looked around the room.

"What's new at the paper?" she asked.

"Oh, little Donnie has a new pet. Being the managing editor, he has his pick, and he picks them younger and younger. This one's about twelve. Some J-school protégée. He's letting her write long features. Helping her over the rough spots."

"What a nice man," she said sarcastically, nibbling on a pretzel in spite of her diet.

"He asks about you, as if I know. I say that you're fine. You have your highs and lows, but essentially you're fine and soon you'll be married and raising little weathermen and weathergirls."

"I hear that you're sleeping with Carol."

He didn't blink. Just took another sip of his sour. "Yes. Sleeping. That's what we do. Such a bore."

She finished her drink and held up her glass and the bartender brought another. Greg put his hand on top of his glass.

"I'm working on a story," she said to change the subject.

"Yes?" he asked. "Are you going to bring us a white Christmas?"

"I may bring an insipid ass like you a black and blue Christmas."

He turned to face her, to deliver the full force of his frustration at the fact that she continued to reject him, even when she called him in the middle of the night: "I write a daily newspaper column. I write about drugs and cops and the mayor. You're a fucking weathergirl."

She got up, throwing a twenty and a ten-dollar bill on the bar.

"I know when to get out of the rain."

18

Wednesday, December 24th, Christmas Eve, and the looming holidays seemed painfully unwelcome. Headlines about murder hung over the city like low clouds. The citizens went about their business with a vaguely suppressed edge of hysteria. The killings inside the Police Task Force headquarters upset the frail sense that some few places were utterly secure. Even the streets felt unsafe. The cold and gray mist didn't add any cheer.

It was one of those brittle, gray wintery days when people fought their way through the streets, heads down, grim, advancing into the wind. Of course Jack didn't feel the bite of the weather. He was overheated with emotion, immune from the climate. It wasn't only the inexorable decline of Natalie that drove his temper high, although that was no small factor in his mood; there was also this latest command from Inspector Monahan, ordering him off the case. The inspector's voice had been flat and hard on the phone. "I'm sorry," he'd said. It was the pink-slip tone of a made-up mind. "There's been a shootout in the Task Force headquarters. A suspect in the threats against the United States Attorney attempted to kill Sanders. Got hold of a gun right in the headquarters. Lucky thing he was killed before he could get to Sanders. Bad part is that he killed one of the Task Force. Detective named Cohen. Jack, I want you to lay off this investigation. These people are very touchy just now. One of their own has been killed. You can understand. Let's not give them any more grief."

Before Jack could absorb the news, Inspector Monahan had hung up. Not that there would have been any appeal. It was odd. Before the call, Jack might have toyed with an excuse. He was growing afraid that the evidence of his eyes might be wrong. Maybe the whole investigation was marred by a tiny gyroscopic mistake that was taking him further and further away from the truth. Maybe he was in the grip of a terrible momentum plunging him towards an incorrect conclusion.

But, no, that couldn't be true. He saw what he saw and he knew what he knew. He might be thwarted and frustrated, but he wasn't wrong and he wasn't out of possibilities. There were the Task Force tapes. He would look at them, study them, jar loose some constipated memory. There were clues and links, all dangling in front of his eyes like bits of string: the Korean deli, the homeless man, the killing in the park, the threats against Sanders. Somehow the threads all ran in different directions. An array of confusing clues. It was all random and wildly out of control. But suddenly, with Monahan's fiat ordering him off, Jack was recharged, bouncing with energy and new ideas. Now that he was barred, he would keep going. It wasn't all sheer perversity.

Moe had to move fast to keep up with him. They were half-running along the west side of Amsterdam Avenue. "I can't fucking believe it," cried Jack.

Moe couldn't hear. The wind had bottled up his ears. "What?"

Jack stopped, turned and poked a finger in Moe's chest. "Do you buy it?"

"What? Buy what?"

Jack turned and picked up speed and Moe came rushing after him. He grabbed Jack's arm and pulled him into a pizza parlor on Amsterdam Avenue. A few jittery addicts saw them come in, read them correctly as cops, and retreated nervously to the rear, dancing up and down, looking over their shoulders, trying not to bolt for the door.

Moe got two cups of coffee and brought them to a table. The steam rose in his face and felt good. He had seen the addicts and written them off as street weight, as victims, no immediate threat to society. He looked around and was struck by the exhausted, gloomy atmosphere inside the pizza parlor. The holiday streamers wishing everyone a Merry Christmas and Happy New Year were hung with worn, dull tinsel. The cardboard Santa on the wall was smudged with tomato paste. The decorations only served to remind the customers of the hollow insincerity of the holiday sentiments. The drug addicts in the back fighting to stay calm seemed more appropriate to this deadly season.

Leaning over the table, Jack spoke in a furious whisper. "Do you buy this shit? Do you really believe that crap about the shootout? This *gavone* is going to assassinate the United States Attorney inside of the Task Force headquarters? That makes sense?"

Moe shrugged. Of course he didn't believe it. But there was very little that he believed anymore. He had been a cop for too long. He weighed stories according to their style, not their plausibility. If the department said that someone was killed trying to murder the United States Attorney, he asked for the whole story, he pressed for details, as a connoisseur of rounded fiction. The tales were invariably presented with a reasonable beginning, a mysterious middle with its fluctuations of suspense and false leads, and an inevitable satisfying ending. Moe had conspired in his own share of false reports.

He knew how it worked. He was curious, not for the truth of the story, but for the art of the invention, for the undertone of fact that might indicate the truth. Somebody had been killed in the Task Force headquarters. No doubt about that.

The mobster had probably killed Detective Cohen—that made sense. Too many reliable witnesses to doubt that part of the story. But the rest made no sense. Frankie-the-Fox had been a wiseguy, a mob stalwart. True, his elevator didn't go all the way to the top, as Moe well knew. He had been in court years ago when Frankie answered charges that he sold a stolen car to an assistant District Attorney. But it didn't make sense that a full-fledged henchman of Don Iennello would try to shoot his way out of the inner sanctum of the Task Force. Not when the man could count on high-quality lawyers leaning on sympathetic judges for bail. He would definitely not try to assassinate the United States Attorney without a souped-up getaway car waiting at the elevator. No. Moe did not believe the story, despite Frankie's mental shortcomings and the tale's artistic symmetry.

"The guys at the Task Force believe it," Jack said. "Besides, it's one less murderer. He was a cold bastard, that Frankie. I ran into him a few times on the street and I could always see him looking me over, checking to see if I was wearing a vest. You know? Looking for a spot to hit. Not a nice man. Too bad about Cohen—I knew him from the Shomrim Society. A real *shtarke*. Could knock down walls. Having him along on a job was like bringing Godzilla. Used to play handball at the gym. You should have seen him. Fucking neck like my waist . . ."

Jack stopped, looked up and out beyond Moe, above, at some revelation he was having. He almost lifted out of his seat. "It's connected," he said.

"What's connected?"

Jack slapped the table. "All of it. The Korean deli, the

killing in the park, the threats against Sanders, the shootings at the Task Force. It's all one big fucking crime."

He started to get up, but Moe grabbed his arm. Moe was strong—Jack had forgotten that he worked out with weights every day—and he put Jack back in the chair.

"You are having a spiritual fantasy." Moe looked around, making sure that the junkies were out of earshot. "Look, let me explain something to you. People always want to believe that some intelligence, some superior force is guiding things along some logical path. That way, if you figure it out, you can control things."

Jack was nodding, not really listening. He knew that he saw someone driving by that night. He knew that the face of the man he saw would connect, when he saw the Task Force tapes. And there were other things. "Where did he get the gun?" Jack said. "Huh? What's he doing with a gun in the fucking interrogation room?"

Moe shook his head. "Life is random. No. No. Not just random. Perversely random. There's no connections. Just coincidence. Things happen, and that's that. Three people get murdered in a Korean deli and the only connection is that they happened to be in the same place at the same time when some murderer walked in. The murderer wanted a pack of gum and all of a sudden, he had a different urge. He decided to slaughter everybody instead. Somebody wanted to scare Sanders, so they made a phone call and threatened him. The Task Force gets nervous and they pull in one of their targets and warn him that he better not fuck with their chief. Frankie gets tickled by the same crazy urge that hit the guy in the Korean deli and tries to shoot Sanders. Maybe just shoot his way out. Who knows? He grabs a gun. Somebody's gun. You know how careless cops are. Bing! Bing! Bing! Two more dead. No connection. Just thunderstorms in the brain. Emotions. Feelings. You can't count on feelings."

"You through?" Jack was smiling with the patience of a Pilgrim.

"I'm through."

"I'm telling you there's a connection. The gun. It's the gun. I know it. It's all one big, fucking interconnected crime."

"How do you know?"

"I feel it."

Max Gross was only being friendly when he told Bonnie that the crew was hoping she would have something biting to say about the station personnel cutbacks. Jobs were about to be chopped in a brand-new management thrift attack. Bonnie had thrown in with the working-class crewmen and signed a petition against the Christmas firings. The station management was still getting its Christmas bonuses and profit sharing payments, and this offended her egalitarian upbringing. Only the unions were taking a financial hit. Naturally, Bonnie was one of the few employees in the category of "talent" who declared her solidarity with the lunch-bucket crowd. She openly scowled at the station executives and loudly exclaimed their greed, which made them quicken their steps when they saw her in the halls.

"If you really wanna burn their ears, you might mention that they're planning cutbacks and the notices have gone out in Christmas cards. You know, in one of your funny weather remarks," suggested Max as he was pinning on her microphone.

"What's the matter, Max, the union getting soft? Can't organize a picket line? Wanna hide behind my temperature charts?"

He looked at her with wide, shrewd eyes. Suddenly, he was not the benign, grandfatherly crewman who made sure she didn't make a fool of herself on the air, not with sound equipment at any rate. His eyes turned cool and his voice turned hard. It was an old expression; he'd worn it long ago when he fought the union wars and marched on picket lines and gotten his head cracked by company goons.

"Forget I mentioned it," he said.

She knew that she had reacted badly. She just hated being pushed by anyone. So she decided to apologize, but she screwed it up. She was on the air. She pointed to a high pressure system on the weather map and said that it was moving in: "Whatever that means, but it'll probably cost some jobs, just like at our little station, which is under a lot of high pressure to save money because, you know, it's Christmas, and the spirit of Scrooge still wanders the earth, rattling his chains, growing a new link with each layoff. Why do layoffs and firings and cruelty only seem to come at Christmas? Oh, listen, it's only weather."

She took off her microphone and left the studio. "What the hell was that?" sportscaster Conrad Stone asked the anchors. Stone didn't like Bonnie Hudson, but he admired her grit. She was like one of those quirky, lefty pitchers—all sorts of crazy, but talented. "What gets into her?"

The anchors shrugged. Harvey Levy groaned and the lights on the station switchboard began to blink with sympathetic indignation or confusion at her outburst.

"Shit," she said as she grabbed her bubble coat and barged past the security guard. Max Gross held the door open with his body and applauded as she swept past him into the street.

Max stepped away after she passed, and the door closed, blocking Levy from his pursuit. The managing editor looked over at Max Gross, who shrugged.

All the way uptown in the cab she muttered "shit." The driver, a Moslem named Hassan with signs posted in the back banning smoking, cursing and alcoholic beverages, was also a fan of Channel 9 News. His admiration overcame his scruples. "Don't worry," he said when they were passing Columbus Circle heading for Broadway, "it is only the weather." He turned and smiled, sending jaywalkers scattering for the traffic island. Bonnie closed her eyes.

Jack was waiting for her on the northwest corner of 72nd Street and Broadway. Moe had gone to report in at the anti-crime unit. They would meet again that night.

"Listen," Jack began, when Bonnie was still calculating Hassan's tip. "Listen!"

She got out, handed Hassan an extra three dollars and turned, and he was startled. He was happy to see her, with her red nose and involuntary smile and steamy breath that smelled of mint. He took her arm and she went willingly. He led her across traffic, and they walked down Broadway, as if they had a destination. "Listen," he said, marching in quick step. "Are we late for something?" she asked. She had to run to keep up.

Although she didn't understand it, she knew that there were several layers of meaning to this rapid march. At 65th Street he stopped, turned, then crossed four lanes of traffic and stopped on the east sidewalk, waiting for her to catch up. She fell against his arm and started to laugh, not knowing why. "I'd like to sit down," she said, still laughing.

He joined her in laughter and he didn't know why either, although he suspected that it was not something that he should examine too closely. "You know, I've been ordered off the case."

"I figured you were never on the case. Not officially."

"You did?"

"Well, the way you operate seems sort of unusual."

"How's that?"

"Letting me help, for one thing. I know they have policewomen. All of my experience with cops is that they are very touchy about civilian help. They especially hate it when a journalist butts in."

"Well, a weather reporter is not exactly Woodward and Bernstein."

She gave him a cross look.

He led her to a restaurant across from Lincoln Center.
It was the middle of the afternoon and she had finished
an update broadcast. They had no trouble getting a table.
They sat near a window and huddled over hot chocolate,
letting the steam calm them down. They were quiet, as if
each understood that it was a fragile moment. Finally, he
spoke.

"I'm not going to quit the case."

"Good. Me, too."

He told her about the gun. The gun sealed it for him.
That meant some kind of conspiracy. Someone had planted
the gun for Frankie to grab. It had to be a member of the
Task Force.

"I got those tapes," she said. "You know, of the Task
Force."

"So? You find our guy? You find the 'good-looking cop'?"

She shook her head. "Very subjective. Who's to say what
Stavros considers good-looking? And not all the members of
the Task Force were in the clips. Some didn't want to be
filmed. Some were electronically altered."

"I'll look," he said, taking the copy she had made. "I know
what to look for."

They used an empty viewing room in her studio on 67th
Street. He stared at the tape, used the stop-action button,
rewound it, then played it again and again. "What?" she
asked. He leaned closer to the set, leaned back, trying for
perspective. The quality of the tape was poor, especially
when he hit the pause button. A lot of electronic scratches
hit the screen. "This guy," he said, pointing to a blur in the
rear of a group of purposeful men entering the Task Force
headquarters. He moved the slow-forward and the man
squinted and turned away.

"How can you tell?" Bonnie asked.

He nodded. "I know."

They walked out into the wind. "Right now, we have to
find Jimmy Coffee," he said. She nodded, glad to be included in the first team.

They headed north with the same purposeful stride. At 68th Street, they passed an empty lot protected by a chain-link fence. Beyond a break in the fence was a wakeshift shelter. Under the rags, Jimmy Coffee scratched his empty belly. He began to organize himself to go forth and get food. He made a small opening in the layers of cloth and cardboard and peeked out. Jimmy Coffee patted his pocket and made certain that the gun was still there; then he rose from under the crude shelter.

19

Gus Schmidt had his dinner on the stove in the back of his shop. A stew with bits of beef and carrots donated by the butcher and the vegetable man. To preserve his own dignity, the old man always left some Scotch tape or ribbon behind when he took food. Gus ran a novelty shop on 98th Street off Broadway, a narrow corridor half forgotten in the sixty-year exchange of building owners. Over the past six decades Gus had sold a lot of pins and ribbons and string to pay the rent. The rent had gone from $25 a month to $250 a month during the lifetime of Gus's lease. It was a bewildering spiral to the old man, who still thought that the natural cost of a hamburger was a quarter. His mind was locked into an old 1949 menu with twelve full ounces of Pepsi for a nickel. But then, many of his thoughts and memories lingered around that youthful time when his life did not daily seem to hang in the balance.

If the eleven-foot-wide space could have been used for anything else, he would have been thrown into the street long ago. But only bins of attic junk would fit into the area, only dust and the debris that the old man found on his early morning rounds of the neighborhood. When building ownership changed, the new landlord would come around, expecting to find some overlooked opportunity for profit in the space. But invariably he would march back and forth, stare up and down looking for something that wasn't there, then eventually sigh with resignation and leave the old man in peace.

When his wife died sometime in the fifties, Gus moved out of his apartment. Now he lived in the back of the shop where he had a stove and a sink and a leaky, balky toilet. He washed his clothes in the sink. Once a week, he went to his friend Marty's home in the Bronx and took a bath. The local thieves didn't bother to smash his windows anymore. That was the usual punishment for shopkeepers who didn't keep enough spare cash around to pacify the outlaw youths. They found the old man too pathetic and conferred upon him the freedom of his useless shop. Once or twice, strangers came in to rob the old man. They, too, perceived that he wasn't worth the manhunt and left him unharmed. And so he stayed in business, selling the small items in his bins to shoppers who came in mostly by accident and didn't want to leave without spending something as an act of charity.

When Jimmy Coffee came into the shop, Gus began his usual warding-off tactic of shouting and waving to drive a derelict away. "Nothing here!" he cried. "No money!"

Jimmy shook his head. He tried to speak, but his throat was closed. He was hungry; he had smelled the old man's food cooking from the street and he hadn't eaten for more than a day. He intended to offer to work for a meal, but he was choking on his own saliva and couldn't speak.

Gus was almost eighty, small and frail, and became frightened when the homeless man kept advancing, following the smell of the stew, making strange, strangling sounds. "Go! Get out! I got nothing!" He reached behind the counter and grabbed a lead pipe that he kept there for self-defense. He doubted that he could use it. But as the homeless man kept coming, he raised the pipe over his head and prepared to fight.

Jimmy Coffee saw the move for the pipe. He tried to turn around and get out of the shop, but the aisle was too narrow. Bins and cartons began tumbling off the shelves. The old man, seeing his inventory collapsing, panicked and began to shriek. He swung the pipe and Jimmy Coffee ducked and lost his balance. As he went down, Coffee dragged more bins, more cartons with him.

The old man lunged, swinging his pipe with all of his strength. Jimmy Coffee held up his arm, but the old man was quick and the pipe struck him on the arm. Jimmy could hear the bone crack. He realized that he was under a deadly assault. He couldn't retreat. The aisle was blocked by cartons and bins. He was trapped. He thought: "If I don't stop him, this man will kill me." Frantically, he reached into his pocket and pulled out the gun. He had three bullets left; he had counted them. As Gus bent over him, Jimmy Coffee fired blindly and hit him squarely between the eyes. Gus straightened up, blinked, then tumbled backward, dead. He looked almost peaceful, covered by his strings and ribbons.

Jimmy Coffee heard his own labored breathing. He felt his arm throbbing. He wiggled his fingers, but he knew that the bone was broken. Carefully, he rose and leaned against the counter. He still had the gun in his good hand. He slipped it back into his pocket after he was certain that the old man was no longer a threat. "I just want something to eat," he explained, finding his voice. As if something so plain should have been clear. Gus Schmidt just stared at the ceiling.

Jimmy Coffee calculated that he had done the only sensible thing under the circumstances. He had saved his own life. The old man had been trying to kill him. A lot of people were out to kill him these days. Why didn't they just let him die naturally? Couldn't they see that he was old and already dying? He judged that he was at least as old as the old man who lay dead in the aisle. He thought: At least you don't have to go through it. At least I spared you that.

Jimmy Coffee hunted through the shop and found sticks and tape to make a crude splint for his arm. It hurt, but he was accustomed to pain. He could bear it. It was nothing compared to what dying would be. Then he went into the back of the shop, shut off the stove and ate the old man's dinner.

I don't understand, he thought as he dipped some bread into the gravy, sopping up the last of the meal. I have been trying to save myself from these killers, and they keep coming after me. It had begun in that Korean deli. Because he took the food. That had to be the explanation. He couldn't think of any other reason. They were out to kill him for the food. The man in the woods—at first he had thought that he had come after him by accident. He was certain, after thinking about it, that it was because of the food he had stolen. Now the old man. Again, the food. He had only needed one bullet for the old man. But now there were two left, there were more killers. He would need more bullets.

Tommy Day needed help. He had a good plan, one that he could carry out the day after Christmas, which was within the time frame he set for the murder of United States Attorney Marvin Sanders. Between Christmas and New Year's, when the world was less alert, somewhat drowsy. But he couldn't do it alone. He needed tactical support. Someone reliable. He called his oldest ally: Vinnie Insolia. Vinnie always knew where to find things. He would know where to send Tommy. And he could be trusted. It was Vinnie who had first indoctrinated Tommy in mob protocol. And while he was semi-retired now, taking only an occasional job, running errands for the gumbahs on Mulberry Street, Vinnie still took a rooting interest in Tommy's career. He was a voice of wise caution who advised Tommy to be careful as he was walking the fine line between the law and the mob. Either side could turn on you, he warned. For no reason. If they smell a rat. If they need someone to blame.

It was strange to hear this nugget of conservative advice from a man who, in his youth, had been feared as a wild killer without conscience or reservations. Only mob honor counted to him. According to accepted street lore, Vinnie Insolia had once walked into a local hangout and shot his own brother dead for defecting to a rival mob. He had walked out untouched, leaving everyone agape with wonder and dread at someone who would commit such an unthinkable act. Afterward, his own biological family—his mother, father and two sisters—considered him dead. Vinnie lived alone without family, except his own gang members. His only soft spot was for Tommy.

Vinnie and Tommy met for dinner once a month and afterward walked through Little Italy—a display of cultural defiance on both their parts. Everyone in the neighborhood knew that Tommy was a cop, and that it didn't look good for a cop to be seen with a mobster. But the stroll down Mulberry Street showed that he had balls, that he was not afraid to be seen with a wiseguy. That kind of bravado gave him respect from the men who kept track of such things. Vinnie, of course, didn't care what people thought. He had long since given himself up as a dead man. It was the only thing that made life possible.

The friendship was not as difficult as it appeared for Tommy. His assignment within the Task Force was to maintain contact with members of organized crime families. If he saw Vinnie for dinner, it was part of his job. The only thing that Tommy had to worry about when they arranged to meet was that someone had planted a wire to pick up their conversation. He was always careful to arrive early and change tables and drop his napkin and look underneath the table. His hands were always wandering around the back of banquettes, searching for a hidden microphone. He always hugged his friend, feeling for a battery, and his friend hugged him back. He trusted Vinnie as he trusted no one else—but in the end he trusted no one.

After he devised his plan and decided that he needed Vinnie's help, he telephoned and left a message in their usual way: a barber who lived down the street from Vinnie went to his door, knocked and told him where Tommy would be waiting.

Tommy was sitting in an Italian bakery on First Avenue. They often met there. It was out of the way, yet still convenient. Tommy watched Vinnie pause in the entrance, checking out the customers. He was a big man, well over six feet, with shoulders like an ape's. Seventy years old and he still fills up a doorway, thought Tommy. He knew why men like Vinnie were treasured by the mob rulers. Vinnie gave weight to whichever side he stood with. He moved off the top step, spotting Tommy, exhaling, as if he could now relax. He dropped into a seat, his back to the wall, and smacked Tommy lovingly in the face and smiled. "Hey, movie star, you making all the girls happy?"

Tommy turned red. Not many people could make him blush. "I'm pulling my share," he said.

"You don't wanna pull that thing." Vinnie laughed. "Makes you go blind." He yelled, "Carmela, some more of that stuff you call coffee."

The waitress, a dark, thick-set woman with a sour expression, held her palm up to God and came to the table. "That stuff, that stuff!" she mimicked. "You don-na want that stuff, you don-na get that stuff!"

"I'm sorry, Carmela. I had a bad night. Tell you what, I need some of that fine coffee you make. It'll make me sweet again."

She looked at Tommy, then raised her eyes to heaven. "Some friend you got," she told Tommy. "He all-a time need some-thing. Why you not get-ta a wife and let her make you sweet?"

Then she went in the back and returned with a tray loaded down with coffee and breakfast pastries.

"Ah, Carmela, you're trying to kill me!"

"You need to eat, big man like you. Shut up and eat!"

Vinnie ate the sweet rolls and swallowed the coffee, while Tommy sipped and nibbled at his breakfast. Vinnie left a twenty dollar bill on the table and they left before Carmela could make something of it. Then they walked down First Avenue, checking the cars across the street, looking for the telltale sign of a government stakeout: two men wearing suits in a plain sedan. They wound up on 19th Street heading west against the traffic, looking in the cars, watching the doors and entries, not looking at each other—soldiers on patrol.

"So?"

"I need some equipment."

Vinnie always knew where to find things. People trusted him with secrets. "What kind of equipment?"

"Explosives."

The tone of their conversation was ordinary. They might have been discussing where to find a decent restaurant.

"Well, it all depends. You wanna hand grenade it's one thing. You wanna make a parking lot, it's another thing."

"Somewhere in the middle."

Tommy stole a peek at his friend and saw that he was unfazed. To Vinnie, Tommy had raised a technical question, a matter of professional interest. There was no emotion involved.

"Is it true that you once bit a guy's ear off?" he asked.

Vinnie looked at Tommy. Then he went back to making sweeps of the street. "I was trying to get his attention," he said.

Tommy laughed.

"I got a guy," Vinnie said.

"I need someone discreet."

"This is a very good man." That was a ringing endorsement. Vinnie could issue no higher praise. "Tell me what you need."

Tommy ran down his shopping list.

They stopped at an outdoor phone and Tommy stood guard while Vinnie made the call.

"He'll be waiting," Vinnie said when he hung up.

The supplier, Johnny DeTuccio, ran a radio store on East 90th Street on the lip of Spanish Harlem. The radio store was a front. Johnny DeTuccio was, in reality, a major dealer in illegal weapons. The decaying buildings around his store were dappled with graffiti. The security gates on all the surrounding businesses were bent and twisted from the endless attempts to break in, but the radio shop looked untouched. It might as well have been Fort Knox. The neighborhood thieves must have gotten the word that this was not fair game.

It was evening, Christmas Eve, when Tommy Day came to pick up his merchandise. He wore a low-slung hat and an oversized coat. Johnny DeTuccio was accustomed to the quirks of his clients and did not comment. They went through the transaction in the usual manner: speaking in short, ambiguous bursts and watching each other with a hawk eye.

DeTuccio was a tough businessman. He had the goods, but he insisted on his price and he demanded cash. He kept his finger on the trigger of a sawed-off shotgun which was mounted under the counter in the rear of the store, where he conducted his real business transactions. The muzzle of the shotgun was pointed at Tommy Day's belly.

"I assume you have the goods," Tommy said. He was wearing three-inch lifts in order to throw off his identification.

Johnny DeTuccio reached under the counter, pulled out a package one-handed, and put it on the counter.

"Open it," Tommy said.

It was the size of a cigar box, gaily wrapped like a Christmas gift. DeTuccio nodded and undid the bow, then carefully loosened the tape from the bright Christmas paper.

Santa Claus rode across the front. Under the wrapping was a
small box. Inside was a mass of orange pulp, some batteries
and wires and a clock.

"Show me how it works," Tommy said.

DeTuccio nodded. "It's a simple remote timer," he said.
"You set the timer here." He was a bald, sweaty man with
thick fingers that moved with amazing dexterity around the
switches and wires. A violinist with switches and bombs.
"It's really quite simple," he said staring into the tangle of
wires. "All you gotta do is insert this activator, set the timer
and get the hell out of there."

"How much time do I have?"

"Two minutes," he said. "Give or take five seconds."

Tommy tried it, without actually setting the activator. It
seemed easy enough, although his hand trembled slightly.
Not much. Not as bad as most people. DeTuccio picked him
as competent, just seeing how he handled the touchy, high-
risk, M-1 explosive. Most people shook. If they were inex-
perienced they bled sweat. He'll do it, thought DeTuccio.

"Okay, now, I want one more," Tommy said.

DeTuccio raised an eyebrow.

"I want an accelerator-type."

"You're gonna need more wrapping," DeTuccio said, indicating the Christmas paper.

Tommy laid down three thousand dollars in hundreds—
twice the agreed-upon price. DeTuccio counted it, put the
money away one-handed. He nodded. He didn't ask what
the explosives were for—he'd find out on the television
news. He'd see pictures of the debris. He would take some
professional pride knowing that there would not be enough
left to be traced. No signatures in the wiring. Nothing that
could leave him vulnerable. He was a very careful dealer in
death.

"What's the acceleration rate for this second one?" he
asked.

"Make it sixty miles an hour," Tommy said.

"Yeah," DeTuccio said with a rare smile, "I hate speeders, myself."

Then he rewrapped the packages separately, the first one in more Santa Claus paper, the second in candy cane paper, and put them both into a bright Bloomingdale's shopping bag. As Tommy left the shop, DeTuccio sang out, "Buon Natale!"

Tommy took the shopping bag and walked three blocks before he hailed a cab; he got out five blocks from the building where Special Assistant United States Attorney Marvin Sanders napped peacefully, having sent his wife away with his kids to her parents on Long Island. Tommy made his way through the empty streets, conscious of the Christmas shoppers and their gift packages and his own packages of explosives.

"How powerful is this?" he had asked DeTuccio about the first package.

"Depends," DeTuccio had shrugged. "You set it off in an open field and you got a kill radius of twenty feet. You put it in an enclosed space—say a room—and don't expect any mail from anyone inside."

"Will it bring down a building?"

"No. Not unless the foundation is already gone. This is like an anti-personnel bomb. Just kills people. Not even much structural damage, if that's what you're asking."

There were increased police patrols in Sanders's neighborhood. He ducked into an alley to avoid a patrol car. Then he slipped through a hole he had left in the security fence in the rear of Sanders's apartment building and pried open the hatch for the coal chute. Earlier in the day he had made certain that the hatch was unfrozen.

He dropped down into the basement, then made sure that there was no one else there. Homeless derelicts made their way into half the empty basements of the city. No one knew where they would turn up. They had even found a homeless family living in the basement of the Municipal Building.

Tommy had found his hiding place when he searched the basement earlier with his flashlight. Now he tipped the rusted coal chute forward and placed the Santa Claus bomb under an old oily rag. He pushed the chute back into place and stood back and examined it. You couldn't detect it, not if you didn't know it was there. He reached into his pocket and pulled out a tube of chili powder, sprinkling it over the floor to foil bomb-sniffing dogs, if it ever came to that. Then he washed himself off with the Handi Wipes he had left with a supply of fresh clothing in the basement. He changed back into his regular suit and the lined raincoat, and stuffed the old suit, the disguise hat, lift shoes and oversized raincoat into the large Bloomingdale's shopping bag. He looked at his watch and waited.

Finally, he heard the garbage truck working its way down the street. He pulled himself up and climbed out of the coal chute hatch, careful not to soil his fresh clothing, then dumped the shopping bag into a garbage can just as the garbage truck approached. The uniformed cops in the squad car were watching the front of the building and didn't notice him on the side street. Security checks had already declared that area sealed.

Tommy entered through the front door, the candy-cane-wrapped bomb under his arm, nodded to the team of uniforms in the squad car, showed his credentials, then went into the front door of the apartment building, as if he had just returned from his half-day off. Plainclothes Officer Nancy McDaniels was waiting for Tommy, looking cross and impatient, like a suspicious wife.

"Good day?" she asked.

"So-so," he replied, then nodded off at Sanders's room. "How's the brave G-man?"

"Taking his nap."

"Then why don't we take our own?" He grasped her hand and pulled her into the kids' bedroom where she fell gratefully into his arms.

20

Bonnie Hudson had become a typical New Yorker, suppressing the usual shivers of fear. She had learned to grip her purse tighter, wear subdued coats, avert her eyes, and develop a quick, ambiguous way of walking—cautious or unhinged, no way to tell. To survive in New York required aggressive vigilance, as well as state-of-the-art street tactics. But Jack moved strategically between her and the crisscross threats and suddenly she felt safe in the cusp of his deterrent force. The city's vultures circled away from him.

It was noon on Christmas day, a Thursday, and she could tell that he had had another sleepless night. His eyes were bloodshot and he had greeted her with a hollow, haunted smile. She didn't ask after Natalie. She didn't want to open that can of worms. Bonnie had a hunch that she and Natalie might have been friends. It seemed to work that way with men she found attractive: their women were interesting. She felt some pang of sorrow at Natalie's condition. As if they already knew each other, and in a way, they did, through Jack. Through it all, she could hear the voices in her own head: "The body not even cold!" "Not even dead!" "The woman's lying in the hospital, dying, and this one comes after the man! Can you believe it?" All the voices were her own and she agreed with every one. She felt as if she were pursuing a priest, and in many ways it was worse. This one was just starting his grief. He was overwhelmed with guilt and remorse. Like a priest, she thought. Just like the keeper of a sacred flame.

She told herself that she was innocent, that her contacts with Jack had to do with the job, the angle, the story, but deep in her heart she knew better. With so little progress she'd ordinarily have dropped the story. No, what propelled her was something else. Something shameful was going on. In the company of Jack Mann she grew quick and short of breath, half-overcome by an old familiar rush of bewildering emotion. She was out of control.

He felt the same way; she could tell. He broke eye contact whenever it reached a critical stage. He jumped when her hand brushed against his. He was charming and entertaining as they made their way to Police Headquarters looking for Jimmy Coffee. They laughed like lovers at any excuse.

"Moe says he gets off so little, he feels homeless," said Jack. "He practically lives on the street."

She laughed.

He stopped. "My friend Marty," he said, nodding at a man hurrying into an office building ahead of them.

"Cop?"

"Retired. A year ago. Worked at the Motor Vehicles Bureau."

They started walking again and Jack spoke in a not-quite-gloomy tone. "Christmas duty. That asshole Fenster. You know, Marty still comes to work every day. Probably late. Shows up on time, goes to lunch like he's still got a job. Does some errands, whatever they have, you know."

"Why?"

Jack shrugged. "He likes cops. Misses the action. Misses the company. His wife left him ten years ago. Got nothing else to do. So every day he comes to work, brings his lunch in a brown paper bag. If he's gonna take a day off, he calls in, asks the sergeant if he can slide. One of the sergeants, this guy Fenster, a real prick, chewed him out for calling in sick. Said they needed him. Marty got dressed and pulled a late shift. He's pulling a Christmas Day shift today."

"That's incredible."

She didn't understand. Hard to make people understand, he thought.

"Some guys, they have nothing else. Come to work for thirty years, can't just quit cold. They miss it. They have to do something. Or else they wind up on street corners barking at cars."

"Cops," she said, shaking her head.

"Cops," he agreed.

They were downtown, near the courts and the municipal office buildings, in the midst of the Works Department-era cluster of gray structures where all the agencies slogged through the paperwork, moving at the same slow, dull pace. He stopped and said she couldn't come with him.

"Why not?"

"You better wait someplace. I have to use the computer. They don't let civilians into Police Headquarters."

She looked around, making certain that no one overheard. "I'm a journalist," she hissed.

"You got a press card?"

She opened and closed her mouth.

"If you have a press card, fine, they'll let you in. Otherwise, they'll only let you on the ninth floor if you're a cop or a prisoner."

They agreed to meet at Forlini's, the Italian restaurant on Sullivan Street near the courthouse. "You're gonna be buying," she said crisply.

*   *   *

There was a tray of curling sandwiches on a table in the ninth-floor computer center—the remnants of a Christmas party. A small stack of plastic cups had tipped over and spilled on the floor. On impulse, Jack grabbed a small triangle of a salami sandwich. "Help yourself," said the duty sergeant, who had sagging jowls. The technician logged Jack onto the Police Department computer. He was a nice kid, thought Jack, a college boy, clicking with engineering and technical wizardry. Spoke computer-talk, about downtime and bytes and microchips, with a kind of happy jive lilt.

"We got a slow response time today," said the kid, whose name was Darryl. He was a civilian employee working on an advanced degree, and he had fingers that played symphonies on the keyboard. "Christmas and the mainframe just slows down," he said, turning, smiling at Jack. A real smile, thought Jack. Talking shit about computers in the house of cops. He hoped that the supervising cops wouldn't turn him bitter, with their sly racist innuendoes and mean undercurrent of contempt.

"Why does it slow down on Christmas?" Jack smiled back at the kid. "I'd think it'd speed up."

The kid's eyes were glued to the screen. He wore bottle-thick glasses, probably from staring at too many cursors, decided Jack. "Everything slows down at Christmas. You know that. People get reluctant. Wanna go to parties. Probably the computer is hung over from some office shit."

"Uh huh."

"No, see, here's the real reason: guys on line, they call up all kinds of shit. See what's shaking. See what kind of last-minute sales are going on in the toy departments."

"You can find toy sales in a police department computer?"

"Are you kidding? We got a shared-time mainframe and you would be amazed what we could plug into. I could find out about sales, I could find out about almost anything. Listen, makes some sense. If you know where the sales are, you deploy some anticrime units and nail some Colombian pick-pockets. That's where they grow 'em. Got to know where to place your men. If you get the inventory, you find out what's hot. You can play with this baby and find out who's shipping chemicals through town—because they have to notify you—who's shipping arms—because the snitches are plugged in, too. You can tune into how many drug dealers are staying at the St. Moritz and what kind of shit they are doing."

"No shit?"

"Well, you got to have authorized access. You got to know some codes and some access numbers. You got to know where to look and how to look."

"Bet you tap into all kinds of unauthorized programs, Darryl."

Darryl turned his palms up in a show of innocence. "I am just a civilian hacker doing my job so I can work my way to a Ph.D. All I wanna do is get my degree, get a nice job at a big mother mainframe and rule the world. I am on the American killer career track."

Jack laughed.

"Cough me up a name," he said.

"Check. What is the name of this malefactor?"

"His name is Charles Benson."

Darryl started tapping on his keys. A look of tranquility came over his face. The kid really liked plucking the keys.

"B E N S O N, C H A R L E S"

Jack could hear the whirring as the machinery made connections, relaying instructions, taking the return from the master files in Albany.

Then the screen showed: "No file."

"Damn," Jack said.

"Chill, my man," Darryl said. "That's just a cold run. Computer ain't hot yet."

"What are you talking about?"

"Lemme tell you something, between us. These computers are cliff-hangers. Can't stick 'em once and expect results. You have got to work at it. Trick them out. I mean, sometimes they kick out some hot scoop and sometimes they turn real cold. Glitched to shit. You know what it's like? It's like my mom and her TV set. My momma loves her TV. But sometimes it starts snowing on the TV. She does not call a technician. She talks to the set. She slams the back wall of her apartment. She don't hit the TV or the floor in front of the TV. She hits the back wall, which ain't nowhere near the TV, and that picture turns sunny. Why it does that I have no idea, and I am an advanced electronics and engineering student. The thing is, it works."

"So?"

"So lemme hit the back wall on this 5-20 L Model Mainframe Wang computer. Okay?"

"Pound the shit out of it."

Darryl started tapping on the keys with his dancing fingers. They went through all the permutations of Benson. Charles. Chuck. C. Benson. Then they hit misspellings. Besan. Bensan. Binson. "No file."

"Does our man have an AKA?" asked Darryl.

"He does. AKA Jimmy Coffee."

Darryl went to work.

"Search: Jimmy Coffee." Nothing. Search: Cofe or Coffe. "no file." "Search Coffee, Jimmy." No file.

They sat there for a moment, bent into the blinking amber light of the screen.

"I got one more trick," said Darryl.

He began hitting the keys again.

"B E N S O N; C H A R L E S, AKA Jimmy Coffee"
The computer began clicking and spitting out details.
"BENSON; CHARLES, AKA Jimmy Coffee:
DOB 7/23/59
ARRESTS: 6/3/81 17 Pct. 201.7 Penal Code, DOR Summons # 238694-0 AO: PO J. Caulks, 570219"

"I don't get it," said Jack.

Darryl smiled.

"You see, this computer, man, it only hears what you put into it. It didn't hear the first time because we put a comma after Benson. The cop who programmed the case hit the wrong key. He hit a semicolon. The computer was looking for a semicolon. Cops are definitely not into punctuation. Computers are."

"That's amazing. That's fantastic."

"Just gave the back wall a slam. You need a printout?"

"If it's not too much trouble."

Jack knew the lingo by heart. Jimmy Coffee had been arrested for disorderly conduct in the Midtown North precinct of Manhattan on June 3rd of 1981. There were seven other arrests, all on minor charges from vagrancy to public intoxication, all dismissed. He could look up the summons in the Clerk's office and he could go find the arresting officers and maybe someone would remember Jimmy Coffee.

There were clues and leads to follow and Jack felt satisfaction. This Jimmy Coffee had a record as a harmless vagrant. He didn't look like a killer from his files.

"Say," cried Darryl as Jack hurried out to meet Bonnie. "Merry Christmas, hear?"

"I hear," Jack shouted. "And felicitations of the season to yourself."

The teakwood outside of the restaurant was draped with laurel and dappled with red bows and for a moment Bonnie felt a twinge, some seasonal emotion. Everyone rushing through the streets looked flushed and smiling, like Christmas, she thought.

She was just handing her coat to the hatcheck woman at Forlini's, neutral ground to the judges and Mafia chiefs who ate side-by-side in a state of gustatorial truce. The front door opened with a blast of cold air. Special Assistant United States Attorney Marvin Sanders burst in like an arctic wind. He was trailed by a pair of steely bodyguards and a few other men in civilian clothes. With his wife and kids in the safety of Long Island, Sanders had only his staff for a Christmas family. The owner of the restaurant came out to greet him and ushered him through the waiting lunch line. While there were some murmurs of protest at the preferential treatment, no one objected out loud. Even if Marvin Sanders hadn't just narrowly escaped an assassination attempt and been under a death threat, it was commonly understood that his work had transcendent importance and that he should be allowed to break the line.

Not that Bonnie agreed. She thought that everyone should wait his or her turn. Even the President should be made to wait on line like everyone else. She handed over her attaché case to the hatcheck woman with a growl. "Big shot," she said.

The hatcheck girl smiled. Then Bonnie remembered something and took back the case for a second. She removed a small, book-sized package containing Jack's Christmas present. She hadn't known what to buy him. She'd spent an hour in Barney's, going from department to department in a daze of indecision. She didn't want to make too much of it; it would be unseemly. Especially when he wouldn't have a present for her. So she bought him a belt—she guessed at his size. He wouldn't guess that she'd paid $175 for an ostrich belt.

"Merry Christmas," she said to the hatcheck girl.

The room was warm and rang with cheerful "Merry Christmas"es.

The owner of the restaurant seated the couple and the foursome ahead of her, frowned when he heard that he had to put a single person—and a woman, at that—at a table that could be supporting two luncheons, then recognized the weatherwoman. "Hey! You! Don't worry, it's only the climate! Heh! Heh! Did I do it good?"

"Fine, fine," she said, lowering her head, trying not to be recognized. Dignified man like that making an ass of himself, she didn't understand it. The thing that bothered her was the fear that maybe she looked like that on the air. Maybe she was a fool and everyone was too polite to say anything.

"Scotch," she told the waiter, who was smiling like an idiot, suppressing his impulse to greet her. "Double scotch."

When he brought it to her table, decorated with a small, festive tree in the center, he leaned over, and whispered: "It's only the weather!"

She smiled and held up her glass of scotch in a salute, drained it, then asked for another.

Marvin Sanders was across the room, already plunging his fork in and out of a huge plate of lasagna. The two body-guards were at a separate table, watching everyone in the room. One of them was strikingly handsome, with fine fea-tures and penetrating eyes. A lady killer, she thought, who wore his leather holster like décolletage. She could see flashes of it as he dipped into the pasta on his plate. A real good-looking cop, she thought, then turned her attention back to Sanders. She didn't make the connection from the tape—it was too indistinct, and too unlikely. The thing that Tommy had going for him was that his looks were so striking that they absorbed all attention. You didn't associate him with trouble.

The Special Assistant United States Attorney, between gulps of his food, was poking his fork at a thickset, worried-looking man on his left. She couldn't hear the entire conver-sation, but words drifted across the room, like tantalizing odors.

"You're full of shit, Jerry," Sanders told his media advisor, Jerry Casolaro, the man on his left.

Casolaro waited until the waiter left before saying em-phatically, "I'm telling you, Marvin, you have to leave town. Let's not take chances."

"You're the guy who told me to stand up tall! You're the guy who told me I was starting to look like a wimp. Now you want me to look like a coward? You want people to have confidence in a man who runs away at the first sign of trouble?"

"I was wrong. This won't hurt. I'm telling you, it'll help. It'll make people think you're prudent. Sensible."

Sanders shook his head. "I ain't gonna look like a coward," he said. "It's over. The threat is over. They got the fucking guy. I am going to stay here and conduct business."

At the next table Tommy Day felt a surge of relief. Good. Now he could carry out his plan.

Bonnie was still nibbling at her salad when Sanders got up abruptly and left. As he was barging out of the restaurant, he passed Jack, who was looking for Bonnie. Nobody noticed Jack, but Jack noticed Sanders and the coterie behind him. He was aware of the characters who trailed Sanders around. Especially the bodyguards. He noticed the one with fine features. One good-looking cop, that one.

Then he saw Bonnie sitting at the banquette and he smiled and waved. He had a lot to tell her. He had a good idea of the tracks that Jimmy Coffee had followed.

Before he could speak she handed him the package. He opened it and smiled, leaned across the table and kissed Bonnie on the cheek. Then he pulled a crumpled, but nicely wrapped package out of his jacket pocket. She undid the bow carefully. Inside was a scarf. The label said Hermes.

"Merry Christmas," he said.

She couldn't look up.

21

There were 221 members of the uniformed force assigned to the Two-Oh Precinct covering the Upper West Side of Manhattan. The actual precinct house was located in an old building designed to withstand a siege. The style was a variation of the colonial outposts called French Fortress. It was built in the twenties when nervous municipal fathers still feared hordes of Bolsheviks marching with pikes on the bastions of law and order. Build the station houses strong, they ordered. Strong enough to withstand a mob.

But the Bolsheviks never came and the station house remained standing, a gray, grim sentinel sandwiched between high-rent apartment buildings. The architectural intent was not entirely wasted, however. The police remained an undigested part of the community. They didn't mix with the upstanding citizens—the successful MBA's, the corporate sharks, the legal hot shots—but went forth from their fortress like a unit of the Foreign Legion. At night they went

home, to Long Island or Staten Island, or some remote corner of an outer borough. Their closest contacts on the community level were with the criminals or the vagrants. With
them, they had something in common: exclusion.

Malcolm Westfield was one of those natural sentries assigned as a patrolman to the station house. He understood
the relationship between the police and community, and he
kept the streets under a kind of colonial surveillance.

Jack and Bonnie were too early—it would be more than
half an hour until the eight-to-four shift got off duty at the
20th Precinct. Patrolman Malcolm Westfield, whose name
appeared on Charles Benson's last arrest sheet, had agreed to
meet Jack at 4:00 at Teachers, a popular restaurant on Broadway between 80th and 81st Streets, eight blocks north of the
station house. When Jack first called, Officer Westfield was
friendly and helpful. Sure, he said, he remembered Benson,
AKA Jimmy Coffee. A neighborhood character. Got to
know him the way you get to know all the street people in
your sector. You see them around, you learn their habits,
you begin to look for them. He said that he'd be glad to talk
about Jimmy Coffee, as much good as it would do.

Jack and Bonnie were circling the restaurant's block, killing time until Westfield's tour of duty ended. "Too cold,"
Bonnie said, shuddering. "Too damn cold."

"Hey, it's only weather," Jack said cheerfully.

She punched him in the side. It was a sharp blow, and it
hurt. Jack gave her a surprised look.

"No more shopping days," said Jack, walking more
quickly to outrun the cold. "God, what a lousy Christmas."

"Yeah, well, this year I'm giving all my money to charity,"
Bonnie said, rushing to keep up. The words came out in
puffs of steam.

"Let's wait inside," said Jack.

The restaurant was in that twilight between lunch and
dinner. It was a young place, popular with the untenured
faculty of Columbia University a mile north, and with the

local flashy business types. At night there was always a
squad of attractive women cruising the bar. The waitresses
were unemployed actresses and had their own followings.
They were, at the moment, clustered at a table in the back,
their shoes kicked off, slouching. Five of them, looking exhausted from the hectic Christmas lunch hour. There was a
cloud of cigarette smoke hovering over their table. The waitresses all gave Jack and Bonnie looks. They didn't budge.
Christmas had left them soggy and foul-tempered.

The bartender was preparing mixers in a large, industrial-
sized jar. "Bloody Mary's," he explained, smiling. "Very big
at Christmas."

"Yeah, I'll have one of those," Bonnie said, picking out a
stool.

"Virgin Mary," Jack said.

The bartender fixed the two drinks. Then he tactfully
moved to a far corner of the bar to give them privacy. He
was one of those bartenders who read between the lines, con-
struct stories from snips of conversation, invent novels about
their customers from small clues. He looked at Jack and Bonnie. Christmas lovers, he thought. Like couples who meet on
a ship, judging by the fresh glow in their faces.

He came back and laid a bowl of salted nuts like flowers in
front of them, smiled and retreated to his corner of the bar
again.

"You don't wanna be here when Westfield gets here," said
Jack. "We'll be talking cop talk."

She nodded, scooping up a handful of nuts and tossing
them in her mouth like a sword swallower.

"I'm gonna check out some things," she said. "Then I have
the broadcast."

She got up, finished off her drink, then put her hand on
Jack's shoulder. He looked at her in the mirror, and their
eyes were like anti-magnets, pulling away each time they
met. Her hand on his jacket felt as if it could melt through
and burn his flesh.

"Meet you later," he said.

"Where?"

"Here. About midnight."

She stopped at the door, turned to look at Jack slumped at the bar, then decided against it. There was no talking about it now. The whole thing hung suspended by the life-support systems of his dying wife. She turned away and left.

Westfield was youthful, blond, and easy. He clapped Jack on the back, recognizing the cop quality instantly. "Sorry I'm late," he said. "We had a small Christmas thing."

"Doesn't make up for working Christmas."

Westfield shrugged. "Somebody's gotta keep the peace."

Jack liked him.

"How long you been on the job?" he asked.

"Nine years."

"No shit? You don't even look twenty-five."

"Thirty last October. Don't trust anyone over thirty. I remember that from someplace, but now I believe it."

Jack laughed and Westfield ordered a whiskey and water, looked around, checking out the restaurant. A good cop always wants to know what he's up against.

"You hungry?" asked Jack.

"No. I can't. Besides, I promised my girlfriend Chinese." He looked at his watch.

"On Christmas?"

"My girlfriend's Chinese."

They both laughed.

"Okay," Jack said, "business. Tell me a little about Jimmy Coffee."

"Lemme ask you, you workin' this case?"

Jack had been afraid of this. It was unusual for a plainclothes cop to be tracking someone. It had the odor of someone working a private contract, and Westfield, given some time to think it over, had picked up on it.

"Yeah, I'm working the case, and my superiors know

about it, but it's not on the clock. I'm working discreetly for borough command, but I'd prefer if we kept this informal."

"You mind if I see your ID?"

Jack sighed, pulled out his wallet and showed him his badge and the Police Department identification card with his picture. Westfield studied it, then handed it back.

"The reason I ask is, see, after I talked to you, I asked around and it seems that the Organized Crime Task Force has been checking up on this guy, too. Not too aggressively, but asking."

"Yeah, I know."

"Not that it makes a shit of difference to me, but if you know those people in the Task Force, they tend to get very touchy about territory. They definitely do not like city cops fucking with their caseload."

Jack nodded. Then he leaned closer, drawing Westfield closer. "I know all about the Task Force," said Jack. "You been on the job, so you know about them, too. They couldn't find a fart in a windstorm. You know what I mean."

Westfield laughed. He nodded and raised his glass to the bartender and asked for a refill. When they were alone again, he said, "What the fuck, how can I help you, pal?"

"Tell me about Jimmy Coffee."

"Jimmy's one of the summer people."

"One of the what?"

"Summer people. You know, we have summer people and winter people and all-year-round people. Most of the summer people live on the street in the summer, then spend the winter in jail. Soon as the snow starts to fly they get themselves arrested—some six-month term for burglary or attempted arson or assault. Something so they have a warm cell in the winter."

"Coffee's one of those people?"

"Not exactly. He isn't crafty enough to get himself arrested. You saw his record. He isn't mean. He just migrates naturally. Moves back and forth across town like some nomad. He spends the winters on the East Side, you know, they have much warmer shelters over there. A lot more friendly churches, a lot more heated public places. If you're gonna live on the street, you're much better off on the East Side in the winter. That was the way he explained it to me when I busted him for disorderly conduct. Summers, though, he drifts back to the West Side. Better parks and open spaces. You can look at the river and scrounge more food. People on the East Side tend to discourage street people in the summer."

"What kind of guy is he?"

"A loner. Doesn't trust anyone. Keeps off to himself. Doesn't share. Most of the people on the street around here share their food and their wine. Not Jimmy. That doesn't make him popular. A real loner. Most of all, though, he is crazy. Crazy as hell. Goes off on wild tracks, like how he was really a doctor but he couldn't take the pressure, or a judge seeing how people lived on the street. And he is smart. He'll say some things that are amazing. Talks about religion and God and says that he graduated from Columbia."

"He did go there."

"I believe it. He is smart, like I said. Recites poetry. But then he starts to babble, you know? Asked me if he was black when I was taking him in. Like he really didn't know if he was black or white. He wasn't just busting my balls. He really didn't know. Asked me how old he was. He said he thought he was very old, and you know the guy was in his twenties. The guy definitely was not playing with a full deck."

"Where did he hang out?"

"On the traffic island. The benches. But he'd get hungry and you could catch him on the line at the food kitchens. One on 72nd Street, another on 95th Street. That's out of the precinct."

"You seen him lately?"

"No. Not lately. Like I said, he's summer people."

                    *   *   *

The apartment above the gadget shop on Prince Street was
barred and triple-bolted and defended by a heavy-metal rein-
forced door. There were signs plastered on the door, warning about traps and alarms. It wasn't that there were jewels
or a lot of cash hidden behind the layers of steel. It wasn't a
paranoid reaction. It was that this was the apartment of Vinnie Insolia, who didn't want anyone touching his things. Not
that he kept anything incriminating inside the apartment.
There were no illegal guns or compromising diaries. He simply had an aversion to being molested.

Insolia had a bag of groceries in his hands as he began the
climb up the long flight of stairs to his apartment. Inside the
bag were two large hero sandwiches and a six-pack of beer
and a bag of pretzels. He was tired and feeling his age and
wanted to spend a quiet evening watching television. But
something made him stop halfway up the stairs. It wasn't a
sound or a shadow. It was a sense of disturbance. Something
he couldn't even define. He put the groceries down carefully
and reached under his coat and came out with a .38-caliber
pistol. Then he began advancing up the stairs.

From the landing above his apartment, he heard a voice.
"It's only me, Vinnie."

Insolia recognized the voice: Tommy Day. He kept his
gun out anyway. He moved back into a shadow, moving his
head and throwing his own voice. "Come on down," he said.
"Slow."

Vinnie Insolia had been part of too many ambushes: Set a
guy up with someone he knows, lower his defenses, invite
him into the trap. If Vinnie died—and one day, he knew,
that was coming—he didn't intend to go alone. Someone was
going with him, even if it was his protégé.

Tommy came down slowly, moving in the light so that
Vinnie could see his outstretched hands were empty. Vinnie
kept looking up and down the staircase in case someone was
moving in stealth for a kill.

It took a moment, but Vinnie was finally convinced that Tommy was alone. "You shouldn't come here," he said climbing the last two steps.

"Can I get my case?" asked Tommy.

Vinnie watched him retrieve his attaché case. He shook his head. Cops were like bankers, he thought. Then Vinnie opened the door and checked out the apartment for intruders. The debris he had left as booby traps was intact. The window shades were at the exact length he had left them. He looked in all the closets, all the rooms. He did it every single time he returned home. Then he took off his coat and hat and opened a beer. He opened one for Tommy, who followed him inside.

"So what are you doing here?"

Tommy looked around. He believed that there were no taps or wires in the room. Vinnie could have checked and re-checked, but you could never be one hundred percent certain. Still, he had no choice and he took a chance.

"I need you."

Vinnie had that look on his face—somewhere between disappointment and skepticism.

"This is very important, Vin. Listen, maybe we better take a ride."

Vinnie shrugged and gazed over at the bag of uneaten food, the puny Christmas tree with the blinking lights, then climbed back into his coat, reset the booby-trap debris scattered around the apartment and accompanied Tommy onto the landing.

"I hate to miss the service at St. Pat's," Vinnie said.

Vinnie's big Lincoln was parked in a commercial garage off Avenue of the Americas. The attendant had it out in five minutes. Vinnie and Tommy strapped themselves in and headed north through a dusting of snow.

"First snow," said Tommy.

"Yeah. It ain't like when I was a kid, though. They had real snow. You could get snowed in. I remember my old man couldn't get to work. And they closed the schools."

Tommy stared out at the little flakes of snow falling like tiny sequins, bright in the headlights, then melting on the sidewalk.

"I remember some major fucking snowstorms," said Vinnie. "You had piles of snow around the house, twenty feet tall."

"Come on!"

"No shit. I'm telling ya. Twenty fucking feet. We'd ride sleds down the snowpile. It'd take a month to melt. Sometimes the coal trucks couldn't even get in to make a delivery."

Vinnie drove, and Tommy tried to imagine a twenty-foot drift. He tried to picture Vinnie Insolia sliding down on a sled. Outside holiday bunting looped the streets together. There were seasonal bells on the lampposts. In the bakeries along the avenue, the green and red theme of the season was reflected in the cakes. On the corner of Eighth Street, a scrawny Salvation Army Santa Claus rang a bell and every once in a while someone dropped a coin in his pot.

"It doesn't seem to get like that anymore," Vinnie said.

"So, kid, what gives?"

Tommy told him. He outlined his plan. He spoke in the flat, unemotional tones of a professional, but hard Vinnie Insolia felt the hair on his arms stand up in a kind of salute at the boldness of the scheme.

"That's some plan," said Vinnie after he heard it all.

"It's got a chance."

Vinnie was silent, thinking it over. Tommy was sensible enough to let him weigh the odds.

"I'm not saying that I don't wanna help," said Vinnie. "I just hafta point out that I'm not as young as I used to be. I could get into a situation which could be sticky."

Vinnie looked over at him. Tommy nodded.

"I'm trying to tell you, kid, I won't be caught. You know what I'm saying?"

"I understand."

The car picked up speed. "Hey, take it easy, Vin,"

Tommy said, looking down at the attache case. Vinnie eased up on the gas.

"There's some other things, too," Vinnie said. "I may take a few people down with me, but if they get me, even if I'm dead, they put me together with the Don. You know what I mean? Maybe even you, because, let's face it, they know we're not strangers."

"I'm not worried about it," said Tommy.

Vinnie cut south again. He dropped the big Lincoln back at the garage and he and Tommy said goodnight. Tommy felt a jolt of sorrow as he stood on the sidewalk watching his old friend, his benefactor, walk away.

He waited until the attendant was back inside his booth, hovering over the space heater, watching a game show on a portable television set. Then he slipped back to the second floor and searched for the big Lincoln. He found it parked by itself near a corner. He took the package out of his attaché case and began connecting the wires and timer. He hooked it under the driver's seat in a spot almost impossible to find.

Then he walked out of the garage, making certain that the attendant wasn't looking, and took a cab back uptown to the apartment of Marvin Sanders.

22

When Bonnie arrived at the station to get ready for the 10:00 broadcast, young assistant producers were running back and forth from the wire room with fresh bulletins. Baby-faced executives in sober pinstripes stood frowning ominously in the back of the studio, their smooth chins cupped in their uncalloused hands. Holiday anchorman Tony Canasto was standing in the middle of the studio crooning softly, "Ohhhh, ouuuhhh, OHHHH!" Harvey Levy, the managing editor, was sitting in the corner of the studio, his legs propped on a monitor, shaking his head. "Damn!" he said. His face was broken into happy moons by a broad, daffy grin. "God damn!"

Bonnie studied the scene. Had to be a major breaking story. A big-time assassination. Maybe a plane crash. She had never seen a major breaking story at a television newsroom. Election nights and convention coverage; fixed battles. Planned. Orderly, if somewhat hectic. But nothing like this complete, utter, wall-eyed madness.

"What gives?" she asked Max Gross.

He smiled with his usual detached amusement. "They just got the ratings," he said.

"That bad, huh?"

"No. No." He shook his head. Smiled again. Laughed. "On the contrary. We have, my dear child, broken out of last place."

"No kidding?"

"As you know, we've had a lock on last place for years. Can't remember when we weren't tenants of the basement. Held it with pride. Nobody lost in the ratings with as much good cheer as we did. Nobody occupied last place with our style and dignity. All of a sudden, we're fourth in the market. Can you believe it? My God, now, we're out of last place. We're actually ahead of 11 and 5. Fox is on the run. We're even beginning to worry the local flagship stations."

"Is this good news or bad?"

"That's a very good question. And hard to say. Last place had a nice, comfortable safety. You couldn't get worse. Let's face it, it was restful. Like home. Now, now we have a position in the world. A history to uphold. Now we have something to lose."

"Yeah, well, I can see that this is bad news for me. They're gonna get all nervous and conservative. They'll want a professional weatherperson. Maybe even a meteorologist."

"I wouldn't worry about it."

"You wouldn't? Why not?"

"Well, from what I hear—and I make it my business to eavesdrop on all the important business—the focus group reports seem to indicate that this sudden surge of public interest in our little station has a very specific cause."

"What's that?"

"An irreverent and spunky new member of the cast."

"Please don't tell me it's Tony. Anybody but that ignorant asshole."

"It's not Tony. It's you."

"Huh?"

He nodded. "They're gonna put you in for an Emmy. Maybe even a Dupont."

For a second, the studio spun as if she had just swallowed a large, potent martini. She experienced the quick, intoxicating effects of an imperial blessing. And the surge of power that went with it. Suddenly, in that one wild instant, she understood completely the temptation—and corruption—of power. She could walk over to Harvey Levy and tell him to go screw and he would regard it with tactical amusement: a joke, a teasing comment. He would not balance, as he always had, whether or not to fire her. Now she had weight.

The heady possibilities lasted only a moment. She was still Bonnie, still a journalist with an enduring mistrust of power and authority. But she noticed that as she walked deeper into the studio, there was a stuffy deference in her wake. Not a hush, but a different kind of awe.

"Calm down, Tony," she said, and the old anchorman had new lines on his face when he looked at her, wonder at the new force to contend with. He was pathetic.

"How are you, Bonnie?" Levy asked. He had bounced out of his chair to follow her to makeup.

"I'm afraid it's gone to my head. I want my own hairdresser and wardrobe mistress and a trailer. Could I get a hot tub in my trailer?"

"I can only guarantee your own personal broken leg." He stalked off, grabbing Gene Harman, the station manager, under the arm and pulling him away.

"I want to congratulate her," Harman said, trying to pull free.

"Not a good time. Wait 'til the swelling goes down."

When it neared time to go on the air, everyone retreated to the booths and marks and chairs and a hush fell on the set. Conrad Stone, the sportscaster, leaned over and said to Bonnie grudgingly, "Nice going." He can't help it, she thought.

He regards this as a touchdown. The man cannot help looking at life like a football game.

As the countdown began, Tony Canasto was miserable. The entire edifice of his beliefs and certainties had been shaken. How could this be? She was not telegenic, certainly not in the accepted sense of the term. She was not winning. She definitely was not winning. Matter of fact, she had a kind of twisted nastiness that she took on the air. But the audience liked her. Liked her! They all said she was a breath of fresh air. Arctic air coming down from Canada, no doubt.

He sat there, frozen, and watched the technician pinning the microphone to her sweater, smiling at her, and she, smiling back, as if she had planned it like this all along.

"Okay," boomed the voice from the booth, "ten seconds to air and counting."

The musical theme began at seven seconds and the off-camera announcer began his run-in. "Now, with tonight's late edition of the news, Tony Canasto at the anchor desk, Conrad Stone with sports, and our own Bonnie Hudson with the weather!"

She looked at the announcer, who smiled back at her. The custom was just to say, "Bonnie Hudson with the weather." Now she had become "Our own!" With all kinds of upbeat emphasis. A declaration of management love.

"Two . . . One . . ."

The stage manager pointed to Tony Canasto who opened and closed his mouth. He blinked at the camera, smiled and began to wink. But he couldn't speak. He was vocally paralyzed, trying to dream up some irreverent and biting, yet winning, way of introducing the news. Conrad Stone didn't notice what was happening; he was preoccupied with the late scores in a basketball game on which he had a substantial bet.

The seconds ticked like hammers. Still Tony was unable to find his voice. Bonnie was watching the monitor and saw a tear emerge like a drop of blood at the corner of his right eye.

The director was waving his arms, hissing into Tony's ear-piece. "Good evening, ladies and gentlemen! Good evening, ladies and gentlemen! Good evening, ladies and fucking gentlemen. Say it, goddammit!"

Just then the news director in the booth cued the standby stage-left camera, which was Bonnie. She had a copy of the news script in front of her—a habit left over from newspapers when she read everybody else's stuff—and nodded as the camera came to her.

"Good evening ladies and gentlemen, I'm Bonnie Hudson, wishing you a Merry Christmas; this is tonight's news. Mayor Koch today appointed two new commissioners to investigate the growing scandal that has rocked his administration. . . ."

In the booth, Harvey Levy smiled and punched Gene Harman's arm. The station manager flinched. Levy's punch was harder than he expected.

Levy said: "You see? What a pro! I told you about her. And you said she was dangerous. The woman is pure television. That is a fucking professional. The most professional thing I've ever seen."

Harman nodded, his eyes flooded with an almost spiritual gratitude. "She saved the broadcast."

Meanwhile, Tony Canasto remained at his post, opening and closing his mouth, his face wet with tears. During the commercial break two stagehands tried to lift him—one under each arm—but he emitted a piercing cry of pain and they backed off. So they cut off his sound and there he remained, weeping and flapping, trying to make some sort of lovable sound.

At last Bonnie was delivering the wrap:

"Thank you, good evening, tune in tomorrow for Tony Canasto and the 10:00 news—and remember, it's only weather." Bonnie unhooked the microphone and the staff and crew broke into applause.

Harvey Levy and Gene Harman hurried to the set, their

arms raised to heaven in praise. "You want a hot tub, you got a hot tub," cried Levy.

"Bonnie, for you," cried Max Gross holding up a telephone.

"Excuse me," Bonnie said, grateful for the interruption. I don't want to be one of them, she thought. What frightened her was how easily she had behaved like the best of them. It had come over her like a familiar calm. She had known what to do and she had done it.

Behind her, the staff and cast of the program were breaking into the pile of Christmas sandwiches. A tub of beer was carried in by a team of stagehands. A group of the secretaries wearing Santa hats came slowly in, like a church chorus, singing "Oh Come All Ye Faithful."

Bonnie put her finger in her ear to shut out the noise. "Hello?"

"Miss Hudson? This is Jenny Benson."

It didn't connect. Bonnie was still in the television mentality and had to pull herself back. Jenny Benson. Oh! Jimmy Coffee's sister.

"You don't remember me."

"I do. I'm sorry. I was still embarrassed."

"Don't be."

Jenny Benson had that cold, business-like sound of people steeling themselves to do things that they don't want to do. Bonnie tried to ease into something more casual.

"How are you?"

Jenny wouldn't be pushed. "I'd like to talk to you."

"Sure. When?"

"Tonight. Now."

Plainclotheswoman Nancy McDaniels closed Sanders's bedroom door after checking. "He's asleep." she said. Tommy Day nodded, finished his beer, belched delicately and put down his newspaper.

Close. It was getting very close. He could hear the count-

down in his head. It was getting nearer and nearer and
no one else knew. Only Vinnie. And he didn't know the half
of it.

"Coffee?" Nancy asked.

"No."

He didn't say thank you. Not because he didn't know that
it was called for, but because he didn't want to admit that he
owed anyone gratitude. He would have to work on that. In
the new life that was coming up he would have to show gratitude. He would have to feign humility. He would have to
display all the signs of sensitivity and gentleness that he regarded as weakness and cowardice.

"You haven't eaten," she said.

He looked at her with an expression that she misunder-
stood. She thought it was one of those endless-male-suffering
looks. It was contempt. Such a cow, he thought. Wanting to
smother him with her domestic instincts. Can't function without some pet to fondle. Can't live alone, without human contact or need. A cow.

He thought bitterly, Sanders—this feeble dork wants to
be mayor! The guy can't run an investigation. He can't organize a campaign. He needs five staff members to write a
speech. And even then he stammers with buts and maybes.
Tommy hated weak-willed politicians who hesitated whenever a definite move was called for. He didn't shrink from
doing what had to be done. That's how he knew that he
would be a good congressman. Or senator. Or even mayor,
which was something he'd been thinking about lately.

They were in the living room of the duplex off Fifth Avenue. Nancy McDaniels had begun to pout from the silence
following their few quick sexual collisions. She had expected
more. She ached for more. He hadn't mentioned anything
more and she was too embarrassed to bring it up. She expected . . . she didn't know what. Something. Tenderness.
A sign. Instead, he acted as if it never happened. He ignored

her. As if he had done his duty and didn't want to be bothered anymore.

She picked up her china cup of coffee, noticing that her
hand was trembling. She put it down because she didn't
want him to see her high-strung state. He moved from the
chair to her couch and sat close to her. She could smell his
aftershave, his sweat, his breath. She drank it in. He put his
arm back behind her and she leaned back, helpless to stop
herself. No pride, she thought. I have no pride left. Her
head slumped over onto his shoulder. He put his right hand
under her chin, lifted it, and kissed her tenderly.

He was thinking about the plan. His heart was racing and
she put her hand on his chest and smiled. She grew soft and
pressed herself against him, opening her mouth, tasting him
and moaning softly.

I will have to do this, he thought, although he had no
appetite for it. Not at first, anyway. I will have to appear as
if I have the normal urges and drives and it will break her
guard down. I cannot have her vigilant and hostile and looking for explanations.

And so he reached over and undid the strap of her shoulder holster. Then the buttons of her blouse. She arched her
back and presented herself to him, looking down at the fingers unfastening the buttons with wonder and delight. The
simple job of opening a button became a riotous act of wild
sexual meaning. She felt his fingers as they moved and the
twisting and pressure caught her breath. She whispered,
"Oh, Tommy!"

He could playact if he had to, and he knew that he had to.
He bent down and kissed her breasts through the silk under-
garment and she held his head there for an instant. She will
want me to say I love her next, he thought miserably. She
shrugged the blouse off her shoulders. He took her hand and
led her to the bedroom. If Sanders woke up and found them,
they would be pulled off the assignment, maybe kicked off
the force. He hummed in her ear. She thought that it was
passion.

It was dark in the room, but a little light seeped in through the window. The moon, he thought. "Oh, Tommy!" she muttered, and he put his mouth on hers to shut her up. Don't talk, he thought. Let's just get this over with. He fondled the black silk bra—no doubt for him. She was scented and freshly bathed.

It wasn't that he was indifferent to sex, or that he found Nancy unattractive. Tommy just had this other thing on his mind. The plan. The aftermath. Life would be easy, he had no doubt of that. He would have his staff work out his programs and figure out his votes and he would sit back and count the money. No more worries. No more ledges and killings.

She was pulling down his pants and she saw that he wasn't ready and it made him angry. "It's okay," she cooed. "Don't worry. I'll fix it." He pushed her away with such violence that her eyes bulged. She started to get back up but he pushed her again and she hit her head on the headboard.

"Tommy!" she cried, and he grabbed her arms and pinned her to the bed. He was cutting off the circulation in her hands, hurting her, and she squirmed underneath him and suddenly he was ready and she felt it. He forced his way in. She tried to object, but he pushed her back down again, held both of her hands with one of his and pried open her legs with the other hand. He plunged ahead brutally. Her eyes were wide with fear. She had lost the half-lidded adoration. Now she was simply afraid.

Her fear made Tommy ready, and he pounded away at the helpless woman under him until he was relieved. Then he rolled off, turned to her and smiled. He thought that they had had a good fuck. He was surprised at the look of horror on her face.

The apartment was neat and compact, not what Bonnie had expected. She tried to imagine Jenny dusting all the small, fine pieces of bric-a-brac with those thick fingers. The wastage must have been high.

The tea sandwiches were cut into triangles. Salmon, cucumber and cheese. The tea was strong and delicious. Bonnie was hungry and ate more than her share. Jenny sat across from the coffee table, her hands folded in her lap.

"I didn't have dinner," explained Bonnie, when she realized how she had attacked the food.

Jenny nodded. "I wouldn't have called you, but the police have been back and they're looking for my brother."

"Yes," said Bonnie, "I know."

Jenny looked down at her hands. Her lips were compressed, as if she didn't want to let the words out. "I think they want to kill him," she said.

Bonnie looked up.

"Why do you think that?"

"The way that they talked about him. They said he had committed a lot of crimes. Murders. That he was dangerous. They said they didn't want anybody else to get hurt. The way that they said it . . ."

Bonnie shook her head. "I'm sure they're not going to hurt him."

Jenny started to cry softly. "I think they are," she said. "You see, he has a gun. I saw it when he came by. Charles has a gun." Jenny looked out of the window, searching for some neutral place to rest her eyes. And then she told Bonnie two or three specific places where she might find her brother. "Do you think I should have told the police?"

Bonnie shook her head, tried to smile back. "I know a cop; he's not like the others. He'll bring him in gently."

Jenny lowered her head and began to sob.

"They want to kill him; I know it."

23

Nancy dressed silently, quickly, without looking at Tommy Day, who lay almost blissfully on the bed watching her, his hands cushioned languidly behind his head.

She hates me, he realized. Some of them like me afterward. Some of them are frightened, yet still excited. And some of them hate me. It was not altogether unpleasant. In fact, there was a kind of excited tingle, knowing he was hated. That made everything easier. It's better if she hates me. Uncomplicates the knot. He almost liked her for it. He was, at any rate, grateful.

He glanced at his watch. "If you want me to take this shift, it's okay," he said, not meaning it. He needed his rest, with the time closing in the way it was. But for some reason, he made the offer. He liked the idea of working Christmas night. On his rounds. Like a dedicated Santa.

She shook her head. Even in the dark, with the moonlight ducking behind the clouds, he could see the violence of the

denial. She wants nothing more to do with me, he thought.
Okay, he thought. I get the idea. No need to call a cop.

He got up to clean himself and she flinched, then smiled
woodenly and continued dressing. She only relaxed when
she strapped on the shoulder holster and the .38-caliber
pistol inside. Not that he wanted her to cling and pester him,
not that he enjoyed the calf-eyed worship and the moony
attention. But those things did make him feel . . . human. A
part of the species. He shook off the shudder of alienation
that her rejection caused. He was not quite human; he knew
that. He couldn't help it. There were such people. And, in
the end, in the middle of the night when he couldn't sleep,
he had a vague, dim wish that he could feel something for
someone. But he couldn't, and in the morning light, he knew
it and accepted it.

He passed her silently and went into the children's bathroom and turned on the shower.

Less than twelve hours, he thought as the water struck his
face. He washed himself carefully, meticulously—a ritu-
alistic act of purification. He dried himself off, put on a robe
and toweled his hair.

She was in the living room when he came out of the
bathroom, staring out of the picture window, looking at the
park. It was like looking into outer space with all that black,
impenetrable emptiness, he thought. She seemed a little
calmer. She nodded at the kitchen, where a crack of light
crawled out from under the swing door.

"He can't sleep," she said.

"Guilty conscience?"

She shrugged. Sighed. "Misses the missus."

Sanders came through the door with a plate of sandwiches
in one hand and a glass of milk in the other. He sat at the
dining table and went to work on the ham and cheese.

He looked up and smiled at Tommy. "You hungry?" he
asked.

"No, sir."

"Whenever I can't sleep, I eat. Then I can't sleep because my stomach's spinning like a clothes dryer all night. Can't win."

He grinned with a mouthful of food.

Tommy went into the kitchen and came back with a bowl of potato chips. "I'm not tired, either."

"You mind if I ask you something?" Sanders used that midnight tone in which people let down their guard and utter revealing questions out of sheer exhaustion. He stopped eating, wiped his mouth hard with a napkin, and rubbed his hands together.

"Ask away."

"You think it's over? You think anybody's still out to get me? Tell me the truth."

Sanders was frightened. Not that he was sweating or drooling. He even smiled a little, as if he were embarrassed at his own selfish curiosity. But he was bottomed-out scared shitless, thought Tommy.

"You really have nothing to worry about," Nancy said.

Sanders gave her a look that shut her up. It was a look that said that he was asking Detective Tommy Day, the man who saved his life, not some plainclotheswoman with no real experience in the mob killer line of work. She turned away from the window and settled back in the couch and allowed Tommy to answer.

He looked back at Tommy, whose face broke into a smile. Tommy said, "I think it's all over. In fact, I'm certain."

Jack and Bonnie felt the time pressure, a clock ticking somewhere. It was past midnight, Friday, December 26th, and the Christmas frenzy was over. "The sister said that he's out there and he's hungry and that sooner or later he's gonna hit one of these shelters for a meal," said Bonnie as soon as she met Jack at Teachers. The restaurant was stuffy and loud and there was a flat, post-Christmas sag in the air.

They collected their coats and left.

Jack had not been idle. Patrolman Westfield had introduced him to a few community affairs officers. "Listen, I've been talking to cops all up and down the West Side; everybody knows this guy. He stands out. He's tall, he's demented and he wears those gloves without fingers, a homeless fashion statement. Also, he carries books."

They were on their way to the first shelter suggested by Jimmy Coffee's sister. It was located in an old Episcopal church on West 75th Street. It was closed and locked, but there were lights inside. Minimum-wage sentries—men just off the homeless rolls themselves—stood guard over the twenty homeless men who slept there each night. Outside of the shelter, a few bloated men were wrapped in burlap and curled over metal gratings. Jack shook his head. Homeless even among the homeless, he thought. How did it get like this? When he was a kid there were vagrants. Every neighborhood had had its share of unhinged derelicts—alcoholics, confused mental cases. But when did the homeless become a virtual tribe in our midst?

Bonnie brushed by the cluster of homeless locked out of the shelter. "Shouldn't we tell someone about the gun?" she asked Jack. The gun made a difference. Jack thought about it. Maybe it changed the way he thought about Jimmy Coffee.

"I called my inspector. Monahan. He was confused. He was home, it was Christmas. He didn't want to hear this shit. Said to call the Task Force in the morning. He got real regimental when I said that I was still working on the case. Said that I better know what I was doing because he was not backing me. Real cold. You know? He likes me, but he got very chilly. I think maybe I'm going too far."

"Does that mean you're not a cop anymore?"

He looked down at her worried face and smiled. "I'm a weathercaster."

"Not funny. I wanna know if that shield still works."

"I'm a cop. All cops are allowed to act when they see an obvious threat."

"And this is an obvious threat?"

"I regard this as hot pursuit."

The head of the shelter was a well-meaning socialite, one of those do-gooder members of the idle rich now employed by the Human Resources Administration. It was her night to stay late and she was a formidable woman. She knew about Jimmy Coffee from his name and description. He was in for lunch the other day, maybe yesterday, she couldn't be certain.

They were seated over a table in the rough kitchen. The table was covered with cracked and slippery linoleum.

"Was there anything unusual about him?" asked Bonnie, sitting back from the table.

"No. Just Jimmy with that frightened they're-coming-to-get-me-look."

"Did he have any weapons on him?" asked Jack.

The woman paused and looked at Jack with a weary indecision. She didn't know how far to go in cooperating. On one hand, she depended upon city financing. On the other, she was by instinct mistrustful of the ruling class since, as a member, she knew what they were capable of. She felt protective of those men sleeping in the bay of the church.

She stared at Jack and said evenly, "We don't search our clients."

He nodded.

"There are things that a man should have, even in dire circumstances, even at some peril. He should have as much dignity as we can allow. He should have a certain amount of respect. . . ."

"Yeah, but he shouldn't have a gun."

Jack could see her eyes flare. "You take some risk when you do this work," she said. "We all take some risk to live in society. Otherwise, it's fascism."

"Or chaos."

"We don't search our clients," she said in a low, settled voice. "We are not prepared to go that far."

232 Ken Gross

"I wonder if the people who get shot feel the same keen indignation about civil rights."

It had a crisp, hard sound when he said it.

Bonnie tried to intercede. "You know, what we're trying to do is protect Jimmy. I mean, if he is wanted and someone believes that he's armed, there could be big trouble for him. I mean, frightened people don't always stop to be polite."

She was smiling, but Mrs. Agnes Van Zandt, the head of the shelter, was glaring at Jack. "And how are you going to take him in, Officer? Are you going to read him his Miranda rights and then offer him a ride in a taxi? Or will it be some technical variation of murder?"

Jack was not the brute killer that she imagined, but she was pushing him. He couldn't stop his rise in temper.

"Lady, you have no idea what you are up against. You think that these people you put to bed are victims of social injustice, that they are nature's noblemen who are one lucky break away from curing cancer. It's not that way, lady. These people—most of them—are half-crazed and violent. They've got one other thing that makes them very dangerous."

"And what is that?"

"A gun."

She let them look at the bay with the homeless men in their beds. A few were still awake, clutching their shoes and overcoats against theft, sipping wine under the covers, maintaining the endless vigil that becomes the occupation of the homeless. There was no one who fit Jimmy Coffee's description.

"Thank you," said Jack at the door, shaking the hand of Mrs. Agnes Van Zandt. He was unable to hide his skepticism and she didn't bother to mask her smile. Bonnie chattered inanely about what fine work the woman was doing and how satisfying it must be to provide shelter and nourishment to such unfortunate people.

"Yes," Mrs. Van Zandt said, speaking more to Jack than to

Bonnie. "But people in my family have felt an obligation for years. Missionaries. Had a great-uncle eaten in Borneo. They didn't eat my great-aunt because she died of malaria. My grandmother was active in the suffragettes. We are all obliged to contribute something to society, don't you think?"

"I do," chimed in Bonnie. "I certainly do."

"And you, officer?"

"I think you are a very nice person with very decent impulses."

"Thank you."

"And I think there are guys sleeping in that very church who would slit your well-meaning throat for a bottle of cheap wine."

He started to leave, but she grabbed his arm. "So do I," she said. "So do I." This time her smile was radiant.

They walked out into the cold. "I think we ought to get some rest," he said.

She nodded.

"Besides, it's stupid to try to find this guy in the middle of the night. Wake up somebody normal, and they'll go after you. If he does have a gun and he is nuts, he might shoot us."

She nodded again.

"Let's get some sleep and meet in time to catch the breakfast trade."

"Okay," she agreed. "Here, or which shelter?"

"The one on 95th Street," he said. "We'll hit that one and then work our way downtown. Meet me there at about eight. Is that okay?"

"Fine. That's when they start breakfast. Good time to look. They're thinking about coffee."

"So are we."

"The beverage."

Jimmy Coffee was sitting in a doorway on 95th Street, eating his second peanut-butter sandwich. They'd offered to let him sleep in the shelter, but he didn't want to get trapped with his back to the wall. He'd eaten the dinner and taken two sandwiches, an apple and three containers of milk. He'd circled the block a few times, like a dog covering his own tracks, then had nestled into this empty storefront.

At midnight, a squad car had come by, shined a light at him, then crawled away.

The light had frightened him. He'd reached under his coat and held the gun. They're onto me, he'd thought. The hunters know about me and they're sending people in after me. When the car had moved away, Jimmy Coffee had been convinced that they were trying to lull him into a false sense of security. They'll be back when I let my guard down.

He had to do something about it. This was survival. He crossed Broadway and joined a group of derelicts on a bench who were passing around a gallon of wine.

"Where'd you get this, Shorty?" asked one of the hags in the group.

"Up around the college, you know the college?"

"You mean the school."

"That's right. The school. Some of those kids was having a party and I comes by and I says, listen, fellas, you're young kids and I'm just a bum. . . ."

"You ain't a bum," protested a tall, spindly man called Smoke with sunken cheeks and an advanced case of cancer. "Just down on your luck."

"Sometimes, Smoke, you gotta be humble. Let them call you a bum. Whatever."

The bottle moved carefully from hand to hand. They treated it with the tenderness appropriate to a precious baby.

"You ain't no bum."

"I know that. But if I call myself a bum, it makes them feel bad. Then they hafta feel all sorry and like they have to make it up to me, being that I'm a bum and they're high-class college students."

Jimmy Coffee had to let go of the gun in order to grasp the

bottle with both hands. He was confused and afraid, but he knew that he had to be careful with the bottle. Nothing that anyone said made any sense to him.

"Are you gonna tell us how you got the damn bottle, Shorty? Cause if you don't, you don't get anymore."

"Well, like I say, I tell 'em I'm a bum and I ain't got nothing—not a place to stay, not a friend in the world, no family, nothing."

"Well, that's the truth."

"So they feel sorry for me and they start to give me money. They're stuffing my pockets with bills. They give me food. And then I see this gallon jug just waiting there for the party. 'You mind if I take a lick a that?' I ask. By now these boys are feeling so bad that they give me the jug. Not to mention that the girls are startin' to show up for their Christmas party and they gotta look a little bit generous."

"You are a genius," said Smoke, falling back onto the bench.

"So they say, 'Here, take the bottle, old man,' and I am very grateful and very happy and I take the damn wine."

They all laughed at the trick.

The jug grew lighter and the derelicts grew unsteadier. Jimmy Coffee felt the soothing buzz of the wine. He walked away.

Jimmy Coffee steadied himself against a wall, then forced himself to move on. He thought that he was heading south, towards his sister, but at 86th Street, he looked up and through the haze and confusion he saw the street sign that told him he was heading in the opposite direction. He passed a clock on a bank. It was 3:30 in the morning and the wind off the Hudson River was going through the city like a paper cut.

"Are you okay?"

Jimmy Coffee stopped, looked around and saw the policeman standing outside of his patrol car. There was no one else on the street. I could kill him, thought Jimmy. He nodded.

"You want me to take you to a shelter?"

Jimmy shook his head. Not a shelter. They took your clothes and threw you into the shower. They'd find the gun and arrest him.

"How about it, fella, it's real cold out tonight."

Jimmy Coffee forced himself to become coherent.

"Going to my sister's house," he said.

He headed north and felt the policeman watching him. He had his hand on the gun, if it came to that. It was him or me, he'd tell everyone. They'd see that. Him or me.

24

Sometime after five in the morning the sound of the city underwent a complete and rumbling change. The occasional bus or car was replaced by the deep, growling engines of the garbage trucks and the delivery vans hurrying to beat the morning rush hour. Like an old man with a cough, the city was hacking and clearing its throat, thought Vinnie Insolia, lying in his bed and chain-smoking cigarettes. Today is the day after Christmas and the whole city will be in a state of rest. A post-holiday slump. The tourists will still be in town, flooding the stores, looking for bargains, stumbling giddy into hansom cabs. Radio City Music Hall overrun with people from Kansas. Pilgrims from Queens and Brooklyn converging on the ninety-foot tree in Rockefeller Center. There will be gridlock everywhere. Vinnie blew a smoke ring at the ceiling and admired Tommy's sense of timing. The kid knew his business. A window of opportunity in the heart of the season. No, Tommy wasn't gonna get caught stupid.

The aftermath of Christmas. Best time. Not quite New Year's Eve, but not an ordinary day. A day when odd things could happen. Smart fucking kid.

Time for him to move. He groaned and poured himself out of bed. When he was young he would have leaped up, jumped like the crack of a whip. Now everything was an effort. Now he never knew what was going to turn up sore when he moved. He was old. Too old even to appreciate the wild thing that he was about to do. Too old to savor the monkey wrench he was about to throw in the works. Just a bone-weary laborer in the field of crime.

He looked in his closet and picked the most conservative, inconspicuous suit. Nothing memorable. Of course, you always had to make allowances, think ahead in case you got picked up, so you made certain that there was nothing in the pockets. No bank statements or receipts.

He cleaned out his pockets, then remembered his blood pressure medication. He took it every day, and he swallowed one now, dry, without water. He hated it. Tethered to the Tenormin and the laxatives and eye drops and the headache pills. When he was a kid he got a jump start on the day and went out and raised hell. Now if he moved too fast, he'd get palpitations. He'd steady himself against walls and listen for his organs, as if he could hear the engine running. He'd wait for the breakdown, his teeth clenched like cement. He'd walk carefully so that he wouldn't trip, and young men would call him "sir" and he'd want to break open their skulls, shove his fist in their faces and mash their noses into pulp, tell them exactly how many young men he had sent to hell.

Now he had to spend twenty minutes every morning on the toilet, careful not to squeeze and break a hemorrhoid. He had to take his time and brush his teeth and sit in the tub and take a shower afterward and allow his body to adjust to the slowed rhythm and motion of the late day.

He picked up the floorboard in the closet, ignoring the jolt of pain in his back, and took out a fresh gun and a box of ammunition. He put one gun in each pocket. Then he took out the fully automatic grease gun, along with an extra clip with room for forty-five rounds of .30-caliber ammunition. He put the gun and the clip in a gym bag and closed it tight.

Then he sat down and sipped his decaffeinated coffee. He felt the bathroom urge and looked at his watch. He didn't have time, but on the other hand, he had no choice; he wouldn't be much good if he had to stop at a strange bathroom on the way. So he removed his jacket and his pants and sat for a moment, until a long, wet sigh of flatulence relieved the pressure. He shrugged back into his clothing, rinsed the cup in the sink, set his traps, then hoisted his gym bag with a grunt and left.

Jack awoke, wet with perspiration. He didn't know where the dream left off and life began. He didn't even remember closing his eyes. It was still dark outside, but he sensed that he was late for his rendezvous. He rushed into the shower. When he came out, breakfast was waiting. Barry sat at the corner of the kitchen table. Jack looked at his watch. It was twenty after five. "I'm a little late," Jack said softly, as if Natalie were still home, as if he could disturb her in her hospital coma.

"Please, Uncle Jack, take a minute." The plea carried the unspoken weight of Barry's sorrow. They had slept through the night and knew that there was no change in Natalie's condition. Someone would have woken them. Barry kept picking up the phone to see if the dial tone was there, checking that it still worked. Natalie was dying and Barry was a lost soul without her. He was afraid and needed some reassurance that he was loved somewhere by someone, and Jack recognized the need. So Jack sat down and ate the bran cereal and drank the freshly squeezed juice and sipped the steaming coffee. He chewed and tried to smile, but his smiles came out like grimaces now.

"Uncle Jack, we should have got a tree."

Jack shook his head.

"I'd've put it up," said Barry.

"Not this year," said Jack.

Barry looked down at his plate. "Aunt Natalie always loved a tree."

Jack couldn't say what he was thinking—yes, but she's not here now. He could only nod and mutter after a moment, "Christmas is over. It's too late, Barry." He had to blot out Christmas thoughts. The memories were too painful.

The air between them was brittle with emotion.

"I have to go," Jack said. Barry nodded. "I'll call you at the hospital," he said as he grabbed his coat and fled his own morbid home.

Was it the alarm? Bonnie poked her head out from under the blanket. Then the phone rang again. She picked it up, but held it away from her head, afraid of the news at such an hour.

"Bonnie?! Bonnie!"

It was Harvey Levy, sounding emphatic, but not angry or frantic.

"What, Harvey? What is it that you have to call about in the middle of a wet dream?"

He was quiet for a moment; she could hear the wheels turning. "Do girls have wet dreams?"

"Certainly. I was swimming at the beach. What did you think I meant, you creep?"

"Bonnie. Listen. You ran out so fast, we wanted to talk to you."

"Not at 5:30 in the morning, Harv. I'll be in later today."

"When?"

"Later. Before the broadcast. Have some coffee for me. You know how I like it."

Then she hung up, not bothering to speculate about what it was that had gotten Harvey up this early. Nothing threatening, or else he would have snarled. It was nearly time for her to get up anyway. She plunged into the shower, lingering for a moment under the hot, sensuous spray. It had been a while, she remembered. Sometimes you put your body on hold and attended to other business and then something came along, something ordinary like a hot, tingling shower, and reminded you that you had unanswered cravings, unstimulated drives.

Of course, she had no desire for just anyone. Only one, and he was distant and preoccupied and an emotional timebomb. Very dangerous. She looked in the mirror and saw the worried face looking back at her. What did he think of her? Not accepting. That's what he would think. Definitely not your legendary sidekick who would attend to fires while he went out and took care of business. A sharp-eyed stalker, looking at him like an X-ray. He was not used to it. She could feel him squirm under her eyes. Not that he didn't enjoy it. It was just strange for him. He was accustomed to being the watcher.

She dried her hair and thought about the story. Today she would find Jimmy Coffee. She was certain of it. She felt a premonition. He was moving north, heading for one of the food kitchens, hungry and cold—and dangerous. She stood on the plastic cover of the commode to unplug the hairdryer and felt the cover crack under her weight. Her first worry was her weight, but then she got annoyed at the flimsy construction of the commode. As she climbed off the broken seat, she was annoyed at the cheap plastic world in which she lived and paid too much rent.

Another thought crowded into her mind: Jimmy Coffee knew her face. He had looked straight at her when she crossed the street. And she had seen something in his eyes. An unsettled rage. An unfocused, wandering gaze, definitely looking for something upon which to fix. Like the guys who march through subway cars deliberately bumping shoulders, trying to provoke something.

She made a mental note to tell the superintendent, if she

could ever find him, about the commode. He was a phantom presence. Every day there was a note on the mailboxes with a phone number to call in emergencies.

She didn't have time for this. The warm gray slacks and the bulky matching cotton sweater. The winter shoes and a hat. She tried not to think about what she would say when she came face to face with Jimmy Coffee.

He awoke in an alley full of people. They were half-dead, snoring and complaining in their unrestful sleep, buried under blankets and cardboard boxes. The space between the buildings stank of urine. Jimmy Coffee checked to see that his gun was still there. Then he peeked out from his covering of boxes to see that it was safe. You couldn't just get up. You might see someone stealing a man's shoes. That might lead to a fight. Or you might witness a murder. That might lead to a second. No, when you woke up homeless you had to be careful that you were poking your head out into a world that was not looking.

He rose and felt the rumble in his belly. He had to get food. He urinated against the wall and then slipped out onto the street. It was still very early and only the puffy starters were out: the Wall Street types in their cashmere coats and silk scarves, waiting for a cab; the workers opening shops, with that blank, numb look people have when they are operating on automatic pilot.

He could smell something in the air. Something baking. He knew that he was close to one of the free kitchens, but he wasn't certain where it was. He turned and tried to sense a direction, but he was lost. He might have been in China. It was too cold to stand still. He began walking, heading south, away from the food kitchen on 95th Street. On Broadway he saw the people starting to come out in numbers, plunging one by one into a hole in the sidewalk. It took him a moment to realize that this was the subway.

Then he saw a trio of homeless men heading in the opposite direction. They had a purposeful look. Jimmy Coffee turned and fell into their slipstream and headed north to the food kitchen.

There was no traffic to speak of. Just the usual prowling police cars and the stumbling garbage trucks and early morning vans delivering fresh bread and milk. Vinnie Insolia made certain that he stayed within the speed limit. He drove his old Lincoln carefully, slowly, but not too slowly. The trick of being inconspicuous was the proper attitude: not caring. Not overcorrecting. Not clenching the steering wheel when moving past a police car. Over the years, Vinnie had perfected the art of indifference. But now there was this new factor of age and the unresponsive parts he could not ignore.

Vinnie pulled over on 14th Street, parked, locked the door, and ran into an all-night deli. He bought a roll of antacids, then resumed his ride. It was after six and he was early. That was fine. Better to be early and lower the pace than be late and rush into something already taking place.

He thought dreamily, I could be heading upstate. I could do it. Just keep driving and make for the mountains. I could rent a cabin near Lake George! I could spend New Year's Eve in some strange inn, warmed by a fire. I could drink hot toddies and eat turkey and ham and watch the people coming in from the snow.

But he had a job. A mission. Maybe later. Maybe afterward. If everything went okay. He looked over at the bag holding the gun and then turned back to the road. Think of the job and nothing else. But his mind, like his disobedient body, wandered back to the mountains.

25

Tommy had lain awake all night staring at the luminous dial of the clock. But at 5:45, unable to prevent it, he had closed his eyes. It seemed only a matter of seconds, but when he opened them, it was 6:20 A.M. Tommy felt the churning panic of being late, although he had not missed anything; he had no other destination, and he had plenty of time to do what he had to do. But he was late for his mental preparation for the kill.

The couch was lumpy and uncomfortable, but he was the duty officer and had to be out here in the living room while Nancy slept in the bedroom.

He went into the kitchen to put up coffee.

Marvin Sanders was up, wearing his robe, waiting for someone to come and make the coffee.

"Some bodyguard!" Sanders said.

Tommy nodded, then measured out the coffee, and sat down with the United States Attorney, waiting for the coffeepot to speak. It felt a little odd, sitting with Sanders, considering what was going to happen. But it would have been unnatural to go back into the living room. Tommy tucked his shirt into his pants and ran a hand through his hair like a comb.

"Can't sleep?" asked Tommy.

Sanders shook his head. "They wanted to pull you off, you know. Lukash said it was all over, and you could go back to your regular duties."

"You don't agree."

Sanders's hand shook a little and he stuffed it into the pocket of his robe. His day-old growth of beard made him look haggard. "I spoke to our guy, Highway—that was his code name—I spoke to him just before he got shot. I heard him. I know what he sounded like. I could hear the terror in the man's voice. I know that he was frightened of something very specific. Someone. I can tell the difference. Lukash didn't talk to him. I did. I was the last person he ever spoke to. The last person in the Task Force, anyway."

No, thought Tommy. You weren't. I was the last person in the Task Force that he spoke to. I heard the terror, too.

"You can't drive yourself nuts, Mr. Sanders."

"Get the coffee."

Tommy filled two mugs, placed one before Sanders and poured sugar in his own. As he stirred the sugar into the coffee, he almost felt sorry for Marvin Sanders.

"Right now, being mayor doesn't seem like such a big deal. Right now, a nice peaceful vacation in Europe seems like a much better idea. With my family. Where nobody knows me. Eat in good restaurants. Sleep in nice hotels. See some plays in London."

"If you don't mind my asking, why don't you do it?"

Sanders waved his hand, and lowered his head. "Oh, my people changed their minds and want me to stay. They think it'll make me look like a coward, like I'm running away."

He meant his public relations expert, Jerry Casolaro. Everything that happened went through Casolaro's political/media calculator. What would this mean to the political standing of Marvin Sanders? How would this affect his Q-rating in the public approval polls?

Tommy had his own psychological edge. "But don't most people think it's all over? How can that be running away, I mean, if it's all over? You didn't leave until we got the guy at headquarters. That was pretty brave, right there I mean, exposing yourself and all."

Sanders raised his head, and there was a smile on his face, running from ear to ear. "That's right!" He got up, banging the table happily.

Nancy emerged from the bedroom, dressed but sleepy. "I thought I heard something," she said. "Is everything all right?"

"This young man just saved my life again." Marvin Sanders slapped Tommy on the back.

On Fifth Avenue, at a few moments before seven, doormen were out polishing knobs. Superintendents were sweeping the sidewalk. Chauffeurs waiting for the corporate sharks or celebrity charges to appear for the day were listening to the radios in yacht-sized limousines. The apartment house doors were marked with holiday wreaths, spruced up with red bows. It looked festive and prosperous along Fifth Avenue, where the city's business and government and media elite owned multimillion-dollar apartments and lived like Middle-Eastern royalty.

At 81st Street, outside of the building where United States Attorney Sanders lived, two uniformed officers in a sector car had two more hours before their shift ended. They were in the midst of an argument that had started out sounding trivial, but was becoming a real threat to their ability to work together. The argument seemed to be about which one should go out into the cold and bring back coffee, but there was more to it. The white cop, Patrolman Steven Sloan, thought that they should flip a coin to see which one of them would walk to Madison Avenue and get the coffee.

"Why is that?" asked Patrolman Leonard Jackson. "Why should I go? Didn't I go yesterday?"

"Yes," Sloan said, "you went yesterday. The reason you went yesterday was because you lost the toss."

"So then why shouldn't you go today?"

"I will, if I lose the toss."

"That don't make no sense. I already went once."

"Listen, Jackson, this isn't a football game. It was a bet. Plain and simple. You lost the bet. Yesterday is over. That means today we start out even. We start from scratch."

"You can scratch my ass, Sloan, I am not fetching you no coffee. I did my share yesterday."

At that moment of hot impasse, Vinnie Insolia drove by, surveying the lay of the land. The cops were quarreling, he noticed. They weren't paying attention. A stroke of luck. He saw the wall between the sidewalk and the park. That's where he could hide. Beyond the wall, just as Tommy said, there was the bush that would shield him. He noticed the path where he could make his getaway, just as Tommy outlined. He circled the block, then parked north on an eastbound street. They would think south afterward, he decided. They would look at the flow of traffic and think south. They wouldn't think to look north. Not for a while.

He parked the car, removed his bag, then locked the car carefully, double checking the handles. He lifted the bag with the guns and walked slowly into the park.

The traffic from Long Island was making the worst jam of the year. After-Christmas sales and business. Jack was stuck on the ramp leading to the Midtown Tunnel for an hour. He looked at his watch. 7:30. He was supposed to meet Bonnie at 8:00 at the coffee shop on 92nd Street. He wouldn't make it. The police radio was making a welcome racket. It would help when he pulled into the lane marked for buses and emergency traffic. No telling when he would reach it, although it was only a couple of hundred yards ahead.

He could see the sad, drooping Christmas tree atop the toll

booths, with its sagging ornaments. How could a tree survive the assault of so many car exhausts? The toll takers themselves had the sallow, sick look of coal miners. But on this, the day after the saddest Christmas, the only thing that Jack could think about was Natalie. And the growing mass of doomed junkies. And the fluid sea of homeless.

Jimmy Coffee. He didn't kill Iennello's man in headquarters. He didn't make a threatening call. Homeless beggars didn't phone in death threats. They hadn't got the resources to do all the things that Lukash was ascribing to this one. Like a dozen others, they had a file on Coffee. Even if he was a university genius with some wires on the fritz. If Jack's theory was true, then Jimmy Coffee was being manipulated, or a diversion, or a straw man. Why would anyone bother to use such a device? What was the real purpose of all this killing?

Jack felt a stab of pain in his chest. Heartburn. Ate too fast. No, he realized, not too fast. Nothing went down now. Everything got stuck in his throat, like a sob.

"I'm hungry," insisted Jimmy Coffee. Pastor Harold Morris had come across a lot of hunger, especially lately. People needed to be fed.

"We'll be open for breakfast in an hour," he said, smiling beatifically, trying to close the door so that the cold air wouldn't drive up the heating bill. He had to shut in the heat. The church elders had been on him about the heating bills. They were on him about the food bills, too. But he couldn't cut the food bills, in fact they kept increasing, so he turned down the heat. He had been under pressure to close the kitchen. Let the city run it, the elders urged in their parched manner. They were offended at the unbalanced books. The old minister shook his head. No, we won't close the kitchen, he'd said with more toughness than anyone thought he had. We'll feed the hungry as long as we can, as long as I have breath. The elders had argued that the people in the neighborhood complained about the food kitchen clients. They foul the neighborhood, said the elders. They sprawl on the street and defecate in the doorways. Pedestrians can't walk two feet without being accosted for change. It was driving property values down. There was talk of closing the church, food kitchen and all.

Pastor Morris dug in his heels. On this he would not be moved. They were God's children. He had become a minister to do this, he said staunchly. To feed the hungry. There was no simpler nor more compelling message from Christ. Take that away and the edifice of faith would not stand.

"I'm hungry," Jimmy Coffee repeated.

"I'll give you some bread for now and then in an hour we'll have breakfast," said Pastor Morris. Jimmy waited, his foot planted in the door, allowing the winter air to blow through the heating bills, while the minister went into the pantry and fetched two slices of buttered bread.

Vinnie Insolia entered the park across the avenue and waited, walking slowly, until there were no pedestrians in sight, then ducked into the bushes and dropped behind the wall. He unzipped the bag, wiggling his fingers to make them work in the cold air, then removed the .30-caliber modified Uzi. He screwed the silencer into the front and slammed the long clip of ammunition into the slot.

He counted up from the ground floor, although he knew which windows belonged to Sanders. Twelve floors. Could not be too careful. He sighted without the weapon first, just poked his head up far enough to see. A woman walking her toy poodle saw him and jumped, then rushed ahead. Bad, he thought, but not fatal. Just another New York anecdote. This man was hiding in the bushes when I walked past; good thing I had Bootsy. He looked up and down. The coast was clear. The cops in the squad car were ahead of him, yapping, not paying attention to anything in their rear.

There were lights on in the third picture window from the

left on the twelfth floor, but the curtains were closed. He could see a shadow. "That's all you need," Tommy had said. "Just spray the window—don't worry about hitting anyone." Vinnie no longer felt the cold or the danger. He reached down and picked up the Uzi, aimed it at the window and teased the trigger. There was a small belching noise and a streak of flame out of the front. Up on the twelfth floor, the picture window shattered. From this angle, he couldn't have hit anyone if he was trying. But it didn't matter.

The glass came down like rain and Vinnie emptied two more bursts up at the window. The uniformed cops had come out of their car, but they were in that first stage of confusion, belly down on the ground, ducking the shower of glass and the incoming fire. They peeked out, having established their own cover, and, thinking that the falling glass was where the problem began, took defensive stands facing the building. It never occurred to them that the fire came from the park. Their attention was up, towards the window, and they shielded their eyes from the falling glass.

Vinnie unscrewed the silencer and replaced the Uzi inside the gym bag. He stepped out of the bush unnoticed. A jogger was running in place, staring up at the window, as Vinnie walked deliberately out of the park, heading for his car. Nothing to it, he thought. Retired old villain, and I can still do a good day's work. He slipped the key into the lock and opened the door of his car.

In the apartment, Marvin Sanders lay on the bathroom floor where Tommy had thrown him. He'd been shaving when the first burst of gunfire had torn through the picture window. He'd started to come out into the living room, thinking that someone had knocked over the etagere. He'd begun to say, "Hey, what was that?" when Tommy grabbed his neck and threw him to the carpeted floor. The second burst of gunfire then stitched a line across the living room ceiling.

"What the fuck is that?" cried Sanders, squirming under Tommy.

"Shut the fuck up!"

Nancy came in, gun drawn, ducking low.

"Get the front door," Tommy commanded. She looked confused. "Block the front door. In case anyone tries to get in."

Tommy had his own gun out and was waiting for that last, final burst of fire, which hit the side of the building, chipping away cement and sending the patrolmen downstairs under their patrol car.

"This is bad," Tommy said. He grabbed Sanders's hand and pulled him up. "Stay low," he ordered, then led the way out of the apartment and into the service staircase. Nancy went first, checking corners. Sanders was a docile, obedient captive. When they got to the basement, Tommy said he would cover the rear. "Keep him in there," he told Nancy, pointing to the old coal storage room. "I've scouted this and it's secure. Sit him down, keep him calm, and I'll get help. First lemme check it out."

Gun drawn, Tommy went combat-style into the storage room. He made scuffling sounds with his shoes and pulled the chair over to the coal chute. The door was closed and Nancy and Sanders couldn't see inside. Tommy reached in and found the Christmas package under the oily rags behind the chute. He pulled off the paper, opened the container and triggered the bomb. He had two minutes to get out.

"Okay," he said, hurrying out, "take him in there, don't let him move, and I'll be right back with an army."

It seemed strange to Nancy, but she didn't argue. She was a cop and obeyed the instructions of her superior. She took Sanders's hand and went through the door into the coal storage area. When she pulled open the knob, the timer Tommy had rigged began to tick. She pulled Sanders over to the chair—the only chair—and like a good cop, she stayed close.

Two minutes later, Tommy came out of the building and

confronted the two uniformed policemen, asking them if anyone had radioed for help. As he did, all three of them were knocked to the ground by the blast from the basement. A tongue of fire licked out of the old chute and part of the building wall buckled. Tommy knew that nothing could live through that.

26

Vinnie heard the muffled sound of the explosion after he turned onto Madison Avenue. He was travelling north through a thin mist of traffic when the shock made the car sway. His foot fell harder on the accelerator as he instinctively tried to put as much distance between himself and the apartment as possible.

He thought: "It worked!" A complicated plan. Not like walking up to some contract target and blasting away. That was his style. You took a guy on, you looked him in the face and you killed him. There was a certain amount of satisfaction in the eyeball-to-eyeball settling of accounts. But he knew that was old fashioned. It was not personal, although what else did he have to show for a lifetime of standup crime except his unbroken code of honor?

Ah, but it's stupid, he thought. Who's gonna know except the guy you put away? Who's he gonna tell what a noble character killed him, according to the ancient rules of engagement? Stupid. Tommy's got it right. Cold-blooded. Strictly results. Like the chilly business guys in English suits who take over companies and destroy everything; they don't give a shit about anything except the bottom-line kill. Fuck the dead jobs. Fuck the economic casualties. Fuck everything. He'd seen these guys when they met with the Don. Come up and have dinner at Rao's in East Harlem, the Don in his rumpled sports jacket and tieless shirt buttoned to the neck surrounded by killer thugs and the businessmen with their thin, underfed English charm, picking at the veal and slugging the wine. They liked the Don, and the Don was amused by their squeamish, indirect tactics. They were killers, though. There was a sympathy between them. They understood each other. The businessmen liked to flirt with danger, and the Don liked to flirt with respectability.

Vinnie smiled and shook his head. Tommy Day was the best of both. Or, maybe the worst of both. He continued to be impressed by the clockwork efficiency of Tommy Day.

The needle of the speedometer hit sixty miles an hour and, like clockwork, an inertial switch planted under Vinnie's seat activated a timer. Vinnie Insolia was at 102nd Street and he could hear the sirens of the emergency vehicles on Park Avenue moving south, away from him, towards the scene of the blast. It was over. His work was done. He could keep driving north, head for Lake George, give himself a vacation. He had plenty of cash. He eased back on the accelerator, his sense of excitement now under control. The deceleration didn't stop the timer under the seat, a silent digital mechanism running down to zero. It had been activated when the speedometer hit sixty miles an hour.

There were quick openings in the traffic once he got through the tunnel, and Jack Mann slipped and sidestepped like a running back between the cars and trucks. It would not be easy moving across Manhattan. He was late and worried about all the changes that he saw coming in his life. He was troubled by the fact that he was thinking of himself, not her, not Natalie. But the loss. He made insincere vows; he would live in a monk's cell and do humble penance. He would become an observant Catholic and go to Mass every day. He would perform acts of contrition and say endless Hail Marys and Our Fathers, and he began under his breath in the traffic along Third Avenue, his lips moving with the automatic prayers, the other drivers looking in and thinking that he was cursing the gridlock.

There was steam coming out of the manholes; people were puffing through the streets, and cars spewing poison. It was a city racing and panting towards a frenzy of New Year's.

As he was dodging a truck on Third Avenue, Jack heard the citywide alert:

"There are reports of gunshots and an explosion in the One-Nine Precinct," said the usually laconic police radio voice, now turned up a notch. "Emergency Services respond to 81st and Fifth. Organized Crime Task Force personnel within range also respond."

At that location it had to be Sanders. He slapped his flashing light on the roof, turned on the siren, and mashed down on the accelerator, but he had to brake quickly. The traffic heading up Third Avenue wasn't any better in an emergency.

Bonnie kept looking at her watch, comparing it to the clock on the wall of the Broadway coffee shop, a few blocks from the food kitchen. It was 7:40 on her watch and 7:42 on the wall. The waiter came by and filled her cup with coffee. He was a young guy, not bad looking in a trashy kind of way, with too much hair, of which he was very conscious. One of those male sluts who hang out at upscale bars and pretend that they're stockbrokers. She smiled at him, to keep him sweet, then resented herself for using cheap gimmicks to cushion the day.

Where the hell was he? They were going to miss the breakfast line at the food kitchen. Jack was not the sort who

showed up late. Not him. It would have to be some sort of
calamity. Oh, well, she thought uneasily, maybe traffic.
Maybe it's just traffic. She dipped her spoon into her half
melon and kept glancing at the watch, then the clock.

What would she do if he didn't show up by eight? Deci-
sions had to be made. She couldn't just sit there and let
Jimmy Coffee escape. But, on the other hand, she didn't
want to confront him alone. There was the look of his face.
It was all rubber and definitely dangerous. She was not sui-
cidal. Maybe call Harvey and have him send one of the stur-
dier stagehands as a bodyguard? No, she wasn't ready to let
Harvey in on the story yet.

It was 7:51 on the watch and 7:53 on the wall.

At 107th Street, Vinnie began to appreciate the implications if the kid had thought of everything. Tommy had given
himself an alibi—he was outside with the uniformed policemen when the bomb went off. There was no one left who
could finger him. No one except Vinnie.

The blood drained from his face and his heart started to
thump like a drum. He stopped the car in the middle of
Madison Avenue, setting off every horn behind him.

"Christ!" he cried as he tried to leap from the car. He
snapped back, restrained by the shoulder straps. He fumbled
with the release, his hands all liquid. And as he hit the button, unhooking the seat belt, the bomb under his seat went
off. It was a powerful bomb and it turned everything in Vinnie's car into twisted shards of metal and scorched leather. It
turned Vinnie into flaming specks of flesh.

There were no emergency vehicles available for a while.

They were all engaged in a hot run to 81st Street and Fifth
Avenue.

Jimmy Coffee was in the middle of the breakfast line. The
hungry and homeless assembled at the street-level door to the
basement soup kitchen. It led straight down a few steps to

the basement, sparing the parishioners direct contact with the increasing clients of the food program. The entrance to the church rectory was fifty feet down the block to the right, near the corner of West End Avenue. The entrance to the church proper was on West End Avenue—wide and inviting rows of stone steps that led to the arched doors. By the door to the basement, the breakfast line was tightly formed, but even the shabby regulars sensed something strange about Jimmy Coffee and left some extra space around him. They could tell when someone was running along the edge.

Pastor Morris emerged from the rectory door down the block, shivered a little as he studied the bent figures on the line, walked over, and opened the soup kitchen door early, he said because of the cold weather. At 7:55, the men and women began filing in, down the stairs into the basement.

Bonnie came along as the line was being swallowed by the basement door. She turned and looked over her shoulder. No Jack. She stood across the street for a moment, trying to decide what to do next. She forgot the danger and the excuses, crossed the street, and tacked herself onto the end of the line. The people at the rear turned and scowled. She did not look homeless and she did not look hungry. Bonnie glared back, and kept in line.

Pastor Morris shook their hands, one by one, as they entered the church. It was his habit, as it was to murmur a few consoling words. When Bonnie came to him, he held her hand and smiled. "Yes, dear, how are you?"

"I'm fine, Father," she replied, looking past him, trying to spot Jimmy Coffee. "Actually, I'm a reporter for Channel 9 news and I'm working on a story."

"We don't care, my dear. As long as you're hungry there's a plate of food for you here."

The minister closed the door behind Bonnie to keep out the draught and stood on the sidewalk breathing into his hands, stamping his feet, awaiting the latecomers.

*   *   *

Sanders's building was on fire. Smoke snaked out of the basement windows and crawled up the brick walls. Inside, as drapes and curtains caught fire, there were little pops when the heat caused little explosions. The fire was working itself up through the vents of the building.

The streets were jammed with police and fire department emergency response units for blocks around the Sanders's apartment building. Ambulances inched along the sidewalks to pick up the injured tenants. A handful of burn victims who'd run through the flames stood in shock on the sidewalk. Emergency service technicians and policemen were wrapping blankets around the victims' shoulders. Half a dozen bystanders injured by flying glass or brick were bleeding and being led away to help.

Jack found a parking spot on Madison Avenue, then ran to the scene of the explosion. His tin shield flopped from his topcoat pocket. The police lines had already been thrown up. He saw Deputy Inspector Monahan, who was telling a uniformed squad to make a basement-to-roof search of the adjacent building.

"But that doorman says he can't let us in," answered the sergeant. "Says he's got orders not to let anyone in."

"Then break the front door open," replied Monahan.

Standing back, listening, breathing hard, Jack wasn't sure just what he was doing here. Monahan, who felt an enduring affection for Jack, saw him, motioned him over and began walking toward the burning building. Jack could see the black scar of the basement blast. It smelled of battlefield cordite and flame. Cops in flak jackets and combat helmets were drawing rifles and running airborne style into blocking positions at the intersections and around the park exits. Three squads were sealing off the adjoining buildings.

"Did they get him?" asked Jack.

"Him and one of his bodyguards," Monahan replied, putting his hand on Jack's shoulder. "I hope you're not still tangled up in this case. It's really a mess. The only one who got away was the other bodyguard." He motioned over toward the far sidewalk.

Jack looked and saw Tommy Day talking to Lieutenant Lukash. Tommy was shivering, standing in the cold. He had an Emergency Medical Service blanket wrapped around his shoulders. He couldn't go back into the building to get his coat because of the fire. As Tommy Day turned to leave, Jack saw his profile and it struck him like a jolt. It was the night of the Korean deli murders and he was half out of the window of a police cruiser heaving into the night—and a car was going by. An unmarked police car. He remembered that police car and the driver's profile. And the profile in that unmarked police car was the profile of the man talking to Lieutenant Bob Lukash. It was the same handsome face that he had seen in dim, quick shots on Bonnie's tapes.

He tried to tell Monahan, but the inspector was busy dispatching units, emptying the building, arranging for shelter. There was too much fire and too much confusion. If the assassin was trapped in the area, that was the first order of business. Monahan waved Jack away—couldn't he see that the inspector had his hands full?

When he turned back, Tommy Day was gone.

The soup kitchen on 95th Street across town from the fire was overcrowded, and there was some grumbling as newcomers waited for the early arrivals to finish eating and leave room for them at the tables. Jimmy Coffee continued to sit, although he had finished his scrambled eggs and coffee and toast. He crouched over the plastic plate. She was standing there, at the far end of the room, looking over the rows of hungry people. It was 8:20.

He knew her immediately. She was the one crossing the street. He didn't know who she was, but he knew that she was tracking him. He felt under his coat and shirts for the gun. The man on his left side felt his elbow. "Watch it, shit-for-brains."

Jimmy Coffee looked at this scab-encrusted little man. His fingers were freckled with warts and he smelled like a sewer. His greasy hat was pulled low over his face, but Jimmy could see that the face bore scars from fresh cuts and old wounds. The little man pushed a mass of wet egg onto his plastic fork with his filthy hand, then stuffed it all into his mouth. Something snapped in Jimmy Coffee. Maybe he sensed that he had come to the end of things. Maybe it was the casual insult from such a creature. In any case, he could not take any more. He stiffened in his chair, lifted his left arm and knocked the man off his chair. Then he stood and pulled the gun. People began scrambling for the door. Jimmy planted both feet over the terrified little man and aimed the gun at his head.

"Sorry!" cried the little man, egg spilling out of the sides of his mouth. "Please! Very, very sorry!"

Jimmy Coffee threw back his head and roared. "Aaaahhhhh!!!!"

And the little man cringed and began to cry and tried to make himself even smaller. Jimmy kicked the little man in the face, knocking out three loose teeth, sending forth a geyser of blood. Then he vaulted over the table and made for Bonnie. He grabbed her by the hair, but she pulled away and ran through a rear door that led into a corridor.

Jack was outside of the church; he'd come across town to meet Bonnie. Plenty of time to catch up with Tommy Day, now that he knew who he was, now that he felt an instinctive certainty that he was the killer. He was walking up 95th Street when the flood of men and women came pouring out of the basement door. They were running, but some of them still held their plates of food.

He stopped one old man chewing on a bagel. "What's going on?" he asked.

"Guy with a gun." The old man pulled away, taking another bite of the bagel.

Jack deliberately took the service revolver out of his ankle holster and fought through the stream of outbound eaters, making his way down into the basement. He came through the door just in time to see Bonnie fleeing through the door at the rear. Jimmy Coffee was right behind her. Jack was swimming against the flow of traffic, but he fought to catch up.

Tommy Day sat for a moment and savored the long shot of whiskey. Then he stepped into the steaming shower. He had dismissed the detective who had driven him home, saying he would grab a cab downtown. He wanted a moment alone. Perfect, he thought, as the warmth of the whiskey spread through his body. He hadn't even felt the cold, not until the lieutenant pointed out that he was shivering. It had gone so well, he didn't feel the weather. He had heard the radio report of the second explosion, the one that meant he didn't have to worry about Vinnie anymore.

He stood in the hot shower satisfied that he had covered all his tracks. He was home free. He would finish his shower, dry himself, then go downtown and make a report. No one would question his version. All the people who could were dead: Sanders, Nancy, Vinnie. The hot water felt good. He used three towels to dry himself, sighed, then finished off the whiskey. He dressed slowly and carefully, slipping on his favorite coat—the cashmere wraparound. Maybe he could run for mayor, he thought as he waited for the elevator. He would be a hero, a good candidate. It could be his stepping stone for the senator's job. Mayor. It sounded manageable.

He gazed out of the hall window that looked down on 95th Street. The street was pretty quiet, only some sour addicts and winos heading for the avenue—eating things, strangely enough.

Pastor Morris was in his office in the rectory basement adding up accounts when he heard the commotion. He stepped out into the corridor that ran behind the soup kitchen and connected it and the rectory to the church. As Pastor Morris walked into the passageway, he got between Bonnie and Jimmy Coffee. He waved his arms at the gunman and begged for mercy. Jimmy Coffee fired one of his two remaining bullets into the minister's face. Bonnie ran for her life. She dodged through the office door, out the other side, pounded up the stairs, and raced out into the street. Jimmy Coffee was not far behind, screaming and crying for help, afraid of the "assassins."

As Bonnie came flying out of the rectory, Jimmy Coffee with his gun on her heels, the pedestrians scattered for cover. Jimmy Coffee burst out into the daylight, squinting at the sudden glare. He raised the gun, looking for a clear shot at Bonnie.

Tommy Day, in the lobby of his building, heard some muffled something outside the front door. He didn't think much of it. A fight, no doubt, between the ragged beggars. Someone wanted an after-breakfast nip at the bottle of Thunderbird. He would do something about that when he became mayor. Citizens had a right to leave their homes without being molested.

This is what he was thinking as he emerged from his building into the winter sunlight. Bonnie saw him and came running across the street, begging for protection.

The homeless man looked up and his vision cleared. The first thing that he saw was the wraparound cashmere coat.

It was the same coat that he'd seen leaving the Korean deli on the night of the murders. So I didn't imagine it all after all, he told himself, starting to lower the gun, taking aim. They were after me!

Bonnie, panting, reached Tommy just as Jimmy Coffee's gun drew level. Tommy pushed Bonnie away and reached down for the pistol in his ankle holster. He fumbled with the catch. Jimmy Coffee fired. The last shot from Jimmy Coffee's gun struck Tommy in the neck.

Jack had followed through the basement to the door leading into the rectory office. He had seen that there was no hope for Pastor Morris, then pursued Jimmy Coffee through the office, up the stairs, and into the street. He saw him fire and hit Tommy Day, and the coincidence of seeing the detective there left him momentarily paralyzed.

When he regained control of himself, he went after Jimmy Coffee. "Hold it! Freeze!" cried Jack, down in his combat crouch.

Jimmy Coffee turned, the gun still in his hand. One more assassin, he thought. He knew that he had no more bullets, but maybe he could frighten this one. He took aim at Jack, who didn't hesitate. He unleashed a quick three-shot volley into Jimmy Coffee's belly.

Bonnie got up, then fell down on her backside. She wasn't hurt, but was dizzy with fear.

Jack kicked the gun away from the homeless man. He crossed the street and went to Bonnie. He couldn't see any injuries.

"Are you all right?" he asked.

Her eyes were huge and took a moment to focus on him. "Yeah. . . . Yeah, I'm all right. Oh God, Jack. I was scared."

He helped her up, and held her a minute longer than was necessary. She smelled good.

Then he walked over and made sure that he hadn't hallucinated Tommy Day's face. Maybe his obsession had taken control of him. But he wasn't mistaken. The man looking at him with terror was the detective from the Task Force; it was also the man he'd seen riding up First Avenue the night of the killings. He turned away and called to the onlookers: "Call Nine One One!"

Epilogue

Natalie died in March. She never emerged from her coma, and one rainy night, the alarms on the monitors at her bed began to ring. She looks no different, thought Jack, looking down at her corpse.

They buried her the next day, which was the custom in her religion. She was not an observant Jew, but she thought of herself as a Jew and Jack respected what she thought. The mourning period was not intense, or, at least it didn't seem so, but it dragged on. Jack's bouncy personality did not seem to recover.

Barry tried to find work, but he drifted. He sold small amounts of marijuana, fenced some stolen goods and gained weight. Jack bailed him out of trouble, and Barry still lived in the house. In spite of all the failings, Barry was his last link with Natalie.

Moe took a leave of absence and started work on a master's degree in English at Columbia University. He intended to write a book exposing the Police Department. Jack and Moe met once or twice a week for a movie or a meal and did not discuss Natalie.

One night in May, Jack and Bonnie met for dinner at an Italian restaurant in Greenwich Village. Nothing had changed. Except that they were suddenly awkward with each other.

"What *are* we going to do about this story?" Bonnie asked.

He shrugged, tried to look away. "The department wants to drop it," he said. He smiled.

"Wait a minute," she said, starting to work up some smoke. "That miserable, murdering bastard is going to get away with this?"

Tommy Day had hardly gotten away with anything. If anything, he suffered in some far circle of hell. He was paralyzed from the neck down, could only breathe with the help of a respirator, and was withering away in his wheelchair.

"I'd hardly call that getting away with it," said Jack.

She nodded angrily. "It kills me that he's a certifiable hero!"

"There's no proof," he said, holding his palms up in the air. "We know what we know, but there's no proof. Sanders is dead. The Mafia guy is dead. No evidence."

"I know. I know. But a hero cop!"

After coffee, she seemed to soften. "How are you getting along?" she asked.

"I cope. I survive. I'm not sure."

"Would you like to see me?"

"I would. But not yet. Not yet. I watch you on the tube and whisper secrets to you. I admire you greatly."

The next day Jack Mann put in his retirement papers. That night, he sat alone in the dark and watched the late news on Channel 9.

"Hero Detective Tommy Day was released from the hospital today," said anchorman Tony Canasto, in his revived perky voice. "You may recall that Detective Day was critically wounded by a homeless psychopath who went berserk at a soup kitchen on Manhattan's Upper West Side. Detective Day remains paralyzed and unable to speak."

"Sad fate for a brave cop," chimed in the anonymous female co-anchor. "His shield will be missed."

"Now for some happy and sad news right here. Our own Bonnie Hudson is moving on to a brand-new job, delivering the morning weather on a major network. Well, Bonnie, it must be a good feeling."

"No big deal," said a scowling Bonnie Hudson. "It's only weather."